ASHA ANDERSON

–

THE DRAGON

DUSTIN ARCHIBALD

For Tracy, who believes in me.

THE NOT TOO DISTANT FUTURE

The day is surprisingly warm, the previous night's rains evaporated by the constant summer sun. City doves soar on rising air currents, while far below the streets hum with summer activity. A red mini-van slowly moves through the traffic, carrying its two passengers home.

"He did not!" Asha Anderson *exclaims, her voice high and light.*

The sun is warm on her face, filtered nicely through her brand-new, oversized, and oh-so-very-cool sunglasses. Today is her birthday. She is fourteen and has been shopping to celebrate. Thrown carelessly on the seat behind her are the packages she has brought from their trip.

"He did so!" her mother says, laughing.

She sits behind the steering wheel of the van, one arm resting comfortably on the edge of her window sill. She has long black hair, like her daughter; dark brown eyes, like her daughter; a bright white smile, like her daughter. In fact, were it not for the

1

age difference, they could be sisters.

They have spent the day in the city of Ascension's Cross; it's a first for Asha, she has never been here. Light glints off every window, every mirror, every whitewashed wall. It dances in the water fountains; it plays in the ripples.

"Right there in the parking lot?" Asha asks, turning to look at her mother.

"Well, by the dumpster."

"Ewww... nasty!" Asha giggles, wrinkling her nose.

"Well, when you gotta go you gotta go."

"I'm so going to ask him."

"He'll probably want to show you the spot," her mother says, slowing the van down to stop at a red light. "Is that smoke?" she asks, distracted by something past Asha's window. A short distance away a faint, dark cloud grows over the homes and shops that line the street.

Asha watches the dark column curl skyward. It certainly looks like smoke. She's about to tell her mother when a blurred, tangled mass of bodies streaks past their windshield.

Amongst the confusion Asha recognizes police Captain Alexander Stoneman. His navy blue armour is torn, revealing bloody gashes on his arms, chest, and legs. He waves his arms frantically, sunlight gleaming off his steel gauntlets. His jet-propelled boots fire full blast, pushing him and his attackers through the street. Two of his opponents have clamped their arms around his waist, two more have hooked themselves around his legs, one straddles his chest hammering fists into his face; a very large man with a bald head has him in a tight choke hold. Captain Stoneman battles them furiously, driving blow after blow into whoever is in his reach. Even in the van, Asha can feel the heat of their battle.

Buildings have been set ablaze, billowing black smoke into the once-pristine, blue sky. Street lights lie twisted and torn, sending sparks into a spraying fire hydrant.

Captain Stoneman frees one of his arms and throws an opponent into a store window.

This can't be happening, Asha thinks.

Today is her birthday. She's fourteen. She's on her way home. There will be cake. And presents. And movies. And friends. This can't —

In the haze of fire and smoke outside her window she sees a dark mass move. The shape looks familiar, almost human.

"Mom!" Asha screams, pointing out her window

Her mother snaps her head to the side, her eyes wide with shock, a look of horror stamped on her face.

"Stay in the van!" she orders, opening her door.

Asha tries to protest, to beg her mother to stay, but her voice is trapped in her throat and all that comes out is a pitiful croak.

She watches her mother sprint past a shop, then a house, then another, and another.

Ignoring her mother's command, Asha opens her door and stumbles out of the van. The air is thick with smoke. Choking, she follows in her mother's footsteps, watching her stop before the dark shape that has fallen to the street. When Asha finally catches up she is met with a horrendous sight: the black shape nearly unrecognizable. She supposes it is a woman but only because of the form of a charred dress. Every part of the body is covered with ash.

A cat cries its fury against the confusion, but something is wrong with the sound. The cry is too high, too loud, like it has been warped by the howling of the fires. It is only then that Asha realizes she is surrounded by flame.

The houses are alight, as are the grass and the sidewalk and the trees. She feels the heat engulf her like a smothering blanket.

It's not a cat crying for rescue but a child.

She reaches for her mother. Her mother knows how to stop it.

Her mother can save them. Asha grabs wildly, the smoke blurring her vision, invading her lungs so that she doesn't dare to breathe. Groping desperately she finally catches her mother's arm.

She looks up, but instead of seeing her mother's eyes focused on her she sees them looking to the burning house before them and Asha knows that something is wrong. Her mother starts moving toward the house and Asha is glad she's still holding her tightly.

Her mother looks down, surprised, as if she has only just realized her daughter is there.

"Call 911," she says, then tries to go forward again, but Asha holds on tighter.

She shakes off Asha's hand with a small flick of her wrist and runs toward the inferno.

"No!" Asha screams, reaching out.

Her mother mounts the front steps, fire licking her legs.

"Mom!" the girl cries.

She can only see her mother's heel, the rest of her lost in the fire.

"Mo —"

An explosion tears through the street and Asha is lifted off the ground like a paper bag in a hurricane wind. She is in the air, watching the sky tumble below her and the ground flow lazily above. With a crack her back hits the pavement, forcing the poisoned air from her lungs.

A second explosion rips through the air, sending shards of metal over her head. Above her a pie plate-shaped disc slices through a power transformer and she wonders why the disc is screaming. The transformer falls and it is screaming, carrying its rage down upon her.

Before everything turns black, she hears something that she knows is impossible. When it all ends Asha swears she can hear a fourteen-year-old girl crying.

1
SIX MONTHS LATER

Asha sat shivering in the front passenger seat of the van. It was snowing again, the flakes barely visible in the low morning light. In the parking lot, Asha could see other vehicles' lights shining through the dimness. She didn't see anyone in those vehicles; they probably had remote starters, their owners comfortably waiting in their apartments.

The driver's side door swung open, letting in a cold gust of winter air that flipped her hair into her face. Her father slid into the driver's seat and slammed the door after him.

"Whew!" he exclaimed. "That'll wake you up."

He was a tall man, about six feet, so he had to squeeze into the seat. This morning his short, brown hair was covered with a bright red toque. Beneath his winter jacket he wore his light grey uniform.

After stowing the snow brush in his hand he fastened his seatbelt and turned to her.

"Ready?" he asked.

No, she was not ready; she was not ready for any of this. A pit of uneasiness had grown within her. Asha merely shrugged.

With a nod, he put the van in reverse, pulled out of their parking spot, and left the parking lot, driving through the alleyway that joined the apartment complex with the main street beyond. He stopped at the intersection, waiting for a gap in the traffic. Vehicle after vehicle zipped by: trucks, vans, most of them small cars. How many were there? Hundreds? Thousands? Asha couldn't even guess. The van lurched as her father hit the accelerator and swung into traffic.

This area of the city was called the South Crescent, named for how close it was to one of the many ring roads that circled the city. Everywhere Asha looked lights shone, breaking through the gloom of the early morning. Street lights lit up the roads below, store signs blinked and flickered, houses leaked light through their windows. It was no wonder Ascension's Cross was called the City of Lights.

Asha had never seen anything like it. The first and only time she had been in the city it had been summer and daytime; she hadn't even considered what it would look like in the dark. When they had moved into the apartment it had been early evening and she had spent the last few days unpacking boxes.

A flicker of silver flashed outside her window. Through a row of trees she caught a glimpse of a long tube, disappearing and reappearing in the gaps. For an instant it disappeared completely then it shot above the treetops. It was a metal, pill-shaped pod with dark glass windows, twice the size of the van. The track it ran on wasn't supported by anything; it simply stretched on and on, rising higher and higher so that it was soon elevated above all the houses and stores.

"I think that might be the LR2," her father said.

She knew about the city's Light Rail system, which she would be riding most days. It was a web of tracks which carried people to anywhere they wanted to go throughout the city for free. She had only ever seen it on television and never this close.

Up ahead, riding on a section of track that crossed high above the road, appeared a train of nine other pods, each connected front to back. She imagined if it were sunny outside they would glint brightly, but now they were dull, their tinted windows giving them a somber look.

The pod on her side followed a track that curved sharply to meet the track the larger train was on. The single pod was going way too fast; it was going to hit the junction just when the train did. Asha sucked in a startled breath, they were going to collide. At that moment, though, the four pods at the back of the train slowed, not much, but just enough for the lone pod to merge in ahead of them. The front five pods reconnected with those at the back. A moment later they were out of sight, disappearing into the early morning gloom.

"Did you see that?" Asha asked, astonished.

"Pretty slick, eh?"

She could only nod.

Asha watched to see if another train or pod would appear on the tracks but nothing came and, with nothing to distract her, Asha could only dread what lay ahead. With every bend in the road her breath got shorter, her heartbeat louder. Every bump and noise seemed harsher than the one before. She felt hot and wondered why she had worn a winter jacket in the first place.

Then she saw it: a gleaming tip of glass rearing up ahead of her. With each passing moment that tip grew taller, reaching to the sky. The van continued ahead, despite her willing it not to. The glass tip became a building and she could make out windows, hundreds of them, each lit up.

They turned one more corner and then she saw it fully: Veda Zhi Memorial, her new school. It rose high above the street in a swirling cone of glass. Hundreds of students rushed to the main entrance, hunkering against the wind. Seeing them she felt as if a lead weight had dropped into her stomach. How could she possibly ever fit in here?

The van came to a stop in front of the massive building. She had to crane her neck to even see a part of it.

"Nervous, kiddo?"

Startled, Asha turned to see her father looking at her, an expression of mild concern on his face. Asha pushed her glasses farther up her nose.

"Not really," she lied, turning away from him.

"They have everything waiting for you at the administration desk. You'll meet me here after school?" he asked. "Like we talked about?"

Asha nodded.

"You sure you don't want me to come in with you?"

"No, I'm fine," she lied, again. She opened the van door and sucked in a sharp breath as the cold wind threw snow into her face.

"Good luck — " he called, but he was cut off when another gust blew the door shut. She waved, watching him drive away.

Asha turned back to the looming building and walked to the main entrance, dodging the other students. She followed a couple through one of the many double doors and came to an abrupt stop.

The main entry opened high above her head in a towering arc. There were no lights that she could see. Instead, the walls emitted a pleasant yellow-white glow. The floor was made of white marble that reflected the light. Far off in the centre of the room a gigantic, blue cylinder rose to meet the high ceiling. She stared in awe as what looked like a whale floated through it.

She was jolted out of her daze by a rough bump from behind followed by a loud shriek. Asha spun around to find a blonde girl holding a paper cup away from herself; her hand was covered with coffee.

"Watch where you're going!" the girl yelled.

"Sorry!" Asha said, instinctively. "I didn't —"

"Didn't mean to just about ruin this outfit?" the girl demanded, indicating her white coat, pants, and boots.

"I wasn't —"

"Paying attention?" the girl snapped. She took the cup with her other hand and flicked the coffee of the first, a curl on her upper lip.

"I'm just — "

"GET OUT OF THE WAY!" the girl ordered.

Asha turned to the side and the girl stormed past her.

"— new here," Asha finished quietly, watching the girl push her way through the crowd.

She had only been here a few minutes and already she was lost and confused. How was she ever going to find her way in this place?

She looked around and finally spotted the main administrative desk to her right. She slowly made her way over, brushing past hurrying students, to find an older woman sitting behind a tall marble counter. A girl Asha's age stood beside the woman, filing papers.

"What can I do for you, dear?" the woman asked, looking down on Asha over the rim of her glasses.

"Uh... I'm Asha Anderson... "

"Ah!" the woman exclaimed, smiling brightly. "We were told you'd be coming today. I'm Mrs. Bergess." She held out her hand; Asha shook it reluctantly. "If you need anything, anything at all, go ahead and ask. If I'm not here, one of the other admins can help out."

"Uh... actually... I... um... " Asha hesitated, looking around.

"You want to know where to go next," Mrs. Bergess finished for her. "Don't worry, dear. We have everything ready for you. Crystal, can you grab that folder?"

The girl handed a folder over to Mrs. Bergess, eying Asha curiously. The woman pulled out a small bundle of papers and handed them over. On the top was a class schedule with a school map beneath it.

"Thanks, but... " Asha muttered, heat rising up under her shirt collar. She didn't think there was going to be any way she would be able to find any of the rooms in time for her classes, even with a map.

"Got that covered, too. We have someone to show you around," Mrs. Bergess said. "Here she comes now." She pointed over Asha's shoulder.

Asha turned to see a tall, Chinese girl walking toward her. She was a good head and a half taller than Asha.

"Hi, Mrs. Bergess," the girl said.

"Lily, this is Asha Anderson," Mrs. Bergess introduced her.

"Lily Donovan," the girl said, sticking out her hand. Asha shook it warily. "Got everything?" she asked.

Asha nodded.

"Okay, then. Let's go," the girl said and walked away.

"Thanks," Asha murmured to Mrs. Bergess and then hurried to catch up to the girl. "Who was that girl behind the desk?"

"Crystal DeBourg," Lily said. "She's there for work experience."

"Work experience?"

"It's a class option you can take. The school's pretty easy to get around," Lily said leading her toward the blue cylinder, Asha taking two steps for one of the girl's long strides. "All the classes are in the outer wall. Grade Eight is on Level One. Some classes on Level Two and Three. The other higher grades up to Grade Twelve go up from there."

As they approached the cylinder Asha stared up at it, straining her neck to see it disappear through the ceiling high above. All through the blue, dark shadows moved.

"It's basically a big computer screen wrapped around a pillar," Lily stated matter-of-factly. "It's updated by a computer in the administration desk. At the beginning of the year they had it look like a long hallway. Problem was all the new kids kept running into it. Left a lot of forehead marks to clean up. The main gyms are in the centre. One on this floor and six others as you go up."

"The centre of what?" Asha asked

"The Tube."

"The Tube?"

"This," Lily said, pointing at the cylinder, "is the Tube."

Asha couldn't understand how the girl could be so casual about it. The fact there was more than one gym and that each was housed in the centre of this "Tube" boggled her mind.

"Where'd you transfer from?"

Asha looked over to see Lily giving her an appraising look.

"We moved here a few days ago. From a town called Faller, a few hours out of the city."

"I've never heard of it. Small town?"

"Yeah, we only had one school."

"How many people?"

"About four hundred."

"This school has something like four thousand students."

"That many?"

"It's really not much. Four hundred's still a lot of kids."

"No," Asha corrected her, embarrassed. "Our town had four hundred people. We only had one school. Kindergarten to Grade Twelve."

"Really? Did you like it there?"

"It was okay."

"Why did you move here, then?" Lily asked, still staring at her.

"Just because," Asha muttered. Lily seemed nice, but Asha did not want to talk about it; not about the move, not Faller, any of it. Not ever if she could help it. "What about you? How long have you been here?"

"My mom and I moved here from Acheron at the beginning of the year."

"Bet that was a long drive."

"Nah. Flew down. Her new job paid to send us over. Flew all of our things. This city is pretty much the technological hub of the country, maybe even the world. Nearly every new scientific advancement from manufacturing to military tech either starts here or has some stage of it developed in this city. Compared to that,

Acheron, even though it has about the same population, seems somewhat backwards. I mean, most vehicles there still run on gasoline or diesel. Can you imagine?"

Asha tugged nervously at her jacket; her dad's van ran on gasoline.

"So when my mom got a job offer to work here we had to come," Lily continued. "She does scientific research and development, been doing it for years."

Asha thought Lily's mom must have a really good job for a company to pay for them to move to this city. Acheron was practically on the other side of the country, far off to the east coast. Ascension's Cross was just East of the Rocky Mountains, although a fair bit farther North than Acheron.

"Why did you move here?" Lily asked again, turning to her. "It's kind of late in the year. After all, it's December already."

"Uh... shouldn't I get to class?" Asha suggested, trying to change the subject.

"What? Oh yeah, let me see your schedule."

Asha fumbled with the stack of paper in her hands. She managed to pull out the schedule and handed it over. Lily looked over it for a second, concentrating. When she looked up she was smiling.

"You're in luck, we have all the same classes, except Linguistics."

"You're in... we're in... how old are you?" Asha blurted.

"Fourteen. Why?" Lily replied hesitantly.

"I... I just thought you were... older."

"Yeah, I get that a lot," Lily said, then turned and walked away.

Asha wondered if she'd said something wrong - it's not like she had meant to insult the girl - then hurried to catch up.

They walked in silence, Asha twisting and turning to avoid colliding with students.

"Veda Zhi is kind of a strange name for a school," Asha said, trying to start up the conversation again.

"It's named after the woman who founded it," Lily said. "In her will she left a huge sum of money - I'm talking millions - for the construction of the school and more just so the school can buy new equipment every year. So if something new comes out the administration tries to get it. This school is supposed to always be the cutting edge. She wanted to help students out, give them a great learning experience."

"I'd say she got what she wanted."

"Did you know it only took them three months to build it? That includes tearing down the school that was in this location before. They had shifts running day and night. It was pretty impressive, I hear."

"How do you know all this?"

"I read it."

They stopped at an open door.

"8A," she said, turning to face Asha. "Homeroom and Social Studies. We have Social Studies this period."

Asha peered into the room and was immediately struck by its odd pie shape. The back of the room was a curved wall of frosted glass; each of the side walls angled in toward the front. The ceiling and walls gave off the same yellow-white light as in the main lobby. At the front of the room sat a woman behind a large wooden desk poring over a stack of papers. The rest of the desks in the room were, thankfully, empty.

"Come on," Lily said, leading Asha to the teacher.

The woman had long red hair pulled up into a bun and pale white skin. Despite the chill in the air, she was wearing a bright white t-shirt.

"Ms. Lowen," Lily announced. "This is Asha Anderson."

"Hi, Asha," Ms. Lowen greeted her and extended her hand out. "I've been expecting you."

Asha reached to shake her hand but an arc of static electricity shot from Ms. Lowen's to her own. They snapped their hands back at the same time, Asha shaking her arm; Ms. Lowen laughed nervously.

"Happens to everyone Ms. Lowen shakes hands with the first time," Lily chuckled. "Although you seem to have gotten a good one."

Asha massaged her hand, still feeling a tingle in her fingertips.

"Everyone says I have an electrifying personality," Ms. Lowen joked.

Asha forced a weak smile.

"And she always tells that joke after," Lily said rolling her eyes.

"Everyone's a critic," Ms. Lowen sighed. "Anyway, Asha. Do you have everything?"

Asha nodded, then added, "Everything except my books. We

didn't know what I'd need."

"I'll give you the list after class. Until then, how about you pair up with Lily? There's a desk free beside hers," Ms. Lowen said, pointing at a desk in the front row.

Lily beamed.

Asha took her seat, thankful to finally be still. All of this had happened so fast her mind was racing. She doubted she could even find her way back to the main entrance.

They hadn't been seated long when the class began to fill up. Students came in the door, looked at Asha with a sudden curiosity, then looked away and hurried to their seats. She would have been glad to crawl under her desk and never be seen again.

A boy stepped through the door. He was short, almost as short as she was, and very skinny. He had an awkward look about him that was only made worse by his messy blond hair and too-short pants showing bright white socks. His ears stuck out from the side of his head. He looked at her as he entered looked away, then abruptly looked back again, his mouth agape.

A couple of large boys entered the room right behind him, scowling. The biggest one gave the blond-haired boy a shove from behind, causing the shorter of the two boys to laugh out loud.

"That's Trevor McKnight and Andrew Hastings," Lily whispered to Asha. "Pretty much the biggest jerks around."

Two girls followed the boys; one of them was the girl from the administration desk, the other she didn't know. They were chatting with someone behind them. When they parted, revealing the other person, Asha's heart fell; it was the blond girl from before, the one she'd spilled coffee on.

She looked at Asha with piercing blue eyes then whispered something to the other girls. They whispered back and giggled, then rushed to their seats.

The buzz of the room grew louder and Asha knew everyone was whispering about her; no matter how hard she tried she couldn't ignore them.

"Okay, settle down," Ms. Lowen said, standing up from behind her desk. The buzz stopped altogether. Asha suspected they were all looking at her but didn't dare turn around. "As I'm sure you've noticed we have a new student today. This is Asha Anderson. I'm sure you'll all give her a warm welcome to our school.

"So, moving along," she continued, "last week we started our topic on China. This week we'll be looking at some of the philosophies and religions that have come out of China. We'll learn about how these have affected not only their country but the rest of the world, as well: Buddhism, Taoism, Confucianism — yes, Lily?" Ms. Lowen said, staring beside Asha.

Asha looked over to see Lily nearly jumping out of her seat, her arm stretched high in the air.

"It's actually pronounced 'dow-ism'," Lily replied. "You pronounced it 'tay-oh-ism', but that's not right. In this spelling the 'T' is pronounced more like a 'D' although it's not really a hard 'duh' sound, more like a 'tuh' sound really. See, even though the words might look like English words they've been translated from the Chinese characters. The translators do their best to approximate the sounds, but they aren't quite the same seeing as the languages developed over thousands years, which, of course, is only to be expected," she finished, looking particularly happy with herself.

"Thank you, Lily. I see you've been paying attention in Linguistics," Ms. Lowen said, looking slightly bemused. "Yes, we'll be looking at traditions like Buddhism, Confucianism, and Dow-ism to see how they have affected the country and the world around it... "

Ms. Lowen continued her lecture, often interrupted by Lily's waving hand, but Asha couldn't focus. She felt the eyes of everyone in the class boring into the back of her head; she hunkered down lower in her seat, wanting to disappear.

*

After the first class Lily guided Asha through the school. The building was massive. Asha couldn't count the number of rooms they passed. They had some classes on the second floor (you reached them by going into an elevator and telling it which floor you wanted), but most of them were on the main, which suited her just fine for the time being.

At lunch time Lily and Asha sat alone in the cafeteria, a large circular room with two kitchens, a very busy wait staff, and little cone-shaped robots called Resident Custodians — RCs for short — that tried, but failed, to keep the room tidy.

After lunch Lily took Asha to her locker which was, thankfully, right next to hers. Asha figured she would need Lily to guide her around the school for the next year and was grateful they could meet at the same spot all the time. The blond boy from her first class appeared on the other side of her locker, threw in some books, slammed the door, gave her a wink, and hurried off.

"Who is that?" Asha asked Lily.

"Who?"

"The guy with the locker next to me."

"Mick? Yeah, he's a strange one."

"What do you mean?"

"He's a little too happy. All of the time."

Asha wondered if that was such a bad thing.

*

At the end of the day Asha found herself at her locker once more. She had a pile of homework already, but at least the day was over.

"How are you getting home?" Lily asked, closing her locker door and leaning against it.

"My dad's coming to pick me up," Asha replied confidently for the first time all day.

"Did you want me to wait with you?"

"That's okay."

"It's no problem. I can wait a while longer. My mom's probably here to pick me up already, but if your dad's going to be late we can work on some of that homework until he gets here. She won't mind."

"No, I'll be fine, thanks. If your mom's waiting you should go."

"Are you sure? It'll be no problem."

"I'll be okay, really."

"Okay, but only if you're sure."

Asha gave a small laugh and said, "Go. I'll be fine."

"I'll see you tomorrow then? I can meet you here if you'd like and I can take you around again."

"That would be great," Asha said, relieved. She had been worried about finding her way.

"See you tomorrow then," Lily said.

She gave Asha a worried look then turned and walked away.

Asha gathered up her things then followed Lily's path, hoping it would lead to the main entrance.

She was nearing the exit when someone behind her yelled, "Hey, Asha!" She turned around to see the blond-haired girl, the girl from the administration desk, and their friend approaching her. She stood frozen in place as the girls approached her.

The blond girl glided up to her and stopped. She was taller than Asha — everyone here seemed taller than her — and looked down her nose at her. They stood staring at each other for what seemed forever. Then the other girl's stern look broke and she smiled.

"I'm really sorry about this morning," Asha apologized. "I guess I shouldn't have stopped in the door with all the kids coming through."

"Forget about it," the girl said, waving her hand. "My clothes are fine. This is Crystal DeBourg, and Chastity White. We're kind of the unofficial welcoming committee around here. I like to meet everyone and make sure they're settling in fine. Getting into a new school can be rough so I try to make it just a bit easier. So how was your first day?"

"Fine"

"And Lily's been showing you around the school? Pretty nice, right?"

"It's okay," Asha shrugged. Despite her initial uneasiness she found herself smiling.

"Okay?" Keri demanded. "It's amazing! Do you know how many gyms this place has? And the cafeteria! And the pool!"

"A swimming pool?"

"Yep," Keri replied, a grin on her face. "All this must be quite a shock coming from a small town and all."

Stunned Asha asked, "How do you know where I moved from?"

"Oh, word gets around," the girl replied. "It's really not such a big place once you get to know everyone. Plus, you're the new kid in town so that helps. Just a word of advice, though, no one wears those anymore. You might want to get something better."

The girl was pointing at Asha's hooded sweater; it had seemed a good idea this morning but now that she had pointed it out, it looked old and worn.

A look of bright realization spread across Keri's face. "Did Lily tell you about the skating rink?"

Asha shook her head and repeated, "Skating rink?"

"Yeah. Figures Lily wouldn't tell you about the pool and the rink. She's not exactly the active type."

Asha bristled at the statement. She had started to like Lily.

Keri considered her for a moment, then continued, "We're headed up there now. Just have to get our skates."

"Up where?"

"The roof," Keri pointed at the ceiling.

"The roof?"

"Yeah, the roof. Don't worry, it's safe."

"Actually," Crystal said. "Isn't it a bit cold out? To go to the skating rink?"

"Are you serious?" Keri demanded. "It's perfect. What's wrong with you?"

Crystal shrunk back.

Asha was on the verge of saying yes when she remembered her father. "I can't," she said. "My dad's going to be here soon."

"Come on! It'll only take a minute. Besides, there's lots of people I want you to meet. They're up there right now."

The other two girls nodded, excited.

Asha hesitated. She was happy Keri was talking to her, happy anyone other than Lily was talking to her, but she didn't really want to go on to the roof. Still, the girls seemed nice and she wanted them to like her.

When she agreed Keri's smile brightened. "Great! Take the elevator to the top floor right now and go up the stairs to the roof. When you get up there just tell everyone you're with me. We'll meet you after we get our stuff."

Asha nodded and the girls turned away.

"Oh, wait!" Keri said, turning around to face Asha. "There's a code on the roof door. Four-two-four-two."

"Four-two-four-two," Asha repeated, then the girls hurried away.

She rushed to the elevators and got into the first one that opened.

"Top floor," she commanded the control panel at the front. The panel beeped an acknowledgement; the elevator hummed as it rose higher and higher.

The elevator doors opened and she looked around. She was in a large hallway. To her left numbered doors spread down the hall. To her right, at the end of the hall and past some more doors, was a single door marked "Roof Access". Asha hurried to the door and climbed the stairs behind it.

It was a short climb before she found herself in front of a large steel door. Sure enough, there was a number pad beside it. She punched four-two-four-two on the pad and it beeped. There was a slight pause. A green light blinked on the pad and then a click sounded as the mechanical lock unlatched. She took a deep breath and let it out, trying to calm her nerves. She took another deep breath, and, gathering herself against the oncoming cold, pushed open the door.

The outside light nearly blinded her. She had expected the gloom of a cloudy sky and falling snow, not the light of a midday sun. She shut her eyes tight, but even then she could still see the brightness. She stumbled through the doorway, hearing the calls of other kids a short distance away. She blinked a couple of times trying to adjust her eyes as she stumbled farther onto the roof, shielding her eyes. Behind her the door shut with a click.

For a moment the brightness lingered, but then it quickly faded as if the sun had been covered by a large swatch of clouds. Asha looked around to see where the rest of the kids were. No one was there except a flock of doves crowded on the far ledge of the building. Asha walked around the door entry, expecting to find the kids and the skating rink on the other side. There were vents and ducts. There was a tall radio tower. There was a four foot high guard ledge that ran around the edge of the roof. There was no skating rink.

I must have taken a wrong turn, she thought and hurried back around to the door. One of the other doors probably. Besides, who would build a skating rink on the roof? It must be inside.

She grabbed the door by the handle and tried to turn it. Her stomach gave a lurch when she realized it was locked, but then she saw the number pad beside it. She punched in four-two-four-two. There was a moment of silence then a red light blinked on the pad. The code hadn't worked.

She tried it again. Red light.

Panic rose up in her chest. She punched in the code again and again and again. Red light, red light, red light.

"No no no no no," Asha muttered, her voice starting to tremble.

She tried four-two-two-four. Red light. She tried every combination she could think of. Red light each time. She pushed the numbers randomly. Red light.

"NO!" she screamed and pounded the door with her fist.

I'm going to freeze up here! What if no one comes?

"OPEN!" she screamed. "OPEN! OPEN!"

The tears streaming down her face froze to her skin. She pounded on the door with her palms. "OPE —"

There was beep and a click; the door lock unlatched.

Keri's come! She found out I went the wrong way and came back! Asha thought, stepping back from the door.

She would have to come up with an excuse, like she took a wrong turn or something, but at least she wouldn't have to —. It wasn't Keri holding the door open; it was a boy with messy hair and ears that stuck out.

A moment passed then the boy asked, "You coming in or what? It's freezing out here."

"M... Mick?" she stammered, digging his name up from somewhere in her memory.

"Yeah. Me, Mick. You, Asha. Me, cold. You, cold?" he said, pointing his finger alternatively between the two of them.

She stepped past him into the entry. He slammed the door behind her.

"First day and already you want to pitch yourself from the roof. That's got to be a record," he said, rubbing his hands to warm himself up.

"What? No, I just... " Asha blurted. "... got lost," she finished, turning away from him and wiping the tears from her cheeks.

"Right," he said, doubtful, before walking down the stairs. "Well, we should get down to the main floor before they lock us up here."

"Would they do that?" Asha asked, following him.

"Maybe," he replied, shrugging his shoulders.

He led her down the stairs to the elevator where he pushed the button to signal the elevator.

"I thought I was going to be up there forever. How did you find me?"

"I was following Keri and her brood and Trevor and Andrew out the door as we were leaving — "

"They were leaving?" Asha demanded.

"Yeah," Mick replied, giving her a cautious look. "They were leaving and I was behind them, keeping a safe distance, you know. I couldn't hear everything they were saying, but they were laughing and I heard one of them say 'skating rink.' So I decided to turn back and see if I could help the poor schmuck they had pranked this time." He looked over at her and then hastily added, "No offence."

Heat rose in Asha's cheeks. "What do you mean 'pranked'?"

"They try to get someone new whenever they come in. They tell them there's something fun on the roof then lock them out. Mostly tell them there's a pool up there. Skating rink's a new one but it is winter so I checked."

Asha asked, "So you're saying there's no skating rink?"

"Nope."

The elevator doors opened and the pair stepped in. "Main floor, you rusty scrap heap," he said to the console. It beeped an acknowledgment and the elevator began to move.

"Why didn't that code Keri gave me let me in. It let me outside."

"One code lets you out. Another lets you in. Kind of a security feature."

"Why do they let kids have those codes? It's dangerous up there."

"They don't let us have those codes!" he exclaimed. "That'd be a crack of lawsuits waiting to happen. Bunch of kids running around on the roof. No you have to be real clever to even get the code to get outside. Getting the code to get in is nearly impossible."

"Then how did Keri get the code to get out there?"

Mick chuckled. "She's Keri Shaw," he said sagely.

"You let me in. How'd you get the code?"

Mick gave her a sly grin. "I'm Mick Gallows. I'm the man."

The elevator continued down while they stood in silence. Asha stared at a crack in the wall, a nasty feeling creeping through her. Keri had played a joke on her. That wasn't so bad, though. She thought she was going to freeze up there but she hadn't. And so what if Mick saw Keri and the others leaving? They were probably coming back. They'd get up there and open the door and she wouldn't be there and they'd wonder how she got out -

"Asha," Mick startled her out of her daydream. "I know it's none of my business, but… "He hesitated, his face grim. "Look, I know you might want to fit in here — it's tough being the new kid — but honestly, I'd stay away from them if I were you."

"It was just a joke," Asha said, defensive.

"No, they're not good people."

Asha swallowed hard and looked away from him.

The elevator stopped and the doors opened. Mick let her exit first then he followed.

"Later," he said, then turned and walked away.

Asha watched him leave then slowly made her way to the main entrance and out a set of double doors, preoccupied by what Mick had said. Mostly everyone had left, but there were still a few cars, probably teachers', a truck, and a red van. Asha gave a start. It was her dad's van; she'd forgotten all about him picking her up.

She rushed through the blinding snow, ducking her head against the wind gusts, tore open the door and slammed it shut again when she got in.

"You're late," her dad said.

"Yeah, I kind of got lost," she mumbled.

"Your eyes are red," he said, tilting his head to one side.

"Snow blew into them," she answered, turning away from him.

After a moment he pulled the van into the lane and they began to drive.

"How was your day?"

"Fine," Asha replied, not really wanting to talk.

"How's the school?"

"Fine," she said through tight lips.

"And how's — "

"Dad, I'm fine! Leave me alone!" she snapped.

His face grew stern, but he simply nodded and focused on the road ahead.

They drove home in silence.

2
ATHENA

Three figures gathered around an old oil drum, burning whatever wood they could to keep warm, not that it would do them much good. At some point the location had been a vehicle storage facility; a number of old, broken down vehicles and construction machines littered the place. The warehouse was in such poor condition that the cold winter wind could blow in through any number of broken windows or doors. Of the three men now gathered around the fire only the largest didn't seem to feel the cold. The other two, one short, the other taller, shivered.

"Fifty?" the large man's voice roared throughout the building "What? Did you hit an old lady at an ATM?"

He was an extremely large, hulk of a man, wearing a black t-shirt over his heavily muscled upper body.

"C'mon, Toro!" the short man said. "It's too cold out!"

"It's not cold, Finch. You're weak," Toro growled, grinding his teeth. He pointed at the taller of the two men and said. "What's your excuse, Hitch?"

"Give us a break," Hitch said, rubbing his hands along his arms to keep warm.

"Yeah," Finch agreed. "I mean, we took down Captain Stoneman. We shouldn't have to do this."

The warehouse grew deathly silent. Toro seemed to grow taller, his eyes glowed a fierce cold blue. His bald head glinted in the firelight.

"We?" he asked coldly. "Who took out Captain Stoneman?" he demanded, his hands clenched into massive fists.

"Just chill, man," Finch said, slowly drawing back.

"Did you take him out?" Toro asked, poking him in the forehead with his finger.

"Did you take him out?" he asked, poking Finch in the chest.

"WHO TOOK OUT CAPTAIN STONEMAN?" he roared, knocking aside the oil drum like it was a pop can. The fire spilled out onto the ground but was quickly extinguished by the drifting snow. "I TOOK HIM OUT! NOT YOU! ME!"

"And what a good job you did," a soft voice called from the shadows.

The trio spun around to see the tall, slim figure of a woman emerging from the darkness. She wore a red bodysuit and had long, full red hair to match. The snow about her feet seemed to melt with each step. "Don't worry," she continued, gliding up closely to Toro and looking up into his massive face. "I don't bite, big guy."

"Toro" he growled.

"Toro," she corrected herself.

"Hey, you can't come in here! This is private property!" Hitch hollered.

"Shut up," Toro rumbled, looking over his shoulder at him. He turned back to the woman. "What do you want?"

"I'm surprised," the woman said. "I thought the man who killed Captain Stoneman would be doing much better. I mean look at this place."

Toro straightened his back, pushing his chest out.

"Let me guess," the woman continued. "You took down Captain Stoneman, the police's pet lapdog, and you expected... what? Parades, gifts from thankful admirers, rainbows, and puppies?

"No. It wasn't like that at all. The police hunted you. They found you wherever you hid: in bars, in houses, in places like this. And each time they did, they took one of your own with them. It must make you furious."

Toro stepped closer to her; what she said had struck a nerve because his jaw was clenched, his eyes blazing. He reached out toward her with his massive arms.

"Wait," the woman said, holding up her hands defensively. "I want to sign up."

"Get lost! We don't need you!" Finch exclaimed.

"Shut up!" Toro yelled at the man. He moved closer to the woman, looming over her, and rumbled, "I don't need you."

"Oh, I'm sure I could be of use," she said coyly, tapping her forefinger lightly on his nose. "Besides," she said, turning away from him and walking about the area, "this place looks like it could use a woman's touch. I'm thinking some flowers, a few scented candles... " She ran her finger over the burnt-out shell of a car, turning her lip up with disgust at the oil left on her finger. "... a flamethrower," she added under her breath.

"I get it, you know," she said. "I get trying to survive and having people like the police, like Captain Stoneman, try to bring you down. I get doing what it takes to make it through. I get wanting to show them, all of them. I can help you. We can help each other."

"Get out. Now," Toro said with a harsh finality.

"Fine," she replied airily, walking away. "I was looking for some real men. Men who were willing to take this city for their own. I guess I'll just have to join the Crypt when they get here."

"The Crypt is coming?" Toro asked.

"Oh, yes," she said. "I hear they're ready to take down this city. I have a plan to help them do it."

"She's lying, man," Hitch warned.

Toro and the woman regarded each other for a long time; his cold eyes boring into her own intense green ones. The Crypt was the deadliest criminal organization in the world; they were ruthless, violent, willing to do anything to get their way, even if that meant stomping out competition like Toro and his little gang.

"Ok," he said.

He looked at the other two men daring them to challenge him; neither did.

"I'm Toro," he said, jabbing a thumb at his chest.

"Athena," she said.

"You sign up, there's only one rule. I'm the boss."

Although Athena gave a simple nod, although something in her eyes said she had other ideas.

"Tell me the plan."

"Come a little closer, boys," she whispered, giving them a sly look. "You're going to love this."

3
THE SECOND DAY

The next morning Asha awoke to the soft buzzing of her alarm. She groped around for the snooze button, finally catching it after knocking her glasses to the floor. Glancing out her bedroom window Asha could see the sky was just beginning to lighten beneath a blanket of grey clouds. It looked like it was going to be another gloomy day.

She sat up slowly and brushed her hair out of her eyes. Her room was a total mess, as usual. Her clothes were strewn about the floor; empty water bottles dotted the room; school notes littered the floor even though she had just started yesterday. It hadn't always been like this. In her old house, her room used to be clean: all her clothes neatly folded and tucked away, bottles in the recycling bin, notes from school filed. But then everything changed and now she was stuck in this apartment.

She dragged her blankets off and planted her feet on the only bare patch of carpet she could find. Scanning the floor she found a clean-looking shirt and gave it a sniff. It didn't seem too bad, she supposed, throwing it on and putting on a pair of jeans. She picked up her glasses off the floor and caught a glimpse of the picture on her dresser. It was the picture of her family; her mom and dad and her at the park. They were smiling, blissfully unaware of what was going to happen only a few months later. Asha turned away and left the room.

She walked down the hall, past her dad's bedroom door, which always seemed to be shut now; past the bathroom which always seemed spotless, and into the dull, pale light of the kitchen. The apartment was empty. Her dad had left early, which meant that even though it was only her second day, he wouldn't be able to give her a ride to school. Instead, she would have to take the LR2.

She headed to the fridge and opened it only to close it a minute later, finding nothing she wanted. Instead she grabbed a breakfast bar from the cupboard and gathered up her things for the day. After throwing on a light hooded sweater she took one final look around the apartment, then turned and shut the door.

She walked down the two flights of stairs and into the gloom of winter. The previous day's wind and falling snow had stopped, leaving a fresh coat of white covering everything. She was grateful it wasn't cold today. In fact, if it wasn't for the clouds blocking the sun she would have said it was nice, even for winter.

The terminal stop for the LR2 was only a block away, she had memorized its location from a map. She reached it just as the silver, pill-shaped pod silently pulled up. She had expected a noise, like the rumble of a gas engine or an electrical hum, but there was nothing. The doors opened with a sharp hiss, each parting to the side, revealing a well-lit interior. Asha cautiously stepped inside.

With another hiss the doors closed behind her and the pod began to move, slowly at first, but it quickly picked up speed. Asha scurried for a seat opposite the door. Sitting on the cracked faux leather seat she couldn't help but notice the peeling paint on the walls and the fading graffiti on the backs of the seats. The floor, which could have at one time been polished metal, was now a scuffed and faded grey. The roof and walls curved in, along the top were advertisements. Some were still pictures — "KIRBY KOLA: TASTE THE JOY"; some were animated — "IT'S A BRAND NEW DAY" followed by a happy dancing sun and what looked like a bagel — but most were simply black and empty.

This pod, or car she guessed it would be called, was practically empty. At the back a lone man seemed to be sleeping, his head resting on the glass window beside him. Near the front, an older lady sat knitting, the steady click-clack of her needles piercing the silence of the car.

Asha turned her attention outside to the overcast and cloudy city. The faded tops of white buildings blurred past as the LR2 made its way along its course, following the twists and turns of the track. Every once in a while the car would pass a large, silver, cone shaped metal structure about the height of the train. A couple of times the LR2 joined up with other cars and then it left, heading down another curved track.

As the car came to a halt at the latest terminal, there was a short ding followed by the announcement "LR2 stop thirty-nine."

Asha stood on shaky legs and exited the double doors into a cool blast of winter wind. The LR2 car silently departed, leaving her alone on the sidewalk. Veda Zhi was South of here. She could see the top of its cone shape over the line of houses in front of her; she pushed down a flutter in her gut and walked to school.

The building was still huge, the windows still shone brightly against the dull morning, kids still swarmed the main doors. Reluctantly, she joined them as they flooded through the entrance. Students bustled about, oblivious to her and everything around them. She didn't have the slightest idea where she should be going. Lily said to meet at their lockers, but where were they?

She was thinking about heading over to the administration desk and asking for help when a high-pitched laugh caught her attention. She turned to see Keri Shaw surrounded by a bunch of kids, Chastity, Crystal, Trevor McKnight, and Andrew Hastings among them. Enraged, she stormed over to the group, knocking students aside.

Keri looked up and scoffed, "Enjoy the skating rink, Asha?"

Asha slammed her palms into Keri's chest, making her stumble backward into Chastity and Crystal.

"Ow! What's wrong with you?" Keri yelled.

"What's wrong with me?!" Asha screamed. "What's wrong with you?"

"Relax! What's the big deal?" Keri demanded, a scowl on her face. She was rubbing her chest where Asha pushed her.

"I could have died out there!"

"Don't be so dramatic. Obviously, you're fine."

"No thanks to you!"

"It was just a joke."

"A joke? I could have frozen up there! I could have — "

A jolt of white, hot pain tore through her body. She fell to the floor, unable to breath, her body wracked with tremors. The other kids stumbled backwards. Her back spasmed, her head cracked on the hard marble floor. She screwed her eyes shut trying to block out the pain. A wave of dizziness swept over her.

"What a freak," she distantly heard Keri say.

The pain was in her head; it was in her arms and legs and behind her eyes. Then everything went black.

*

"Asha," a voice called in her ear, a warm hand nudged her shoulder.

She slowly opened her eyes, everything was blurry.

"Are you hurt?" the voice asked.

Asha turned to her side to see Mrs. Burgess kneeling beside her. Lily was on the other side, one hand on Asha's shoulder, the other holding her glasses.

"I'm fine," Asha replied, sitting up. She took her glasses from Lily but didn't put them on. Keri and the rest of the students were gone.

"Can you stand?" Mrs. Burgess asked.

Asha nodded and then, trembling, got to her feet. Students passed by her giving her wary looks.

"How long was I out?"

"Only a few minutes," Lily said.

"I came over when I heard the screaming," Mrs. Burgess added.

"Screaming? Who was screaming?" Asha asked. She hadn't heard anyone, but she could imagine Keri freaking out.

"You were," she replied. "Don't you remember?"

"Me? No, I — "Asha stammered. She hadn't screamed, she couldn't have. She couldn't even breathe, how could she scream?

"It's okay," Mrs. Burgess said. "Your father told us all about your condition."

"Condition?" Lily asked, concerned.

"It's nothing," Asha mumbled.

"Let's go," Mrs. Burgess said, guiding Asha toward the administration desk.

"I'll come, too," Lily offered.

Asha looked at her, stunned. No one ever wanted to be around her after one of her "episodes."

"No, Lily. You can go to class and tell Ms. Lowen that Asha will be late," Mrs. Burgess said flatly, then took Asha's arm and guided her to the administration desk.

Asha was surprised to find that she was able to walk. Normally, after an attack she couldn't walk for an hour.

Mrs. Burgess led Asha through a door just beside the administration desk. Inside the room were four single cots along the far wall, each separated by white curtains. On the side closest to the door sat a simple desk. The light coming from the walls was a muted orange.

"Sit down on one of the cots and the nurse will be in to see you soon," Mrs. Burgess said and left the room.

Asha looked around with mild interest. Posters dotted the walls, one had a cartoon picture of a dazed germ wearing boxing gloves with the words "KNOCK OUT GERMS! WASH YOUR HANDS!" written below it; another with a big X through a cartoon picture of a tough-looking boy with rolled up sleeves and tight fists had text saying "STOP BULLYING NOW "; the oddest of the bunch, clearly not official, showed a stick figure of a bear tearing apart paper with its claws and big, thin letters that read "ONLY BEARS CAN STOP THE SPREAD OF POSTERS!" Besides that, the room was the same as all of the hospital rooms she'd been in before: clean, sterile, and depressing.

There was a sharp rap on the door; it opened and a tall man walked in the room. He smiled as he approached her.

"Asha? I'm Mr. Jones, the school nurse. How are you doing?" he asked.

"I'm fine," Asha said, avoiding his gaze.

He looked at her for a moment, then said, "Okay, give me your arm."

Asha held out her arm and he took her wrist, checking her pulse. Then he let go of her arm and shone his penlight into her eyes.

"Your dad told us about your condition," he said moving the light back and forth from eye to eye.

He turned off his penlight and began to write on the clipboard. He wrote for so long Asha began to feel self-conscious.

"So, do you do this full time?" she asked, trying to break the awkward silence.

"This, Linguistics, and Special Projects," he said without looking up.

"Linguistics? I know someone taking that," she said, her interest piqued.

"Yeah, who's that?"

"Lily Donovan. She's in my class. She's been showing me around."

"Lily? Good. She's pretty smart."

"What's 'Special Projects'?"

"Higher grades can sometimes do Special Projects. Things that aren't part of the standard curriculum. Some people choose to do advanced Calculus, computer projects are high on the list. I have one student who's studying EMPs," he said matter-of-factly. He must have seen the confused look on her face because he said, "EMP stands for Electromagnetic Pulse. It can disrupt the electrical signals in just about anything electronic hey, what the — " he exclaimed and stood up.

Asha started, thinking she had done something wrong, but Mr. Jones walked past her and grabbed the bear poster from the wall.

"That kid," he said shaking his head.

"Who?"

"Mick Gallows. He was in here yesterday. I didn't see this one."

"Mick was here yesterday?" she asked, surprised.

"Yeah, he's in here all the time. That kid could support the entire medical industry by himself," he joked. He put the poster on his clipboard and walked back to Asha. "I think you'll be all right. First few days are always the worst."

"First few days of what?"

"The first few days in a new school can be pretty rough. New teachers. New friends. It'll take some time. Just sit here for a while and take it easy. No need to head back to class right away. Do you want me to call your dad?"

Asha shook her head. There was nothing he could do right now; she would have to tell him tonight.

Mr. Jones nodded and headed to the door.

"How long can I stay here?"

"As long as you want," he said with a smile. Then he opened the door and left.

Asha didn't intend to stay very long at all. She would wait for a few more minutes and then she would leave.

She stayed until noon.

*

When Asha finally managed to pluck up her courage and leave she was stunned by the swarm of students milling about the hallway. She looked up at the clock, surprised to see it was lunchtime.

"Asha!" a loud voice called and she turned to see Lily hustling to meet her. Some of the kids looked around at her, whispering to each other.

"Hey, how are you?" Lily asked as she approached.

"Fine."

"I'm really sorry."

Asha was taken aback. "What for?"

"I heard what Keri and the others did yesterday. I shouldn't have left you alone."

"It's not your fault. I was the one stupid enough to believe there was a skating rink on the roof."

"Still, I could have waited a bit," Lily said, almost pleading.

"Look, forget it. I'm fine. Really."

"What are you doing for lunch? Do you want to go to the cafeteria?"

"I'm not really hungry," Asha said. Truthfully, she wasn't sure she could keep anything down. Her stomach felt queasy and her arms were still a bit sore from the attack.

"Yeah, me neither," Lily agreed. Then her face lit up and she said, "Hey, do you want to go up to Market Street?"

"What's that?"

"It's only a few blocks away, where most of the stores and shops in this area are."

"Are we allowed to?"

"Sure. We can go if we want."

Asha agreed, if only to get out of the school and away from the judging eyes of the other students.

The pair walked slowly down the sidewalk, passing stores whose doors had been shut against the cold and howling wind. Lily had bundled herself in winter coat while Asha had flipped the hood of her sweater up over her head. All around them people hustled in and out of stores carrying bags and parcels; many ran to their vehicles and hurriedly unplugged cords from vertical, metal pillars. Asha guessed that these were charging stations for the electric vehicles. Despite the winter weather the street seemed alive with activity.

"I met Mr. Jones, today," Asha said.

"Oh, really? I have Linguistics with him. What did you think of him?"

"He's pretty cool. He said you were really smart," Asha replied. Lily blushed which made Asha smile.

They were passing an electronics shop when something caught her eye; the store window was covered in video screens of a person she knew all too well. The imposing figure of Captain Stoneman repeated over and over across the face of the store; his navy blue armour covered his entire body except for the steel silver gauntlets over his hands and his steel jet boots. His helmet covered his entire head leaving only glass slits for his eyes. When she had last seen him all those months ago he hadn't been wearing it.

On one screen he was surrounded by fellow police officers, none of them wore a fancy suit like his. He gestured forcefully at a device in his hand, then pointed to the building behind him. Asha guessed this was one of the many times he led the police on a raid or some such thing. Another screen showed him sitting on a set of stone steps, surrounded by dozens of children, all smiling and waving. Seeing him displayed here like this made her feel sick.

"He was part of a police research program," Lily said. "They decided they needed a better police force, to keep up with the changes in the city. So they invested heavily into new technology and training. It took a few years, but they finally came up that suit; he volunteered, of course. He served this city well for years; I think everybody looked up to him. It was a shame he died the way he did."

"Yeah," Asha replied through a clenched jaw. An image of navy blue flashed in her mind followed by a brief sense of fire.

The display before her wavered, then every picture of him spun to reveal the words "THE MEGA SALE".

Asha turned and walked away.

"You got ice water in your veins?" Lily demanded.

"What?" Asha asked, alarmed.

"I'm freezing here and you're dressed up like it's spring."

"It's not that cold out."

"Never mind." Lily shivered again and turned to look into the window of a clothing shop called La Rez. "Hey, look at this!" she exclaimed, pointing at the window.

Displayed at the front of the window, a pair of jeans suspended in mid-air, spinning lazily. The shimmering silver shape of a dragon appeared on the calf; it was serpent-like, its long body stretching from the front of the leg to the back. It twitched and then slithered around the leg, up and around the backside and down the other, stopping on the other calf.

"Oooo!" the girls exclaimed, watching the dragon zip back to the other leg again.

"Go try them on," Lily said, nudging Asha.

"You go try them on!"

"Me? C'mon! You'd look totally hot in them!"

"Could you imagine what everyone would think?" Asha wondered aloud, imagining walking down the hall of the school, heads turning as she passed by, the dragon zipping around her waist or disappearing and then reappearing on her hip. She gazed at the jeans, following the dragon's path as it passed under a tag. Her heart fell when she saw the price.

"Five hundred?" Asha moaned. Asha knew her father could never afford the cost, especially for a pair of jeans.

"Wow," Lily whispered.

They watched the dragon zip around again before it morphed into a butterfly that flapped its wings and then settled on a knee.

"How do they do that?" Asha wondered.

"It's called NanOLED," Lily commented, pulling her coat tightly around herself. "Mom's doing something with them at work. See, they take these little robots — " Lily started to explain but Asha's didn't hear the rest.

It hadn't been that long ago when Asha's mother had taken her shopping on streets like this. She hadn't thought about it much, but now that Christmas was coming, she realized this would be the first Christmas without her mother. The joy at seeing the butterfly flit across the jeans dwindled. The day seemed darker.

"You okay?" Lily asked, concerned.

"What?" Asha asked, startled out of her thoughts.

"You've been staring off into space for a few minutes."

"I was just thinking about — "

"Keri and them?"

Asha had forgotten all about school and what the kids would be saying about her

"What am I going to do?" she whispered softly to herself.

"Don't worry," Lily said. "It'll be all right. Give it a few days and everyone will have forgotten all about it."

Asha wanted to believe her, but Lily was wrong. No one would forget.

"What happened, anyway?" Lily asked, then as if she had said something horrible, slapped her hand over her mouth and mumbled, "Sorry! You don't have to tell me."

"That's okay," Asha replied. She was going to have to explain it to someone sooner or later. "I got into an accident a while ago. Got electrocuted. It messed up my nervous system. It's part of the reason we moved here. No doctors in Faller to look after me."

"What happened?"

"Look, can we drop it? I really don't want to talk about it."

"Yeah, sorry."

"Why do you do that? Apologize when you ask me questions?"

"I don't!"

"You just did."

"I didn't mean anything by it!"

"By what?"

Lily gave a sigh. "Sometimes I ask too many questions. I think it's one of the reasons no one talks to me at the school. Except you, I mean. You're the first student I've had a real conversation with since I got here."

Asha felt a pang of sympathy for the girl. Asha had thought she would be more popular, especially considering how smart and outgoing she was.

"Just don't worry about it, okay? It takes more than a few questions to freak me out."

"Okay. What do you want to do now?"

Asha had no idea. All of her options seemed bleak.

"Maybe we should get back?" Lily suggested.

Asha merely shrugged her shoulders. She didn't want to go but what choice did she have?

Together, they walked back to Veda Zhi.

*

That evening, Asha and her father sat at opposite ends of the kitchen table eating supper. He sat as if in a trance, not taking his eyes off the centre of the table. Asha, on the other hand, repeatedly looked up. She had wanted to ask him the question that had burned in her since before she got home. Twice now she had opened her mouth to ask him, but each time nothing came out. She didn't know how to start, or what she would say once she had started. Finally, as he jabbed a snow pea with his fork, she tried again.

"I had another attack today," she said.

"What? When?"

"This morning at school."

"Are you okay?" he asked, his eyes narrowing.

"Yeah, it wasn't... " she hesitated, "It wasn't that bad."

"Dr. Singh said they still might happen once in awhile. We'll have to get another appointment. I'll set it up tomorrow."

"Yeah," she replied, looking down at the table.

For a moment she thought about not asking him the question, but then she remembered the look of concern on his face. Maybe he would say yes.

"Dad?"

"Yes," he answered. She looked up to see that he had not taken his eyes off her and felt a quick surge of hope.

"Can I have some money?" she asked quietly.

"For what?"

"Some clothes," she muttered, dropping her eyes to the table again.

"What kind of clothes?"

"Some jeans."

"How much?"

"Five hundred," she mumbled. She knew he was going to say no. She knew it.

"Five hundred?" he asked. She looked up to see he was looking at her with his eyebrows raised. "For jeans."

"Yeah," she replied slowly.

"Ash," he moaned, unfolding his hands and leaning back in his chair.

Now she knew he wasn't going to say yes. Normally she would just let it go but this time was different. He needed to understand what they could do.

"No, you don't get it. These are so awesome. They have this dragon that zips around the calf and... "

"Ash... "

"... up the leg and down again and it turns into whatever — whatever — you want them to like birds or ...

"Ash... "

"... a butterfly. Lily says it's Nanoids like her mom's working on — "

"Asha," he said, cutting her off. "We can't afford that."

"But... "

"No." he snapped. He sighed, closed his eyes, and then opened them and looked at her again. "We just can't do it. I'm sorry,"

Asha slumped back in her chair, crossing her arms over her chest.

"Mom would let me," she spat before even realizing she was going to say it.

"That's enough," he warned.

"She would!"

Ignoring her, he stood up and took his dishes to the sink.

"This sucks!" she screamed, leaping out of her chair, knocking it over. She stormed down the hallway to her bedroom and slammed the door.

Why didn't he get it? Why couldn't he understand that if she just got those jeans, things would be better? Maybe not perfect, but at least she would have something special. She wouldn't be a freak anymore.

She fell into her bed, burying her face in her pillow, angry and hurt. Things couldn't get any worse.

5
ONE FINE DAY

The next day Asha left the doctor's office dejected. Dr. Singh was the only specialist in the entire city who could help her and he had just given her the bad news.

It was not what she had been hoping to hear.

She moved along the sidewalk, hunched over and head down, stopping in front of an electronics display store. The news brief on the screens only made her feel worse.

"Prisoners have escaped from VOC," the newscaster said.

VOC, the Violent Offenders Centre, housed the some of the most vicious criminals from the entire country. The prison was located at the northern tip of the city, in the centre of the river that cut the city in two. The prison was surrounded by guards, weapons, and state-of-the-art security systems.

"The breakout happened early this morning and while police have yet to confirm any details, sources at the prison say that the attackers used high-powered weapons to blast into the building. Many of the escaped prisoners have been directly linked to the murder of Captain Stoneman.

"A group calling themselves The Dragon has claimed

39

responsibility for the attack and released the following statement to all media news outlets... "

There was a pause from the announcer. Then the screen showed the black silhouette of a gothic looking dragon. A low, harsh voice tinged with a high rasp spoke.

"We are chaos. We are anarchy. We are The Dragon. VOC was the first. It will not be the last. We are in your offices, your schools, your homes. You will know fear. You will know despair. The police cannot protect you. Your heroes are gone. You are alone."

*

At school, it was all everyone talked about. At every turn Asha saw pictures of the escaped criminals, always followed by the same questions: How had it happened? Was anyone hurt? Where were they now?

She and Lily were walking down the hall when they heard a scream. Together, they rushed ahead to find a group of students surrounding a set of lockers. Through a gap in the crowd Asha saw Keri Shaw flapping her hands frantically.

"Who did this?" she screamed.

Someone, in pitch black paint, had sprayed The Dragon symbol on her locker.

"Let's go," Lily said, dragging Asha by the arm. "Knowing her she'll probably blame it on you."

"How could they get into the school to do that?" Asha asked. "Isn't there security."

"Loads," Lily said. "Cameras, alarms, the works."

Based on the look of Keri's locker, Asha was starting to doubt that.

*

"I'm sure they'll catch whoever did it," Lily said.

The pair were standing outside the school, waiting to go home.

Asha wasn't sure Lily was right. An uneasiness had come over her since she had first seen the picture of the bald man. He had been the one strangling Captain Stoneman on the day her mother died. It was their fight that had started the fire in the first place.

"Make way! Comin' through!" a voice yelled from behind the pair.

They turned to see Mick Gallows sprinting toward them, a plastic bottle splashing his hands with purple juice. Behind him chased Andrew Hastings followed closely by Trevor McKnight; he had a large purple splotch on his jacket.

Mick zipped past Asha and Lily and then wove between the waiting cars. Trevor and Andrew rushed after him, slamming into Lily, not even slowing down.

"Watch it!" Lily screamed, stumbling backwards. Asha shot out her hand and grabbed Lily's arm before she fell back. "Thanks," she said when Asha had pulled her upright.

"What was that all about?" Asha asked, although she could guess.

"Mick likes to get into it with them," Lily replied shaking her head. "He just doesn't learn."

The pair watched until they couldn't see the boys anymore and then started walking again.

Lily kept giving Asha little glances. Every few steps she would look at Asha then quickly look at her feet.

"What? What's wrong?" Asha asked.

"Well... it's just... " Lily stammered. "Do you want to come over for supper tonight?"

Asha looked at her, shocked. It had been so long that anyone had asked her to go anywhere that she thought she had misheard.

"You don't have to come if you don't want to," Lily added hastily.

"No! I mean yes! No, I can come. My dad's working late anyway."

"Really?" Lily asked, her face lighting up. "You don't have to... "

"I want to. I can't wait to meet your parents."

Lily's face grew dark for a moment then she said, "Well, it's just me and Mom right now, but she makes the most awesome pizza in the world. You'll love it. There she is now."

Asha looked up to see a slight woman waving out the door of a blue car. Lily's mom was small, smaller even than Asha.

"Hey, Mom," Lily said as they approached the car. "This is Asha Anderson."

"Asha," Lily's mother said, shaking Asha's hand through the open window. "Lily's told me about you."

"Hi, Mrs. Donovan," Asha said.

"It's just Eva," Lily's mom replied.

"Uh, Mom," Lily said. "Can Asha come over for supper tonight?"

A frown appeared the woman's face and Asha knew it had been too good to be true. Lily's mom knew about her "condition" and didn't want her around. No one ever did.

"No, we can't," Lily's mom replied. "We have to eat at the lab tonight. I've got some more work to do still."

"But tonight's pizza night," Lily whined.

"I know. We'll have to order in," she answered. "And you know how they are about security. I'm lucky to be able to have you there at all."

Lily turned to Asha and gave her a sorrowful look. "I'm so sorry, Asha. I really wanted you to come over."

"It's okay," Asha replied.

"Can we give you a ride?" Lily's mother asked.

"Where's your lab?" Asha asked.

"It's by the Hydro Plant on the south side," Lily answered.

Her dad worked at that Hydro Plant. He was there right now.

Asha took a step back. "That's okay. I can take the LR2 back home."

"You sure?" Lily asked, opening the passenger side door.

"Yeah, I'm good," Asha said, waving a hand in front of her.

"I'm really sorry," Lily called as she got into the car. "I'll see you tomorrow then."

She slumped in the car and then the pair drove off, leaving Asha by herself.

Asha stood alone for a moment then walked downtown, in no hurry to get home.

While it seemed everyone else rushed about huddled against the brisk winter wind, Asha was comfortable in her sweater, with the hood up. Just then a rush of wind kicked up a blast of snow, slamming it into her face. She sputtered and coughed, ducking her head against the gust. Once the wind died down, she found herself looking into the window of La Rez once again.

The jeans were still there, this time instead of a dragon there was a dove, fluttering its wings as it flew about the legs. She stared at it, mesmerized by its grace. She knew it wasn't real, that it was simply a bunch of Nano-thingies running about, but it was beautiful nonetheless.

"Hey, Twitch!" a high voice trilled from behind her. Asha turned to see Keri, Crystal and Chastity coming up behind her. "Looking for some clothes without holes in them?" Keri taunted, stopping a few feet from her. The other two girls giggled, covering their mouths with their gloved hands.

"What did you call me?" Asha asked, coldly.

"Twitch," Keri sneered. "That's your new name."

"What do you want?" Asha demanded, gritting her teeth.

"Nothing," Keri remarked, turning her back on Asha to look at the store window. "I was just wondering what the world's biggest loser was up to. Nice jeans." She was eying the jeans in the window with a unmistakable greed. "Pretty cheap, too," she added with a smug look over her shoulder.

Asha clenched her fists in her pockets. She could feel a thudding in her temples, her cheeks boiling despite the chill. She turned around to walk away.

"Aww," Keri sneered. "Gonna go home and cry to Mommy?"

The other two girls gasped gleefully.

Asha swung around to face them, eyes blazing and her heartbeat thundering in her head. Without warning, a sharp jolt of pain tore through her arm making it shoot to the side. The gloomy day got so bright she had to squint. Then the three girls before her froze, Keri's next words forming on her lips. Even the fur lining the hood of Crystal's jacket stood still.

Asha was forced to the ground by a blast of air as if a giant hand had pushed her down. She had only a moment to think that Keri's boots were awfully shiny before a violent explosion rocked the street. The other three girls screamed as the blast shattered the windows of the shop, showering them with glass. Red flames leaped up, licking at the cars that lined the street.

"Hey, kids!" a voice called from overhead.

Asha rolled over to see a man with long blond hair hovering mere feet above her, supported by what looked like Captain Stoneman's firing jet boots. She knew that she should run, but she was unable to move or even breathe. A shrill scream rose up from behind her immediately followed by two more equally shrill screams.

"What's that?" the man yelled. "I can't hear you, the jets are too loud!"

Keri, Crystal, and Chastity pressed themselves up against the wall of the store; the flame from the cars glowing against their skin. Keri and Chastity screamed then ran. Crystal tried to follow but slipped on a patch of ice. Her feet slid until she caught the dry pavement again and then she was off. Soon all three were out of sight.

The blonde haired man turned his evil grin on Asha.

"No!" she yelled, scrambling to her feet.

Asha turned and ran.

"You're a quick one!" the man called after her. "Well, I can be quick too!"

A loud blast thundered behind her. Asha turned her head, not daring to stop running, only to see him barreling toward her, his boots propelling him down the flaming sidewalk.

She darted down an alley, her heartbeat pounding in her head and the bright light of the world boring into her eyes. She took a left down another alley and a right, but still she could hear him chasing her. She pushed harder, running around a corner into another alley. Her foot caught on the ground and she slammed face first into the pavement. She had only a moment to wonder that her glasses hadn't fallen off before a rush of air and heat pressed behind her. She rolled onto her back to see the man in the jet boots suspended high off the ground, his hair blowing wildly about him.

"Well, that was fun," he laughed. "Pointless, but fun!"

"Get away!" she yelled, scuttling back.

Her whole body pulsed with the beat of her heart, its thumping driving in her legs and arms. She reached around with trembling fingers for something — anything — the touch of the snow like a thousand electric shocks. She groped feverishly, moving her hand to the left, to the right, to the — her hand hit something!

A garbage can lid, she thought grabbing its rounded edge.

"LEAVE ME ALONE!" she screamed.

For a moment he froze as if commanded then she hurled the lid at him with all her strength. It slammed into his chest, driving him backward toward the building behind him. He crashed into the wall and hung for a moment as if on a hook. His jet boots stopped firing then he dropped to the ground and was still.

Asha sat on the ground, stunned. She saw something she didn't remember seeing before: a large circular hole in the ground, big enough to fit a person through.

She turned and looked at the man; his limp body had crumpled up motionless against the wall. The lid seemed to have hit him flat against his chest. Something was off about it, though. It was dark and rusted, not the silver color of trash cans she was used to. It was thicker than it should have been and it had holes in it, big enough to stick a bar or hook in. She looked between the hole and the lid. The hole was big enough for a grown man to fit in and the lid was big enough to cover the hole. The lid was big enough to cover —

Asha scrambled to her feet and fled the alley, leaving the man and the manhole cover behind.

6
THE MALL

A sharp whistle jolted Asha from her daze. She was in gym class, sitting on a bench beside Lily, while other students played a game of floor hockey. Mr. Tan, the gym teacher, who was about six feet tall, shaped like an upside down pear, kept his silver whistle clenched between his teeth. At the far end of the gym Keri, Chastity, and Crystal chatted quickly with a group of other students, Trevor and Andrew among them.

There had been another Dragon symbol sprayed on a locker when she arrived at the school that morning; Keri and her group were most certainly talking about it.

Asha hadn't slept last night at all. Every time she had closed her eyes images of the attack flashed in her mind; the pounding in her head, the man's clothes blowing from the gust of his — Captain Stoneman's — jet boots. Most of all she saw the disc shape of the manhole cover spinning through the air, driving into the man's chest and slamming him back into the wall.

Maybe something had blown the cover from the manhole; gas pressure or something. But she had thrown *something*. Surely she couldn't do that with a manhole cover. Those things were so heavy even her dad would have had a hard time moving one, let alone throwing it.

What was happening to her?

"Sorry about yesterday," Lily said.

"What about it?" Asha snapped.

"Uh... about inviting you over and then bailing... "

"Oh, that!" Asha exclaimed, relieved. "No, it's fine."

"Did you hear about the bombing?"

Asha stiffened.

"No," she lied.

"There was a bombing downtown just after we left. It took out cars, stores, everything. The Dragon has already claimed they did it. Heard it on the news. You're lucky you weren't anywhere near there."

"Yeah, lucky."

"Anderson! Donovan!" Mr. Tan hollered. "You're up!"

Asha looked at Lily, who gave her a shrug. She heaved a heavy sigh, grabbed her yellow plastic hockey stick, and stepped onto the court. Keri, Trevor, and Andrew stepped onto the court as well. Keri whispered something to the two boys and they both grinned.

"Keep an eye on them," Lily warned.

Mr. Tan blew his whistle again and before Asha knew it the bright yellow ball had zoomed past her head and the game began. The play was fast and furious; Asha liked it. She ran and hit the ball, sending it flying whenever she got the chance. Kids bumped into her and she shoved back. She caught an elbow in her stomach and a shoulder knocked against her chin; she kept going.

Someone drove an elbow into her gut and when she looked up she found Lily standing off to the side, the ball resting against her foot.

"Hey, Lily!" Keri yelled from beside her.

Lily turned her head and everything slowed. Asha watched, helpless, as Andrew, who was a few steps from Lily, lunged out with his stick, striking the front of Lily's legs. Then she saw Trevor come up behind her, dip his shoulder down and drive into her back. Lily, who couldn't have seen him coming, tripped over Andrew's stick and crashed down, smacking her head on the floor. A chorus of cheers and hoots erupted from the rest of the class as Trevor took control of the ball and rushed to the other end of the gym, Keri and Andrew leading the way.

Later, Asha wouldn't be able to explain it. She wouldn't be able to explain the fire in her muscles, how her breathing slowed and her heartbeat hammered in her head. All she could see were the three kids hurrying down the court, grinning like crazed monkeys.

Asha sprinted after them, driving her legs hard. She closed in on them, her vision focused on Trevor's back. When she was barely a few steps away, when she could smell his sweat and hear the deep heaving of his breath, she gripped her plastic hockey stick with both hands and drove it cross ways into his back. He flew forward, knocking Keri to the ground. He stumbled and clipped Andrew's feet with his own and they both fell to the floor with a crash.

The shrill sound of a whistle caught her by surprise and Asha looked around. The entire class had frozen; everyone was looking at her.

"Anderson!" Mr. Tan shouted, stomping toward her. "What are you doing?"

Asha shrunk back as he approached.

"What was that?" the teacher demanded, pointing at the heap of bodies on the floor beside her. Keri and Andrew struggled to stand. Trevor sat on the floor rubbing his back.

"They... I... " Asha stammered. She didn't understand what he was talking about. Why was everyone staring?

"Get out," he commanded, pointing this time at the change room door.

"But they... " Asha started.

He couldn't be mad at her after what they had done to Lily. He couldn't. Everyone had seen it; they had laughed.

"Go!" he yelled, jabbing his finger toward the door again.

For a moment Asha stood and looked around at everyone. They all stared at her, some with wide eyes, others with suspicious glares. Asha gave one final look into Mr. Tan's enraged face.

"Fine!" she yelled.

She threw down her plastic hockey stick and stomped away to the change room trailed by the wild laughter of Mick Gallows seated on the bench at the other end of the court.

*

"That lump on your head is getting better," Asha said to Lily

They were at the South Common Mall; not the biggest or best

mall in the city, but it had a nice food court and some of her favourite stores. People milled about, moving in and out of stores in a slow but constant stream. An RC bot zipped between tables, collecting trash.

"Yeah, I keep putting ice on it," Lily replied.

She was eating sushi — or sashimi as Lily had corrected her — which Asha swore she'd never eat based on the fact that it was raw fish. "Mom's been saying she'll have the lab guys give me a CAT scan if it doesn't go away soon."

Asha took a drink of her pop then asked, "And they do this at your mom's lab?"

"Well, HAAS — that's where my Mom works — they do a lot of research. I don't think they'd really put me in one of those, though. Did you have a CAT scan when they were trying to figure out your, you know, condition?"

"They might have. I can't remember."

Asha didn't like to talk about that time in the hospital. Every time she did she got a serious pain in her stomach and her mind went all fuzzy.

"Why did you hit Trevor?" Lily asked.

"He just made me so angry. I'm kind of sorry I did that though."

She wished she could tell Lily what was happening to her. Lily was the smartest person she knew and probably the only person who could help her find answers.

"Why would you be sorry? They deserved it."

"I guess… "

"Is it really bad?"

"What?" Asha asked, confused.

"The lump."

"Oh, the lump. No you're fine."

"Good. On a side note I've figured out who's spraying those Dragon symbols at the school."

"Really? Who?"

"It's Mick Gallows."

"What? That's crazy."

"Just hear me out. The Dragon said they were in our schools. I think they might have students working for them. I read that certain types of kids are drawn to violent gangs like this. They're usually poor, not very intelligent, don't have many friends, and are often bullied. He fits the profile."

Asha didn't want to point out that she, Asha, fit the profile as well.

"Plus, did you see how he was laughing at the end of gym class? He seems unstable."

Lily finished her meal and the pair stood up.

Could Lily be right? It would make sense that he could be the one doing it. If it was him, what could they do about it?

"We should keep an eye on him."

"Are you — "

Asha was knocked from behind and stumbled into Lily, her tray dropped to the floor with a crash. She turned around, ready to confront whoever had run her over, only to find Mick Gallows.

"Sorry ladies!" he apologized. "I was trying to get away from — oh wow! What happened to you?" he asked, pointing at the red lump on Lily's forehead.

"Get lost, Mick," Lily said, glaring.

"Geez, did you know you have a giant zit on your forehead? 'Cause you do,"

"It's not a zit!" Lily exclaimed, turning away from him. "I hit my head in gym class."

"What? When?"

"When Trevor knocked me down. Remember?"

"That was two days ago."

"So?"

"Shouldn't it have shown up before now?"

"It did, I've just been hiding it."

"Behind what, the space station? It's huge!"

"It's not huge! Asha, tell him it's not huge!" Lily cried, rounding on Asha.

To tell the truth, Asha thought it was huge, but wasn't about to tell Lily.

"Nice check, by the way, Asha," Mick said. "Did you see the look on Keri's face when Trevor crashed into her? I wish I had a camera!"

"It's not funny," Lily said.

"Why? You didn't get in trouble did you, Asha? That check was so epic."

Asha was embarrassed to even think about what she'd done; she ducked down to pick up Lily's tray.

"Did you guys hear? They caught the guy who bombed the downtown, just a while ago. Some guy with jet boots," Mick said, excited.

Asha's hand paused, gripping the tray. The man was in jail? Did he say anything about her? About what she had — a white hot pain shot through her arm. It twitched, the tray went flying and Asha dropped to her hands and knees, gasping in agony. Then the food court lit up.

Not again, Asha thought. Not —

An explosion knocked her over with a thunderous boom, slamming her to the floor from the force of it, the air nearly knocked out of her lungs. Pieces of the walls and ceiling rained down, showering her with debris.

A high-pitched ring sounded in her ear. Flames grew around her, licking at her arms and legs. The high pitched ring rose higher and higher. Then Asha understood what it was: people were screaming. She jumped to her feet, coughing out dust.

The place was in chaos; tables were overturned, pillars were knocked down, chunks of the floor were demolished, and everywhere she looked there was fire.

"Take everything!" a loud, rumbling voice commanded.

Asha spun around to see four men not more than fifty feet away, a giant hole blown out of the wall behind them. Dark, black dragon tattoos covered their faces. Two of the men waved guns in front of them daring anyone to move, one carried a humongous gun; the last had what looked like metal arms. She recognized him immediately; he didn't have metal arms at the time but it was definitely him: the man who had killed Captain Stoneman. And killed her mother.

Someone moaned and Asha turned to find Lily and Mick on the floor covered in chunks of plaster and dust. Lily was curled up and crying, arms above her head; Mick was moaning, holding his forehead in his hands, blood pouring between his fingers.

Once again something switched in Asha; her breathing slowed, her eyes narrowed, and her heartbeat hammered in her head. She could feel the muscles tighten in her arms and legs, every part of her on fire. An image of her mother lunging into a blazing house flashed through her mind. Asha turned her glare on the man with the metal arms.

He picked up the RC bot and Asha ran; not away from the men

but toward them. She pumped her legs; once, twice, three times. The man cocked his arm back. The air whipped past her ears. He drew his arm back farther and then Asha was in front of him.

She threw up her hands, slamming them into his chest with all her strength. She felt his chest cave in around her hands then he flew back, crashing into the men behind him. They tumbled through the hole in the wall and into the parking lot beyond, slamming into the pavement, kicking up snow.

Asha didn't wait to see if they'd get back up; she turned and sprinted back to Lily and Mick, who were both still sitting dazed on the floor.

"Come on!" Asha ordered, grabbing each by the arm and dragging them to their feet.

"Agh!" Lily gasped, trying to stand. Her leg buckled and she fell. Asha reached down again, slipped her arm around Lily's waist, and hauled her up.

"Wha?" Mick mumbled.

His head lolled back and he began to topple over. Asha hooked her other arm under his armpits and started moving.

She led them down a hallway to the nearest exit, half dragging, half carrying them. She kicked open the exit door when she reached it, destroying the latch. People were streaming out of the building, screaming as they fled the fire and destruction. Moving quickly, she pulled the pair down the street.

She cut into an alley about a block from the mall and gently let Lily and Mick slide to the ground. Lily rubbed her ankle, hissing with each stroke. Mick sat slumped over; the gash in his head trickled blood down his face, his eyes unfocused.

Asha looked around the alley. It was dimmer now, the clouds obscuring the sun. The brightness just moments ago had faded to the dull grey of the overcast afternoon.

"You guys okay?" Asha asked, crouching in front of them.

Lily shook her head then looked up. Her eyes were red and her face was dirty with grime. "My ankle really hurts," she said, her breath hitching.

"Mick?" Asha asked.

He just sat, dazed. Asha snapped her fingers in front of his eyes. He blinked then lifted his head to look at her. "What?"

"Are you okay?"

He nodded slowly and reached for his forehead, wincing when

he touched the cut. Asha looked around for something to cover the wound with; nothing in the alley looked usable. She noticed a snag in the sleeve of her sweater just below her elbow; something had torn the fabric, although she couldn't remember what. She hooked her finger into the hole and ripped off the lower sleeve, bunching it up and pressing it against his forehead.

They sat for a few minutes, saying nothing. Alarms rang in the distance.

"We have to go," Asha said, standing up. "It's not safe."

"How did you do that?" Mick asked.

"What do you mean?" Asha asked, distracted. She kept looking down the alley expecting to see the attackers at any moment.

"Back there. Those guys."

"I... didn't... "

"I saw you!" he hissed, looking at her with searching eyes.

"I saw, too," Lily said quietly from beside her. She was looking at Asha cautiously.

"I don't know."

An explosion boomed from the direction of the mall making all three of them jump.

"Forget it, we have to go. Now!"

"Help me up," Lily said, holding her hands up.

Asha took them and pulled. Lily seemed heavier. When they were running, Asha thought she could have carried the other girl halfway across the city. Now, she could barely stop herself from falling over. Lily hopped on one foot trying to regain her balance. Steadying Lily with one hand she offered the other to Mick.

"Nah, I'm good," he said, waving her hand away.

He stood up, keeping Asha's sleeve pressed against his forehead. He staggered a bit when he tried to take a step forward and had to grab onto Asha for balance. She wrapped his arm over her shoulders then wrapped Lily's arm over the opposite way and began to guide them down the alley.

"Wait," Lily said. "I gotta call my mom." She reached into her pocket and pulled out a cracked and mashed cell phone. Lily let out a low moan. "She's gonna kill me. I guess I should go home."

"Sure," Asha replied. "Uhh... where do you live?"

"99 South Crescent," Lily replied through gritted teeth.

Asha halted. "South Crescent? That's where I live."

"No way," Lily said, bemused.

"Wait," Mick said, turning to look at the two girls. "You've been, like, hanging out for how long, and you don't know where either of you live?"

"Well, where do you live then?" Lily demanded.

Mick tilted his head back. "South Crescent," he sighed.

Asha and Lily looked at each other, then at Mick, then back to each other. Lily gave a small smirk and the pair burst out laughing. Then Mick started laughing. The three of them trembled together, too tired to stand, too scared to fall down.

Their laughter turned to giggles then finally hitched breaths.

"Come on," Asha said, guiding them down the alley.

*

The trip home on the LR2 was far less eventful and Asha was extremely thankful. She kept Lily distracted from her foot by pointing out the silver, cone shaped structures — "Power and communication distribution nodes, at least that's what my mom calls them," Lily had replied — and gently nudging Mick every time he closed his eyes. By the time the trio left the LR2 station and headed to Lily's house, the sky had already turned a dark grey.

"Where does a guy get metal arms?" Mick asked.

"It's an exoskeleton technology," Lily said. "Generally only used for people who need help moving their limbs. I've only seen basic prototypes. Those were awkward and cumbersome, but that guy's arms were smooth and polished, no sign of gears or electronics. I don't know of any company that makes ones like that."

Lily's home was a fairly large house; it had a main floor, second floor and a dual attached garage beside it. The path to the front door was shovelled down to the cement. Asha couldn't tell if Lily's mom was at home, but she thought not; most of the time Lily's mom worked late.

Asha helped Lily to the front door and was surprised when Lily simply turned the handle and hopped in. The entry lights blinked on when Lily crossed the threshold.

"No lock?" Asha asked.

"The door recognizes me," Lily said through clenched teeth as she gingerly sat down on a bench by the door. "Disarms the system as I approach."

"Yeah, you don't got one? All the cool kids do these days,"

Mick said from behind.

Asha turned to reply that no, she didn't have one, when she saw his pale, white face. The gash on his forehead had stopped bleeding, but he still had blood all over him.

"How are you doing, Mick?" Asha asked, concerned.

"Fine," he said. "Except for this gaping hole in the middle of my head."

"You're not going to fall over are you?"

"If I do will you catch me?" he asked, winking.

Asha gave a short laugh then turned back to Lily.

"How about you?"

"I'll be fine," Lily replied. "As long as I don't try to go upstairs."

Asha looked around Lily's house though she couldn't see much, just stairs leading to the second floor, a large living room, and a kitchen. The place was spotless, nothing was out of place, no pictures on the wall were crooked, even the doormat, dirty in most homes, was completely clean.

A phone rang.

"Can you grab that, Asha?" Lily asked. "The handset is on the counter in the kitchen."

Asha took off her shoes and followed the sound of the ringing into the kitchen. She grabbed the phone and brought it back to Lily.

"Hi, Mom," Lily said, answering the call. "Yeah, I know. I just got back... .Well, my cell kinda broke... . There was an attack at the mall... .Yeah, no, I'm fine, my ankle hurts, I can't walk on it... Asha's here, I took the LR2 with her... Yeah, I'm okay... Are you coming home soon?... The hospital? Maybe, I don't know... Okay... . I love you, too. Bye."

Lily pressed a button on the phone and looked up at Asha, "She's coming right away."

"Do you want us to wait?" Asha asked.

"No. He should get home," she said then, nodding to Mick, lowered her voice to a whisper. "He looks like he's going to throw up, and I don't think my mom would want to clean that."

"Do you think you'll make it to school tomorrow?"

"I don't know, this hurts really bad," Lily said rubbing her ankle.

Asha felt a swell of guilt; Lily was a good person, she didn't deserve this. She must have seen the look on Asha's face because Lily said, "I'll be fine. Take him home."

"Okay," Asha said, reluctantly.

They left the house right away, Asha guiding Mick down the sidewalk.

"Where do you live?" Asha asked him.

"Couple blocks down."

They walked to his house in silence, not that Asha really minded. She didn't think she could take any more noise after what she'd just been through. She just wanted to get home, go to sleep, and forget about everything.

Mick's house wasn't nearly as large as Lily's. It was a simple one storey. There was no garage, but Asha could see a number of cars in the driveway.

"How many people live here?" she asked.

"Just me and Mom and Dad," he said. "And my brother, Richard. And my sister Sarah. And her husband Brad. Sometimes my other brother Keith stays here when he's not at — oh, there's his car, so I guess he's here, too. Man, he'll get a real kick out of this hole in my head!"

Mick took the lead, but instead of going to the front door he headed to the side, squeezing between the cars and the house. He was climbing the steps when the door flew open.

A slight woman with blond hair appeared in the doorway and shouted, "Mikhail Godfrey Gareth Gilbert Gallows! I told you to be home an hour ago!"

"Sorry, Mom, " Mick said, sounding more amused than ashamed. "Got held up at the mall."

"I don't care what happened! We agreed: you come home on time or call if you're going to be late!"

Mick lifted his head, moving his hand away from his forehead. For a moment Asha thought his mom was going to cry, but then her face hardened.

"What in the name of Great Aunt Jessie and the cow she milked for fifty days with two broken hands have you done this time?!" she screamed at him, making Asha take a step back. The short woman's eyes were bulging. She grabbed Mick by his coat with one hand dragged him into the house, stomping as she went. Asha followed timidly behind.

"You're late! You don't call! You come back looking like you've been hit by the LR!"

"Mom — "

56

"Don't 'Mom' me!" she shouted, pointing her finger in his face. "Every time you come home — every time! — if it's not a bloody nose, it's a broken finger or a gash in your forehead!"

"Mom — "

"Do you enjoy getting hurt? Do you — "

"Mom!"

She stopped mid-rant and gave him a stern look.

He hooked a thumb over his shoulder. "This is Asha."

Asha's face flushed as Mick's mom craned her neck around her son. She scanned Asha from foot to head, then, to her surprise, shoved Mick out of the way and advanced on her.

"What happened?" she demanded, pointing at Asha's arm.

"I..I.." Asha stammered. She desperately wanted to explain what had happened but no words came out. She shot a pleading look at Mick.

"Flying spaghetti monster. Meatballs everywhere. It was terrifying," he said, "yet strangely delicious."

"What?" his mother asked, spinning around to face him.

"I was touched by his noodly appendage!" Mick cried, throwing his hands in the air and wiggling his fingers.

"He hit his head. Or... or something hit his head, I'm not sure," Asha said, finally finding her voice. "I think something might be wrong with him," she added in a whisper.

"Oh, there's definitely something wrong with him," Mick's mom replied and turned back to Asha. She didn't say anything else; instead she began looking over Asha once more.

"I think I'm gonna go now," Asha said. She started to back away when the woman caught her arm in a surprisingly strong grasp.

"Not like that you're not."

She dragged Asha through the entry hall, brushing past Mick, who looked both embarrassed and amused, and into the kitchen. She let go of Asha's arm, grabbed Mick, forced him to sit in a chair, and then stormed off into the living room.

Unlike Lily's place Mick's house had a sense of chaos; dishes were stacked in the sink, boots cluttered the floor by the door, laundry was piled high on the couch in the living room. Mick's mom rifled through the pile of clothes on the couch, grabbed something pink, and came back into the kitchen.

"What happened?" she repeated, crossing her arms in front of her chest.

"My head got cut. Asha tore off her sleeve to stop the bleeding," Mick said and held out the blood soaked piece of cloth. Asha's gut gave a slight lurch at the sight.

Mick's mom raised her eyebrows in surprise. "You tore your sleeve off?"

Asha nodded then quickly added, "It was torn anyways," to which Mick's mom raised her eyebrows even further.

"What happened?"

Asha glanced at Mick, but he seemed slightly dazed; she couldn't tell if he was faking it or not but that spaghetti thing was way out there.

The sound of trampling feet echoed through the house; some came from downstairs, others from the same floor. Two large men with blond hair entered the kitchen, followed by a tall young woman with blond hair and a large man with light brown hair. They crowded into the kitchen, took a look at Mick and then at Asha. For a moment they were silent then they exploded.

"What's going on?"

"What'd you — "

"Jeez look at — "

"Mom?"

"Don't touch — "

"Aghh, that hurts!"

"— you have a girlfriend, Mick!"

"Just leave him — "

"Don't be a wuss man!"

"— shoulda brought her over soon — "

"Gross, that thing's all blood — "

"Knock it off!"

"— thing's ma bro — "

"QUIET!" a thunderous voice sounded through the room.

Asha let out a yelp and spun around to see a giant of a man standing in the doorway.

He wore dirty coveralls, had jet black hair, and a great big bushy beard; his dark brown eyes scanned the room looking at each person, pausing on Asha, then finally resting on Mick. He strode over and kneeled in front of him. Moving gently he pushed Mick's hand away from his head and peered at the gash, scowling.

"What happened?" he asked in a low growl.

One by one everyone in the room looked at Asha. She took a step back from the towering crowd.

She swallowed then quietly said, "The Dragon."

If she had thought the room was quiet before, it was nothing compared to now. No one tapped their foot or shifted their weight, no one rustled their clothes, no one even breathed. They all stood rooted in place, eyes glued to her.

Mick's mom clenched her jaw. Her eyes darted between Asha and Mick. She gripped and released the fabric in her hand first slowly then quickly until Asha thought the woman might tear it. Then, as if she had decided on something, she nodded and walked up to Asha.

"Put this on," she ordered, thrusting out the pink sweater she had been holding.

"Hey, that's mine!" the tall, young woman protested.

"Not now, Sarah!" Mick's mom hissed. "Go on, you must be freezing," she said to Asha, holding out the sweater.

Asha did as she was told, the sweater was much too big, although in all honesty she wasn't that cold; she just couldn't bear being ordered around anymore.

"One of the boys will take you home."

"I'm fine," Asha replied. "I can walk."

"No, one of the boys can drive you there."

"It's only a block," Asha said and edged toward the entryway before Mick's mom could grab her again.

"No — "

"Mom," Mick moaned from his seat. "Just let her go. She'll be fine. She got me here, didn't she?"

Asha didn't wait for Mick's mom to reply. She hurried to the door and was at the bottom of the steps when Mick called out to her.

"Can you do me a favour?" he asked.

"What's that?"

"Don't tell anyone about my name?"

Before she could answer, he was pulled inside and the door shut behind him.

When Asha reached the apartment building she punched in the code to get inside; she had to use a key to get into her apartment. They didn't have a punch code like downstairs or automatic door opener like Lily. She entered the apartment and was struck by how empty it was. Compared to Lily and Mick's houses, the apartment seemed deserted. Other than the furniture, the place looked barren.

She went to her room and turned on the light. It was still a mess.

At least this part seems like someone lives here.

The clock on her dresser read five o'clock which meant that her father wouldn't be home for an hour. She sat on her bed and crossed her arms; only then did she remember that she was wearing the sweater Mick's mom had made her put on. She pulled it off; the shirt underneath was dirty, torn, and bloody. She ran her opposite hand over the arm where her shirt was torn but didn't find any cuts. The blood must have been Mick's. If she hadn't got him out — them out — what would have happened?

She had saved them. She had pulled Lily and Mick out of the rubble and debris right after she had slammed those men out of the hole in the wall. An image popped into her mind of her shoving kids in gym class, then another of her throwing a manhole cover into the chest of the man in the alley.

How could she have done those things? What was wrong with her?

7
BIG TIME HERO

Asha stared at the dead frog in front of her, its glossy eyes judging her as if to ask her why it was now lying on a tray on her desk. It smelled of formaldehyde, the vapours making her light-headed.

She sat at the back corner of the room by herself; all the other students sat in groups well away from her. The science teacher, Mr. Speiger, had given the class the assignment to document their observations about the frogs. "We won't be dissecting them this class," he had said and then he had left the classroom a few minutes later. The only observation Asha had made so far was that her frog was ugly.

It had been three days since the attack at the mall and Asha had spent that time very much alone. Lily had sent her a message the morning after to tell her she wouldn't be at school for a few days. She didn't know what had happened to Mick.

A roar of laughter made Asha drag herself away from the accusing eyes of her frog. On the far side of the room a group of students had gathered around Keri Shaw's desk. A second chorus of laughter rose up.

"Hey, Twitch!" Keri hollered.

The group of kids opened up revealing Keri grinning, her frog before her. Beside her, Trevor had an electrical cord in his hands. The end had been cut off, exposing the copper wires.

"Remind you of anyone?" Keri called.

Trevor jabbed the wires at the frog. Its leg shot out.

"Whoa!" the crowd exclaimed.

He jabbed it again and this time the frog bounced. He did it over and over, once even causing a spark. The last time he held the wires on the frog for a long time. Its limbs spasmed; they made a dull thumping sound on the tray.

Asha felt sick at the sight of it. She glared at Keri and turned away.

"Oooo," the crowd taunted her.

Asha heard the scrape of chairs and then turned to see Keri and Trevor stalking toward her desk.

When she arrived Keri bent over, her face close to Asha's. "Do you have a problem?"

Keri's face was so close to hers she could smell the sweet, cherry scent of her lip gloss. Asha's heart began to thud in her chest and in her temples.

"Hey!" a voice called from behind them.

The group turned as one revealing Lily. She leaned on two crutches, her foot bandaged up and raised off the floor.

"Get away from her!" Lily ordered.

She moved to Keri with surprising speed, planting the crutches in front of her, swinging forward on them and landing on her good foot. With two hops she was standing in front of the other girl.

"Leave her alone!" Lily hollered down into Keri's upturned face. "And you," she turned on Trevor and Andrew, pointing her finger at them. "Back off!"

Asha, who was still seated, looked up at Trevor. His smile dropped. Like a snake, he shot his hands forward and grabbed Lily's crutches out from under her arms.

"Give those back!" Lily screamed, wavering in place and finally grabbing onto a chair for balance. She reached out to grab at Trevor, but he skipped backwards holding the crutches away from her.

"Not until you say you're — "

The crutches were yanked out of his hand. He spun around and there stood Mick; his forehead bore a red gouge.

"What happened to you?" Trevor asked. "Training wheels fall off your bike?"

"I think it's about time you left," Mick said calmly.

"Get lost, kid. Before I break you in half."

Mick took a step closer to the boy. "I had my head split open in an attack from The Dragon and you think I'm going to be scared of you?"

The group stood for a long, breathless moment; Lily towering over Keri; Trevor leaning over Mick. Asha gripped her desk and her chair; all the other kids in the class were staring at them.

"What's going on here?"

Mr. Speiger, a tall thin man, pushed his way past the students. He stopped beside Mick, Trevor, and Keri and glared at them expectantly.

Trevor held Mick's gaze a moment longer then, turning to the teacher, said, "Nothing."

"Yeah, nothing's happening," Mick added. His eyes never left Trevor's face.

"Good. Keri and Trevor; I would suggest you find your desks and finish your assignment." When neither of them made a move, he added in a harsh tone, "Now."

Trevor gave Mick a rough brush with his shoulders; Keri gave first Lily, then Asha a disgusted look and stormed off. The class, having sensed a fight brewing but now seeing that wasn't going to happen, went back to their work.

Mr. Speiger gave Asha, Lily, and Mick a quick nod, then walked away.

"What was that all about?" Lily asked.

"They're just being jerks," Asha said. Her heartbeat was starting to slow; she relaxed her hands from the table and the seat. "How are you?"

Mick handed Lily back her crutches, who muttered her thanks. She gingerly sat down in the seat next to Asha.

"Not too bad," Lily said. "I'll be off these crutches tomorrow. I get to miss gym class, though."

Mick grabbed a chair from nearby and sat down beside the pair. Asha looked curiously at him then at Lily who replied with a shrug.

"Yeah, I'm going to gym," he said, leaning back in the chair so it balanced on two legs. "I'm hoping this thing'll split open and spray someone real good," he added, pointing at his forehead.

"That's just gross," Lily replied, disgusted.

"Look, I really have to apologize to you two," he said.

"What for?" Lily asked.

"Up until the mall, I honestly thought one of you two, maybe both, were the one spraying that Dragon nonsense on the lockers."

"Us?" Lily asked, surprised. "But we thought it was you!"

"Yeah — wait! Me? But you two totally fit the profile! You know. Kind of loners, bullied, easy recruits for gangs. I mean, look what you did in gym, Asha."

"And me?" Lily asked.

"You're super-smart. I figured you were the only one who could have erased the security video without being caught."

"What video?"

The video for the times the vandalism happened. It's all been erased. I overheard Crystal telling Keri. She works at the administration desk, you know."

"Well, it wasn't me," Lily snapped.

"Already said I was sorry," Mick said, raising his hands. "Guess I'm back to square one trying to figure it out. Did you know that other schools have had that same dragon graffitied on lockers? It's pretty much across the entire city."

"I hadn't heard that," Asha said.

"Could be a teacher," Mick suggested.

"Why would you think that?" Lily demanded.

"Who else would have access to that video system? Who else could gain access to the school?"

"You're crazy," Lily said, dismissing him. "Anyway, Asha, did I miss anything good in class?"

"Not really."

Asha had no idea what Lily meant by "good stuff", though. To her classes were just classes, except for gym, which she really liked, even though it was the only class she had ever been kicked out of.

"I just can't stand being away for so long. It's like this one time last year I had the flu for a week, and I came back, and I had missed just about everything important. Sure I could do the homework, but there was all this discussion I missed and the exercises. Like in Social — "

"Look," Mick interrupted, "I'm sure your adventure-filled stories about the history of missing useless classes are very thrilling, but we have more important things to discuss."

"Like what?" Lily asked, clearly irritated.

"Like Asha taking out those guys!"

"Shhh!" Asha hissed.

A few students had turned to look at the trio.

"How did you do it?" Mick whispered when the other kids had turned away.

"I..I don't know. It just sort of happened."

"Just sort of happened?" Mick echoed. "That's it?"

"Has anything like this happened before?" Lily asked.

Asha hesitated, debating whether or not to tell them. Both of them were curious, but below that she saw something else: concern. Lily was the most obvious, but even Mick had a worried look on him.

"Yes," Asha admitted.

Their eyes widened at the same time in a way that would have been comical under different circumstances.

"When?" Lily asked.

"A while back, at the downtown attacks."

"That was you?" Mick asked. "You knocked that guy out with a manhole cover?"

"How do you know about that?" Asha demanded. She hadn't told anyone about that.

"They said it was probably gas pressure that blew that manhole cover off. Shot it at him and slammed him against the wall, but it wasn't, it was you."

"Who said that?" Lily asked.

"The police."

Asha tensed. Did the police know about her? Lily and Mick knowing might be all right, but the police? She didn't like that idea one bit.

"How do you know what the police say?" Lily asked.

"My brother's a cop. Didn't you know?"

"How are we supposed to know that?" Lily fumed.

"I thought everyone knew," Mick said defensively.

They were whispering so loudly that students had once more started to look their way.

"Look, just forget it," Lily huffed. "Asha, tell us what happened."

They both looked at her expectantly.

All the students were focused on their work again, although she caught a glimpse of Trevor and Keri's group trying to secretly zap their frog. She looked back at Lily and Mick, expectation written on their faces. She took a deep breath and then told them everything she could remember about the attack downtown.

She told them about how the street had exploded around her. She told them about Keri, Crystal, and Chastity running. She told them about how she was chased, fell, and finally throwing the manhole cover at the man.

"I knew it," Mick said enthusiastically. "I knew there was something else going on there."

"Do you know why this is happening?" Lily asked.

"Were you bitten by a radioactive dung beetle?" Mick asked.

"What?" Asha asked, disgusted.

"Dung beetles can lift fifty time their own weight," Lily stated. When Asha gave her the same look she had given Mick she quickly added, "We learned about it in class."

"I wasn't bitten by a dung beetle!"

Lily leaned in close to Asha and said, "How did you move so fast? I've never seen anyone move like that. It was like two steps and you were right at them but we had to be fifty feet or more away from them."

"I don't know," Asha said. "But is it really so strange? I mean, what about Captain Stoneman? Look what he could do," she added, almost pleading.

"Captain Stoneman was just a guy," Mick said. "Sure he could run fast and break down a steel door with one kick and fly and stuff, but he had a special suit. He had years of police training. I think they even shot him up with performance-enhancing drugs just so he could do all that. But you, you're something different."

"Well at least you're okay," Lily said. She squeezed Asha's hand, the first time she'd ever done something like that.

"What I don't get is why these guys are attacking like this," Mick said.

"They're criminals," Lily answered. "It's what they do."

"Maybe," Mick said, clearly unconvinced. "Oh, hey," he said, snapping his fingers. "You guys want to come over for supper Friday?"

"What?" Asha and Lily asked in unison.

"Yeah, Mom and Dad thought that since we were all in that thing and since it's the last day of school before Christmas and since it's really just you guys and your one parent it might be good... " Mick said, his voice fading when he saw the looks on their faces.

Asha had forgotten that Christmas was next week, she had forgotten that her mother was gone; she had forgotten that her mother wouldn't be with her for Christmas. How could she have forgotten that? How could she have forgotten her?

"How do you know about our parents?" Lily demanded.

"I dunno," Mick replied, shrugging his shoulders. "I thought everyone knew."

Asha barely heard him. She couldn't remember the last time she'd thought of her mother. Had it been a day? A week? More than that? Pushing back tears she brought up the one picture she always did. In her mind she saw her mother sitting in their van. She was smiling, her head backlit with the midday sun, her long black hair framing her face and falling onto her shoulders like a stream of silk. Asha's breath hitched and she closed her eyes. Of course, she had been busy — throwing things at flying men and pushing others through holes in walls could do that — but how could she have forgotten?

"You okay, Asha?" Lily asked, concerned.

"Yeah," Asha lied. "Just kind of out of it I guess."

"Cheer up, kiddo!" Mick exclaimed. He gave her a hearty slap on the shoulder and added, "After all, how many people get to say they're a real life, big-time hero?"

Asha opened her mouth to protest, but the sweet, five-note chime signalling the change of class sang through the room. Students jumped from their seats, dragging chairs and pushing tables.

"I'm not a hero," she tried to say, but her voice was lost in the ruckus.

*

"Where are your presents?" her father asked.

He was holding a fruit tray he had picked up from the grocery store and waiting patiently by the door.

"I thought you were going to get them."

"No, I said you had to pick up presents for Lily and Mick, remember?"

Asha silently cursed herself. If her mom had been around she would have picked them up or they would have done it together. Instead, her dad had told her to pick something up on the way home from school, and she had forgotten.

"What am I going to do?" she asked.

"I saw a place just downtown. You might be able to get something there if it's open."

Asha was irritated by the the disappointment in his voice. If he had wanted presents for Lily and Mick then he should have picked them up.

By the time they got to the downtown area most of the stores were already closed. Her father slowed the van as he looked from one side of the street to the other.

"I thought it was just over — there it is," he said, pointing out Asha's window.

She saw a large store selling women's fashions and another selling sporting equipment; both had been closed for the day

"I don't see it."

"Right here," he said pointing again as he pulled their old, red van over.

The store was an older, one storey house squished between the two larger buildings. The main door was old, the brown paint faded and ragged. There was one small, display window showing carved wooden objects, glass vases, and children's toys. An old sign above the door read "Finders — Keepers: Gifts and Antiques".

"You want me to find something in there?" Asha asked.

"It's about the only place, unless you want to get something from a convenience store."

Asha wasn't sure if he was joking or not.

"Fine," she said, a little more crossly then she intended and opened the door.

A cold blast of wind pushed into her as she hopped out. She slammed the van door behind her, and rushed to the shop door. It took a surprising effort to open it; a bell tinkled when she stepped in.

Asha's glasses fogged up before the door could even close behind her. It was hot inside and smelled of wood and worn fabric. The lights were turned low; once Asha's glasses began to clear she could see flicker of a large fire at the back of the store.

"Hello," a quiet voice said from behind her.

Startled, she spun around and stood face to face with a woman.

"I didn't mean to startle you," the woman said kindly.

She was an older woman, but by no means old. Her hazel hair, which was starting to grey, was tied up in a bun on the back of her head. She wore a long, flowing, red and green plaid dress, a red silk sash was tied at her waist. Calm, watchful eyes gazed at Asha.

"You didn't startle me," Asha blurted.

"You just caught me closing up," the woman said.

"Oh, I'm sorry," Asha replied. She made to move to the door, but the woman held out her arm.

"Don't worry about it," the woman said. "I get all sorts of people coming in late these days. Can I help you find something?"

"I... I don't know."

The woman hooked her arm over Asha's shoulders and gently guided her into the store. "Who do you need a gift for?"

"It's for a couple of... of people I know."

"I see," the woman said, releasing her gently. "What's your name?"

"Asha," she replied.

"Asha," the woman repeated; she smiled broadly. "That's a beautiful name."

"Thanks. I was hoping to just look around and find something."

"No, I don't think so," the woman said; she began to pace between two rows of shelves.

Why had the woman told her to stay if she didn't want her to buy anything? Asha made to turn and leave, but the woman raised her hand and touched a glass globe with her finger; it sang a low chime and glowed with a blue light.

"You can't just look around and find something for... people... you know."

The woman beckoned Asha forward with one finger, her smile enticing. Asha felt a smile growing on own her lips and followed her.

"I try to find the perfect gift for every person who comes in here. Presents aren't things you just throw at people. What good is that? No, presents have to mean something, otherwise they have no value. Two things all presents need: purpose and love. Or love and purpose. I'm not quite such which."

The woman seemed glide, her dress swishing along the hardwood in soft whispers.

"Let's see. Are these two people friends of yours?"

She picked up a jade sculpture of a Chinese dragon, weighed it in her hand, shook her head, and put it back again.

"Yes," Asha started to say but was that the truth? She guessed that Lily might be her friend; Mick she barely knew at all. "No, not really."

"People who are friends but not really. Interesting. You have to understand that to pair people with a gift is tricky business. Especially when giving to more than one person. Lots to consider. Not many choices."

Asha found that last part hard to believe. The farther she moved into the store the more stuff there seemed to be. Hidden behind glass globes and jade statues were steel turtles or ivory drums; kites and woven things hung from the ceiling. Twice Asha nearly tripped over handmade stools. She was surprised at how long the store was, it seemed to go on forever.

At the far back of the store the woman paused, then looked over her shoulder. She stared up at the ceiling and Asha followed her gaze. Hanging from the ceiling Asha saw a steel wind chime.

"Yes," the woman whispered intently and, while still keeping her gaze on the wind chime, rushed to the other side of the room. Asha followed her, doubtful that Lily and Mick would appreciate wind chimes.

The woman stopped before a short counter that supported an ancient-looking cash register. Behind it, a fireplace, glowing warm and bright, cast light on everything around it.

"Ah!" the woman exclaimed. She squatted quickly, grabbed two discs from a hook on the wall, stood up and handed them to Asha triumphantly.

Asha took the discs from the woman, holding them by their soft silk straps; they were smaller than the palms of her hands. Each had a ring of gold around the edge surrounding a black circle of wood.

"These are Obshida," the woman stated proudly.

Asha merely looked at her.

"Little Oracles."

"Okay," Asha replied skeptically.

The woman looked seriously at Asha for a moment then her smile returned and she said, "I'm sorry, I thought you would know. The Obshida are special trinkets. These are the only two I've been able to find. They show you your inner nature. Look."

The woman took one from Asha and held it in her hand. Nothing happened at first but then she caught a glimpse of gold moving amongst the black. She thought it might be a trick of the light but the glimpse of gold swirled around and around until it formed into the familiar shape of an animal.

"A cat?" Asha asked.

"Yes, but not just any cat," the woman said as the cat turned once then laid on an invisible floor. "A lazy one," the woman finished and gave a small laugh.

The woman handed it back to her; as soon as Asha held it in her hand the cat faded away leaving only the black of the wood.

"Hey, it went away."

"You have to be in tune with it for a bit. I mean you can't expect it to be psychic right of the bat, now can you? Trust me, the people you give these to will love them."

Asha considered the discs; they certainly seemed like good gifts.

"Sure, I'll take them."

"Great!" the woman exclaimed. She rushed around to the other side of the counter and, after rummaging around behind it, produced two identical cards and envelopes. They were just big enough to fit the discs into.

"Cards aren't as important as the gifts," the woman said, taking the discs from Asha placing them in the envelopes. "They just end up being recycled anyway."

When the woman handed her the envelopes Asha thanked her and asked, "So, how much for all this?"

"Let's see," the woman said. "Two Obshida, two envelopes. That's one thousand."

Asha's jaw dropped.

"One thousand?" she asked in disbelief. "I can't afford that."

The woman looked at her crossly, then said, "You're supposed to haggle."

"Haggle?"

"You know, barter, negotiate on the price."

"Why?"

"Why not?"

Asha was stunned. Here this woman had spent all this time talking to her about finding the perfect gift, had dropped the bombshell that they would cost a fortune and now she wanted a negotiation?

"Fine, how about ten?" Asha asked, flippantly, knowing the woman could never accept it. It looked like she would have to go to a convenience store after all.

The woman stared at her intently. She tilted her to side and said, "Twenty."

"Fifteen," Asha countered.

"Sold."

"Really?"

"Yes, but you really should have started at one," the woman said with a wink then began adding the items to a cloth bag.

When she was finished and Asha had paid, she handed Asha the bag.

"Thanks... uh... I'm sorry, I didn't get your name," Asha said.

"Hmm... that is interesting," the woman replied. She grew silent as if seriously considering Asha's question. Finally, her face brightened and she answered, "How about Elizabeth? I've always liked that name. I always thought it sounded very royal. Don't you?"

"Right," Asha said, slowly. "Well, thanks," she said and prepared to leave.

"Aren't you forgetting something?"

"What's that?"

"Your father, in the van. You should get something for him."

"How do you know he's my dad?" Asha teased.

"Who else would bring you here on a night like this?" the woman stated, more than asked.

"I've already got something for him," Asha lied. She didn't want to admit it, but she hadn't got anything for him yet.

The woman simply gave her a knowing smile.

"Fine," Asha said. "What do you have?"

They started the whole process over again.

*

Asha's discomfort rose when they neared the house and she saw all the cars in the driveway and on the street, each one plugged in by an extension cord to a metal charging station. Asha was relieved to see Lily's mom's car parked on the street already.

Her dad parked the van and they both got out. A slight gust of wind flipped her hair in front of her eyes, she brushed it aside impatiently.

"Which door do we use?" her father asked.

"Side door, I guess," she said.

"After you," he replied, motioning her to go before him.

The pair wove in and out of the cars, the only one she didn't recognize was a large tow-truck, until they got to the side door. Asha hesitated before pushing the doorbell. A moment later the door opened and Mick's mom appeared in the doorway. She had cleaned herself up quite well compared to the frazzled woman she had met before.

"Asha!" she exclaimed. "I'm glad you could make it. Come in! You're looking well."

Asha gave her a weak smile and followed her inside; the house was warm and filled with the smell of cooking food — turkey, potatoes, bread, and pies. A chorus of laughter erupted from the living room.

"I'm Judy Gallows," Mrs. Gallows said to Asha's dad, offering her hand to him.

"Tom Anderson," Asha's dad said. He shook her hand and gave her a warm smile. "It's a great house you have here. Parking's a bit tight, though."

"You drove?" Mrs. Gallows asked. "But I thought Asha said you only live a block away."

"We do, but we had to get a few things before we came," he said handing her the fruit tray he carried.

"Well, come in. Take off your coats and throw them over there and we'll get you introduced," she said and indicated a row of hooks screwed into the wall.

Asha hung up her coat as well as her father's and followed the two adults into the kitchen. She peered around the wall into the living room; the room seemed tiny with all the people crammed into it.

Lily sat between her mom and one of the large guys she had seen earlier. She looked uncomfortable but her face lit up into a bright smile when she saw Asha. Mick sat on the far side of the room.

"Everyone this is Asha Anderson and her father Tom!" Mrs. Gallows hollered over the noise.

Everyone stopped talking and turned to look at them. Asha's

dad put his arm around Asha's shoulders and pulled her into full view. The big bearded man, Mick's dad, stood up from his chair and shook her dad's hand in a firm grip.

"Great to meet you. Lucas Gallows" Mick's father said. "Heard you telling Judy you had trouble finding a parking spot."

"Not really. We eventually found one in Acheron."

Mr. Gallows let out a loud laugh then said, "Good to see you're doing okay, Asha."

Asha merely nodded. She could feel everyone staring at her.

"Let's see," Mr. Gallows said. "Starting over here is my son Richard. Beside him is my other son Keith... "

"The good son!" the young man said, which made every one laugh out loud.

"Good for nothing son!" Mick yelled.

"You know Lily," Mick's father continued. Asha's dad gave her a nod, which Lily returned curtly.

"And her mother Eva. Have you met already?"

"Not yet," Asha's dad replied giving her a nod as well.

Mrs. Donovan simply smiled.

"Over here is my daughter, Sarah," Mr. Gallows continued. "And that useless lump beside her is her husband, Brad Mauer."

Asha's eyes widened at the insult.

"Not totally useless," Brad said. "Something's got to hold down this cushion."

"I guess you already know the one with the mouth — Mick," Mr. Gallows finished.

"The one and only," Mick said, standing up and taking a deep bow, his arm hooked neatly under his stomach. Asha didn't have the courage to tell Mr. Gallows that her dad hadn't met Mick yet. Her dad merely nodded at him as well.

"Well, I guess that's it," Mr. Gallows boomed. "Let's eat!"

*

The table, which normally would have been way too small considering all the people and food, was layered with an eight foot by four foot sheet of plywood and covered with a large white bed sheet. Asha sat between Lily and Mick.

"Gather 'round," Mr. Gallows said after everyone had taken their seats.

He put his hands on the table, one palm up and one palm down; he took his wife's hand in one and one of Mick's brother's hand in the other. The rest of the table followed his example. When it came to Asha, Lily, and Mick, Asha was comforted to see Lily looked as awkward as she felt. Mick gripped Asha's hand comfortably, but kept his gaze firmly on his father.

Mr. Gallows looked at each person in turn, then smiled broadly.

"Let our bodies be nourished with this food," he began, his voice low.

"Let our minds be open to new ideas.

"Let our spirits be strengthened by this company.

"Shall it be so?"

"Yes," Mick's family answered.

"Are we well met?" Mr. Gallows continued.

"Yes," they all answered, including her dad and Lily's mother.

"Are you hungry?"

"Yes!"

"ARE YOU HUNGRY?"

"YES!"

"WILL YOU HELP WITH THE DISHES?"

"YES!".

"LET IT BE SO!"

There was a massive cheer and then chaos as everyone reached for dishes and food.

Once Asha realized that no one was staring at her, she actually started to enjoy herself. Mick gave the two girls a running commentary on everyone.

Richard worked in construction, mostly structure welding. In fact, he had worked on Veda Zhi. Sarah and Brad both worked at a hospital and were staying with Mick and his parents until they could save enough money to put a down payment on a house. Keith was the police officer Mick had told them about (Asha kept a suspicious eye on him). Mick's mom used to be a receptionist but had retired to look after the family. Mick's dad was, as he called himself, a Jack-of-all-trades. In his life he had been a transport truck driver, plumber, building framer, welder, mechanic, and any number of roles in between. Currently, he was a tow truck driver.

"At least you can get those cars out of your driveway if you need to," Asha's dad joked.

"Won't need to, I'll just sell 'em!" Mr. Gallows hollered. He received a number of "boos" and "bahs" at this.

"So what do you do?" Mr. Gallows asked Asha's father after the jeering had died down.

Asha turned to look at her dad, fork frozen in mid-air.

"Well," her father said, clearing his throat. "I'm a Security and Threat Analysis Operative at the south side division of HydroDynamics."

Everyone looked at him, confused.

"I'm a security guard at the Hydro Plant," he said, grinning.

"A rent-a-cop?" Keith, the police officer, asked. "Did you fail the application to be a real one?"

The table fell completely silent and Asha tensed. This is what she had been worried about; how could anybody like her when her father was a security guard?

"I'll tell you," Asha's father said, looking at Keith. "They were going to accept me, but to be honest, I just couldn't handle one of their conditions."

"What's that?" Keith asked, crossing his arms over his chest.

"I'm afraid I really don't like donuts that much."

There was a pause and then the room erupted in laughter once more. Even Keith gave a hearty laugh and raised his glass to Asha's dad in a mock salute. Asha breathed a sigh of relief

Then Brad, Sarah's husband asked, "And what about your wife? Where is she?" Asha's heart leapt in her chest and she gripped her glass.

Asha's father put his fork to his plate then wiped his mouth with a napkin.

"Can we go downstairs?" Mick interrupted before he could speak. "I want to show these two some stuff."

This was met with a chorus of "oooos." Richard gave him a wink which Mick returned with a sharp punch in the shoulder.

"Yes," Mrs. Gallows replied, calling over the taunts. "Just put your dishes in the sink."

Asha and Lily followed Mick as he placed his dishes in the sink then led them down some stairs to the basement. They turned a corner into a larger room that had been set up with a small TV in one corner. Surrounding it were a couple of couches and some chairs.

"What did you want to show us?" Lily asked.

"Nothing, I just... " Mick hesitated then looked at Asha. "I just wanted to get out of there."

Asha realized he had done it for her. He had seen something she was doing, maybe the look on her face when Brad had asked about her mother, and asked to leave.

"It's about to get real boring up there anyway," Mick continued, stretching out on a couch. "They're going to start talking about work and politics and blah, blah, blah... "

"I wouldn't mind so much," Lily said, sitting down on the other couch. Asha sat down beside her.

"Well, you're strange." Mick replied. "Oh!" he said, snapping his fingers. "I got you guys some presents. They're upstairs. I think you'll really like them."

"Mine too," Lily said. "Actually my mom picked them up, but I picked them out."

The gifts Asha had just picked up were still in her pocket. She reached into her back pockets and handed one envelope to each of them.

"Sorry, they're kind of mashed up," she apologized.

"Hmmm, the butt mashed kind, my favourite!" Mick said, tearing his open.

Lily took hers and gingerly opened the envelope. She held her disc in front of her.

"This is... " Lily started.

"Lame, I know," Asha finished for her. She should have known better than to trust a crazy woman in a broken down old house that was supposed to be a store.

"No, this is great! Look!" Mick exclaimed excitedly.

He turned the disc around. What had once been black now showed a snake curling and writhing around itself. It looked like it was trying to catch its own tail.

"And look at this!" Lily said.

What she showed them looked at first to be a thousand tiny dots of light swarming around the disc. One of the dots of light flew closer to the front and Asha could see it was a bee. "In Grade 6 I did a science report on bees! This is so cool!"

Asha couldn't help the smile that sprang onto her face.

They watched the creatures zip and coil around the discs for a while. From time to time they would disappear completely, as if they had retreated into the black world they lived in, only to return a moment later and resume their relentless journeys. It was so hypnotic that Asha didn't even realize the other two had stopped watching them and were looking at her.

"So, Asha," Mick said from his couch. "Why did you get all wiggy when Brad asked your dad about your mom?"

A jolt ran through Asha and she sat upright.

"Mick!" Lily hissed, scowling at him.

"What?"

"That's private!"

"It's not like I'm going to make fun of her."

"If she wanted to tell us she'd tell us."

"Hey, I'm just curious. I mean we all got weird family stuff. Don't you think it's strange all my family still lives under one, tiny roof?"

"That's not the point."

"What is the point? It's not like — "

"She's dead," Asha said; she clamped her mouth shut the moment it slipped out.

Lily sat wide-eyed and silent. Mick's mouth hung open in mid-sentence.

"I... I'm sorry," Mick said.

Asha felt Lily's tentative hand touch her shoulder.

"You don't have to talk about it," she said.

"Hey," Mick said. "I'm always saying stupid things."

"Then maybe you should shut your stupid mouth," Lily spat.

"It's okay," Asha said. She looked up at both of them, but they were blurry. She wiped her hand across her eyes.

"No, it's not," Lily said. "If you don't want to talk about it you don't have to."

"Yeah, just forget I said anything," Mick replied.

She didn't want to say anything; she wanted to be in her room, away from all this. In spite of herself she found herself talking.

"Last June, on my birthday, my mom and I were driving. We'd just finished shopping and were heading back home to get ready for my party. We'd never been in the city so Mom had decided to take me for a special trip. She had made a triple layer chocolate cake with chocolate fudge icing. Said we'd all probably be sent to the E.R. because of sugar overdose after eating it... "

Asha talked until her throat was sore. Once she started she couldn't stop. She told them about how the men had been beating Captain Stoneman; she told them how her mother had run into the burning house and how Asha tried to stop her but couldn't; she told them how the explosion blew her back and how the power transformer fell on her.

She had been in a coma for three days and when she awoke her mother was gone.

She couldn't leave the hospital for a few days after that. They had to hold her for "observation," whatever that meant, and all that was on TV was Captain Stoneman's funeral. It was a huge affair, hundreds of people crowded into the massive church where his body lay, thousands more packed the streets; there was even an arena that had been filled to capacity where huge screens showed the all that went on. It got to be so much that Asha ended up turning off the TV and simply stared at the window.

Her mother's funeral was much different. There was no parade, no filled-to-capacity church; there were a only a few dozen people at the burial. They all said how sorry they were and people were saying Asha and her father could ask for help whenever they needed. None of it seemed to matter. Her mother was gone and there was nothing they, or anyone else could do about it.

She had spent the next few weeks in a daze. People came and went; she ate food but didn't know where it came from. Sometimes she would wake up and think it had all been a nightmare and others she would wake up and know it was all real. Her father quit his job as a real estate agent. To Asha, it didn't matter.

Then one day she decided to go back to school. Just like that, her mind switched from a haze to the clear intent of going back. Her father tried to talk her out of it, said that maybe she should wait, but Asha wouldn't hear it. He didn't understand.

She arrived at school on a Monday.

"I walked in all proud and confident," Asha recalled. "I thought I could do it."

*

They form a group around her and pepper her with questions. She tries to talk but even more people are coming and she is overwhelmed. She smiles for the first time since her birthday.

It'll be all right now, *she thinks. Everything will be —*
The pain rips through her like a thousand knives slicing into

her flesh. Her legs buckle and she falls to the floor. She has time to hope that she hasn't gotten dirt in her hair, such a silly thought, before another spasm wracks her body. Her arms fly out and her hand hits a girl in the leg. The kids scream and hop back. One of Asha's legs catches a boy in the shin and he howls.

After that, there is only pain and then darkness.

*

"We moved into the city," Asha said. "Dad said we couldn't stay in our old house or our old town; too many memories, everything reminded us of her. It was too painful. Plus, there were no doctors to look after me there and it was a long way into the city. An old friend got him a job at the Hydro Plant and here we are now."

The trio sat in silence. Asha wished Mick would say something stupid so Lily would yell at him again. Or maybe Lily could tell her some scientific mumbo jumbo about why her body kept freaking out.

"I'm sorry, Asha," Lily said.

"Yeah, that sucks. And on your birthday too," Mick added. "So the house was on fire from the fight between Captain Stoneman and those guys. And your mom ran into it to save a baby. "

"Yeah," Asha said. "She didn't save it."

"Wow," he replied, solemn. "Keith told us about that, said there were some people killed in that explosion. I didn't know you were there. That's terrible."

"You know what really sucks?" Asha asked. "They put a statue of Captain Stoneman in the City Centre Plaza and my mom got nothing. I mean, they both died trying to save people, so why not her?"

To this, neither Lily nor Mick had any reply.

*

Asha left the party much happier than when she had arrived. She tried to apologize to Lily and Mick for ruining the party, but they wouldn't hear of it. Mick said it was the best Christmas party he'd had because he didn't have to put up with his brothers and sister. Lily simply told her to not worry about it; she was glad Asha had told her. Asha felt like an actual weight had seemed to be lifted from her.

When Asha and her dad left the house, after many well wishes, and got into their van, he let it warm up for a bit.

"How was the party?" she asked, excited.

When he didn't say anything she looked over at him. His eyes were unfocused, staring blankly before him. She could guess at what he was thinking about. When she, Lily, and Mick had left to go downstairs Brad had been asking about Asha's mom. Asha felt a pang of sympathy for him.

Without speaking, he put the van in gear and drove.

Back at the apartment Asha was still feeling pretty good. She had the presents Lily and Mick had given her in her hands. Lily had given her and Mick miniature planetariums that projected stars; Mick had given her and Lily artificial flowers whose petals changed colours and gave off different scents. She was heading to her room when her father called to her.

"Asha."

She turned around to find him standing with his arms crossed over his chest.

"What's up?"

"Why didn't you tell me about the mall?"

Asha went cold.

"Mrs. Gallows asked me how you were doing after the attack. Why didn't you tell me?"

"I don't know," she mumbled.

"You don't know?"

"I didn't think it was that important."

That wasn't the truth, of course. It was all she thought about, but she knew she couldn't explain it to him.

"You didn't think it was important that I know you were almost killed by The Dragon?"

"I wasn't almost killed," Asha said defensively.

"They told me, Asha. Mick had his head gashed open. Lily hurt her ankle so bad she needed crutches."

"But *I'm* fine. What's the big deal?"

"What's going on with you? You were kicked out of gym class and now you don't tell me about this? Is everything okay? Are you in some sort of trouble?"

"I'm fine."

"It doesn't look that way. You used to tell me when things were wrong but now —"

"Well, I guess having my mother killed and my life in a mess might have changed that," she snapped.

"Forget it," he said; he turned around and walked to the living room.

Frustrated, Asha went to her room.

He wouldn't, couldn't, understand. She had *saved* Lily and Mick. Saved herself. How was she supposed to explain that? How was she supposed to explain what was happening to her when she didn't even know herself?

Asha dropped her face to her hands, pressing the heels of her palms to her temples. She wasn't crying though. Crying, it seemed, she was done with.

8
A GLINT OF SLIVER

Christmas Day arrived sooner than Asha would have liked. The day before Christmas she and her father had put up the Christmas tree, a new artificial one that had needles which could change colour — "From Red to Green and Everything in Between" the box proclaimed — and they had decorated it, both in solemn silence.

The two of them exchanged gifts, although without much cheer.

"Here," her dad said, handing her a present. It was a medium sized box neatly wrapped with a bow on the top.

She carefully peeled off the paper until the cardboard box was laid bare. She flipped off the lid revealing a pair of jeans which she lifted out of the box, holding them out before her.

She was about to say her standard "thanks" when a glint of silver caught her eyes. A silver dragon zipped up one leg and down the other. It twirled around the cuff then started to spin, finally changing into a butterfly that flitted up and rested on the hip.

Asha lowered the jeans and looked at her father. "No way."

He nodded, smiling.

Asha lifted the jeans up again; this time the butterfly did a circuit around the waist.

"I figure you haven't had a lot of nice stuff lately," her father said. "Thought maybe this would make up for it."

Asha nodded. That was an understatement.

"But I thought you said —"

He raised his hand to stop her. "Don't worry about it," he said. "Just enjoy them."

"I'm going to try them on," she said, rushing to her bedroom to test out what was the best present she had ever received.

*

"Where did you get those?" Lily gasped, pointing at Asha's legs as she approached Lily's house.

Lily and Mick were waiting outside her driveway, bundled up against the cold. It was a few days after Christmas and Lily had asked to meet her this morning.

"Whoa," Mick said, his eyes wide.

"My dad got them for me for Christmas," Asha said, beaming with pride. She kicked out one leg and a rabbit hopped around it, settling itself on the cuff. "Pretty nice, eh?"

"I'll say," Mick said, awestruck.

"They're amazing!" Lily exclaimed.

She took off one glove, reached down and caressed the glittering rabbit with her finger. Surprisingly, it arched its back as if to get a better scratch.

Mick reached down and did the same.

"My mom got me a new phone but this… " Lily's voice trailed off.

Asha grew increasingly uncomfortable, standing on the very public sidewalk with two people poking at her leg.

"Why are you here, Mick?" Asha asked, stepping back.

Lily and Mick stood up, Lily reluctantly.

"I was just going for a walk and ran into Lily here," he answered. "What are you guys up to?"

"We were just going to hang out for a bit," Lily said.

"Did you hear about the attack?" Mick asked.

"Another attack?" Lily demanded. "When?"

"Early this morning."

"Where?" Asha asked.

"The West Bridge. They have it all blocked off. "

"Did they catch who did it?" Lily asked.

"No, they just disappeared!" Mick exclaimed.

"How?" Asha asked.

"No one knows but after the attack they just vanished."

"That's insane," Asha remarked.

"I'm going to go check it out," Mick replied with an eager grin.

"*That's* insane," Lily said.

"Why? It's not like we'll be in any danger there," Mick said. "The place is crawling with police."

"Why would you want to go there?" Lily asked.

"I dunno," he said, shrugging his shoulders. Asha wasn't quite sure if he was being entirely truthful; he seemed awfully dedicated not to looking them in the eye. "It sure beats sitting around here all day."

"What's wrong with hanging around here?" Lily demanded.

"Nothing," Mick said. "But aren't you a bit curious about it?"

Asha had to admit, he was right. How could the attackers have just disappeared?

*

Half an hour later they were standing on a hill just off the West Bridge. Like Mick had said, the place was crawling with police. By Asha's guess there were at least ten police cruisers, five fire trucks, and even a few ambulances; zipping through the confusion were little robots that looked like the RC bots from school, though these ones seemed much more rugged.

"You'd never see those bots in any city but Ascension's Cross," Lily said. "I think they might even be prototypes."

Uniformed men and women rushed back and forth between the cruisers. A crowd of onlookers had gathered just behind the streams of yellow police tape. Many of the people hopped up and down to get a better look at the carnage while officers stood before them, impassive and severe.

Behind all the commotion was the West Bridge itself. Asha could see scorch marks along the sides of the bridge, the blast pattern of the explosion fading as it rose. The upright supports, made entirely of steel and towering high overhead, were undamaged. Near the base of the bridge she could barely make out the burnt up husk of an armoured truck.

"I'm gonna go check on something," Mick said then disappeared into the crowd.

"He thinks something big is going on," Lily said.

"What do you think it is?" Asha asked.

"Just another Dragon attack."

The only vehicle that seemed to be in bad shape was the armoured truck. Some of the other cars had scorch marks, like the bridge, and a few were tipped on their sides.

Asha and Lily surveyed for a long while until they saw Mick emerge from the crowd and jog toward them.

"I knew it," he said, gasping for breath, as he joined them. "A bunch of people. One with metal arms. Couple more with guns. Some of them were kids our age."

"What about them?" Asha asked.

"Get this," Mick said, excited. "That tiny two-door car — that one there," he continued, pointing in the direction of the armoured truck. Asha could just barely make out the form of a small car. "They crashed that tiny car into the armoured truck. As soon as they hit — THOOM! — the armoured truck explodes! The truck screeches over and crashes into a long haul truck, a big one."

Asha looked back at the wreckage but couldn't see a big hauling truck anywhere.

"So these guys pile out of that tiny car. The guy with metal arms rips the back doors off the armoured truck —"

"He ripped the doors off?" Asha asked. "How could he rip the doors off?"

"How can you throw a manhole cover through the air?" Lily asked.

"Forget that," Mick said, waving his hands. "The others hop in and grab these bags of money from the armoured truck. They hop out just before a second explosion tears the truck apart! Smoke everywhere! When the smoke clears these guys are gone!"

"Gone?" Lily asked.

"They took the hauling truck!" Mick exclaimed. "Crashed into anything in their way, the thing was loaded down so nothing could really stop it. Took off on the West side of the bridge and no one can find them."

Lily laughed. "How could they be gone? Someone would have seen them."

"I know!" Mick exclaimed. "Something's going on here."

Lily rolled her eyes and gave Asha a look that said *I told you so.*

Asha was tempted to laugh, it was such a Lily thing to do.

"Look," Lily said, turning on him. "Even if there is something going on, what can we do about it? Let the police handle it."

"Lily's right," Asha said. "What do you want us to do about it?"

"How about we go to the other side of the bridge and see what's there to see. If we find anything we'll let the police know."

Lily shrugged and replied, "There's nothing going on here, Mick, so nothing's going to happen. Those guys probably got a ride from someone waiting at the other side."

Mick's smug smile told Asha that he thought otherwise. For her part, while Asha didn't entirely believe what Mick was saying, she was itching to see if he was right. It was as if something on the other side of the bridge was pulling her.

"So how do we get over there?" Asha asked.

"There's a footbridge underneath the main bridge," Mick said.

"I'm not going," Lily insisted, crossing her arms over her chest.

"You just said you would," Mick said.

"That was before I knew there was no way across. And I'm not going to get in trouble just to cross a bridge."

"Asha?" Mick asked, turning to her.

Asha looked first at Lily — she was pleading with her eyes for Asha to stay — then to Mick, whose own hopes were clearly written on his face. Torn between the two of them and unable to meet their stares she looked over the frozen river to the far bank. What was over there was anyone's guess, but she still felt a pull from the other side.

"Yeah, I'll come," she said.

Mick's face lit up but Lily was heartbroken. "You can stay here. We shouldn't be too long."

Lily scowled, then looked across the river as Asha had done; she looked behind her, down the road and back to the LR stop. When she turned back, her lips were pressed together in a thin line, and she was glaring at Mick.

"Fine," she said. "I'll go with you. But if we get caught, it's all your fault, Mick."

Mick shrugged, as if to say what would be would be, then turned and walked toward the bridge. "Don't worry," he said over his shoulder. "If we get thrown in jail, Asha can bust us out!"

Lily whispered in Asha's ear, "He's crazy."

"Yeah," Asha agreed. "But *we're* the ones following him, so who's crazier?"

They made their way down toward the footbridge, it wasn't easy with the amount of people moving back and forth; many times they had to stop and turn around as yellow police tape was put up just as they got to an area. After half an hour they finally managed to get down to the river bank.

"This way," Mick said and led them to a concrete support post. Anchored deep in the concrete were narrow ladder rungs going all the way up.

Mick went up first. It took a bit of convincing, but Asha soon had Lily following after him. Asha went up last. Together the three of them hurried along the bridge. From the east side of the riverbank the bridge hadn't looked that long, but by the time they reached the west bank both Mick and Lily were breathing hard; Asha, on the other hand, hadn't even broken a sweat.

At this end of the bridge, as with the other, there was a huge police presence. Rather than risk being caught leaving the footbridge, Mick led them to another concrete support and climbed down. Once they reached the bank they hurried farther down the river and then climbed up a steep incline, finally cresting the ridge. They had come to a warehouse district.

"We're here," Lily said after she had caught her breath. "What now?"

Even here there were police milling about. Thankfully, this area didn't seem to be barricaded off. The warehouses, like all the newer buildings in the city, were pristine white with lots of glass. The street had been freshly plowed, if Asha had to guess it had been done no more than a couple days ago, but even so she could see the confusion of tracks between all the buildings.

"They must have gone into one of these warehouses," Mick said.

"Don't you think the police have thought of that?" Lily asked, sharply.

"Well where do *you* think they went to?" Mick asked.

"*I* don't think they went anywhere," Lily replied. "They got picked up and drove off."

"Well, where's the truck they stole then?" Mick asked.

"The police probably have it," Lily answered.

"They don't. No one knows where it is. They just disappeared."

"People don't just disappear," Lily huffed.

Unlike Lily, Asha thought Mick might be onto something. This area was the perfect hiding spot for a truck. There had to be a hundred warehouses, each with vehicle tracks coming and going from them. Even if the police had searched them all they still could have missed something.

"Let's just have a look around," she said and walked to their left, away from the police officers.

Forklifts and transport trucks zipped past. She supposed that the police had searched the area, and finding nothing, let everyone go back to doing their jobs. Being Saturday, Asha had expected the area to be pretty much empty, but seeing how the stores were having their massive post-Christmas sales she shouldn't have been surprised.

"How are we going to get anywhere in this?" Lily asked.

Mick led them between two tall warehouses and out into a narrow alley. All the warehouses backed onto the alley, but even here the confusion of tracks gave no clues.

"At least there's less traffic here," Asha said. There were only a few trucks in the alley and none of them had drivers.

"Come on," Mick said and started down the alley.

The alley wasn't as neatly kept as the main streets. Old discarded things poked out of the snow: used oil drums, now rusted out; machine and engine parts; old rubber tires. Items out of place with the white buildings, their exteriors bare graffiti and dirt.

"They use a electrolysis based thread in the coating," Lily said when Asha mentioned the clean buildings. "They run an electric current through it and it zaps off the dirt and paint. It's expensive, but most owners will pay for it since it makes cleaning a snap."

After walking for twenty minutes or so Asha started to fall back behind the others. There was something odd about the buildings; it could have been the failing light but the warehouses seemed to be a bit less white. She didn't know much about the technology Lily had described, but she expected it would work better than this. Just about every second building had graffiti.

"Asha, you coming?" Mick hollered.

It was only then that she realized that she had stopped walking altogether. Lily and Mick were far ahead, looking back.

A glint of silver high up on one of the bay doors caught her eye.

She moved closer to the building, close enough that she could see it was a brand-new door hinge.

"Come look at this," she called to the others.

When they joined her she pointed out the hinge.

"So?" Lily asked.

"The other hinges are rusted out," Asha replied. They were so rusted if someone were to open the doors one more time, they would probably fall off.

"I don't get it, Asha," Mick said. "So they replaced a hinge."

To be honest Asha didn't get it either; something was just off about it.

"Why are all these buildings so dirty?" Asha asked.

"Maybe the owners didn't want to pay for that coating," Lily suggested.

"Or maybe they have it, but it isn't working," Mick added.

Asha admitted these could be good reasons, but something else occurred to her. "Or maybe someone's trying to hide something," she said.

"Like what?" Mick asked.

"I don't know," Asha replied. "But have you noticed that the buildings are looking worse off the farther in we go?"

"Now that you mention it… "

"Why does that matter?" Lily asked.

"You would expect some to be good and some to be bad if the coating systems were failing, or if they hadn't got the coating at all," Asha answered. "But it's almost like they were getting worse on purpose, so you wouldn't notice one out of the lot of them."

"It's starting to look like no one is using these buildings," Mick said. "But all the tracks seem to show they have been used recently."

"And now there's this door with a new hinge," Asha said. "If someone was hiding something and they went in here and busted an old hinge I think the police might have thought it suspicious. What if they replaced it so they wouldn't draw attention to themselves?"

"There are tracks," Lily said, pointing at the ground. "But those could have been made by anyone."

Asha scanned the base of the door; there had to be some sign if The Dragon had been there. Her vision blurred. She wasn't dizzy, but no matter how much she blinked her vision got more blurry.

She took off her glasses and rubbed her eyes, and that's when she saw it. Sitting on top of the snow were large flecks of a dark red, frozen liquid.

"Look at this," Asha said, lowering herself into a crouch and pointing at the ground.

"Probably just oil," Lily said.

"No, it's blood," Mick said firmly. When the two girls looked at him smiled grimly and said, "I've seen enough of it to know."

"Didn't you say some of those people got out of the armoured truck just before it exploded?" Asha asked Mick. "Maybe one of them was hurt."

She stood up and studied the warehouse. It wasn't very large but it could have been large enough to hold a hauling truck. There were no windows at her height; there was only the large bay door and a regular, steel door off to the right.

"I want to go in," Mick said. "I think there might be something here."

"And how are you going to do that?" Lily asked.

Mick walked over to the door and tried the handle, but it was locked

Asha went over to it and tried the handle herself, but it moved no more for her than it had for Mick. She pressed down on the handle harder, steadily, until she felt it start to move.

"What are you doing?" Lily demanded.

Asha ignored her and pushed; a low groan sounded from the handle. It grew louder and louder, a sound of steel bending against steel, until — BANG!

"Asha!" Lily exclaimed as the door handle fell to the ground. "You broke into this building! That's illegal!"

"Technically, it was illegal to bypass the police barrier," Asha replied.

"This is different," Lily shot back.

"Look," Mick said. "We'll only take a quick look around. Then we'll be out. No one will even know we were here."

He led them through the door and stepped quietly over the threshold. The first thing Asha noticed was that it was warm inside; much warmer than she expected it to be, considering the cold temperature outside. The windows along the very top of the building let in small amounts of daylight giving the place a calm, sleepy look. The building was completely empty.

"Let's look around," Asha said. After a sidelong glance at Lily's tense face she added, "Quickly."

There wasn't much to see; more accurately, there wasn't *anything* to see; no crates, no boxes, not even a scrap of paper.

"Nothing," Mick said as he joined Asha in front of the bay door. "I expected with the tire tracks outside that something would be in here, but there are no tracks in here either."

Embedded in the cement floor was a small metal ring, no bigger than the palm of Asha's hand.

"Hold these," she said to Mick, handing him her glasses.

She knelt down and ran her finger over the steel, hooking a finger into the ring. It flipped up easily on one end, the other end anchored to the floor. She gripped it and pulled.

Nothing happened. She had expected the ring to come out, perhaps even to break like the door handle had. Instead, it remained anchored and immovable. She tried a second time, straining with all her strength to pull on it. Nothing happened.

"You run out of gas?" Mick asked.

"I don't know. It just won't budge."

"What won't budge?" Lily asked, coming up behind them.

"This ring," Mick replied "Asha can't do anything to it."

She peered down at it, then looked out across the expanse of the warehouse. She crouched down, took the ring in her hand and turned it.

A low hum vibrated the building and Lily let go of the ring. A dark rectangle began to form in the floor. Lines appeared; starting at the ring, they moved out to either side of the warehouse, then all the way down to the far wall, then back in towards the centre where they met in the middle, making a large rectangle outlined on the floor. The hum stopped.

A loud hiss followed by a gust of air blew out of the crack. The edge nearest to them began to rise silently from the floor. The foot thick edge rose higher until it was nearly touching the roof, a giant door opening on its side, revealing a ramp sloping down into darkness.

"Whoa," Mick whispered.

Asha peered down into the black. The ramp sloped down gradually until it reached a second concrete floor; a little farther in she could make out the long straight edge of something.

"I think we found something," Lily said. "We should go now

and call the police."

"Why don't we take a look?" Asha asked.

"We don't know what's down there," Lily said. "There could be explosives or they could have this place booby trapped."

"Or there could be nothing at all," Asha replied. "It could just be a storage area."

"Someone put a lot of effort into this system. It's much too important to neglect the building and forget about it."

"How about we just go down and see for sure? We'll be in an out in no time."

"Well you're going without me," Lily stated, rigidly. She crossed her arms over her chest and scowled.

"How about you stay up here and keep an eye out?" Mick suggested, handing Asha's glasses to Lily. "Asha, you and I will take a look. At the first sign of trouble we'll get out of there."

"Let's go," Asha said to Mick and walked down the ramp.

She stepped lightly, barely trying to slow herself. At the bottom, just on the edge of the light, Asha was able to see that the line in the darkness was actually a bumper.

"That must be the truck," Mick whispered from beside her. "They must have backed it in."

"If they were in such a rush why would they do that?"

There was about two feet clearance on either side of the truck; as the truck extended farther back, the light diminished dramatically.

They edged their way slowly along the side of the truck. Every now and then there was a piece of metal or handle sticking out that stopped them while they carefully moved around it.

As they approached the back, Asha could see that the truck had a flatbed trailer about four feet tall. It was empty.

"I thought you said this truck was loaded down," Asha said.

"It was."

They moved closer to the end of the trailer, slowly shuffling their feet along, until the trailer ended. Asha could barely make out the back of the trailer in the darkness.

"Did you bring a light?" Asha asked.

"Nope. I wasn't exactly planning on doing anything like — hey!"

"What?" Asha asked, alarmed.

"I think there's something here, just a sec."

There was a scraping sound, like metal on concrete, then Mick exclaimed, "Oh man! This is a gun."

Asha squinted down at what he was holding; sure enough, it was a gun.

"We should get out of here," Mick said. He was worried, almost afraid.

"Okay, let's —"

A shot of pain split Asha's head from the back to between her eyes. She gasped and gripped her temples, pressing her hands into the sides of her face.

A light blasted through the darkness. Then a loud bang sounded followed by shouts. Asha blinked, trying to take in the brightened area; they were near the back of a long tunnel, the end took a sharp corner to the right.

"Let's go!" Mick exclaimed. He was already moving along the side of the trailer, nearly at the truck cab.

"There!" someone shouted from behind her.

She turned to see a pair of boys, barely older than herself, scrambling around the corner, guns drawn and pointed at her. They wore black combat uniforms; they had dragons tattooed on their faces.

There was a bright flash followed by a boom and the taillight nearest to her exploded.

They're shooting at us!

A second boom sounded and a chunk of cement exploded ahead of her. Mick gave a sharp scream.

Like the day in the gym, something changed in Asha. At one moment she was afraid, the next she wasn't. A grim determination had replaced her fear.

She turned and ran toward her attackers. She saw the flash of their guns expanding slowly, dipped down and jammed her foot on the wall. With a push of her leg she launched herself toward them, twisting her body in the air. Grey blurs tore past her, some nearly hitting her face. She dove into the boys, her shoulders catching each one in the chest as her arms wrapped around them.

The three of them fell together in a jumble, Asha landing on top of the two. She hit the ground at a roll and before she knew it she was standing up. She reached down and grabbed one of the boys by his jacket. In a fury, she spun him around, hurling him towards the nearest wall with all her strength. He soared through the air like a rag doll, hitting the concrete with a thud, and falling to the floor, motionless.

The second one raised his gun. A bright flash exploded from the tip and Asha threw herself to the ground. She rolled onto her back and shot out her foot. It caught on the gun, sending it flying into the wall, where the weapon shattered. Asha kicked out with her other foot, driving into the his chest. He hit the wall with a loud thud and let out a grunt before falling unconscious.

Asha laid for a moment, still and silent, the only sound the heavy beating of her heart. She slowly rose to her feet.

The two boys lay crumpled on opposite sides of the tunnel. She wanted to check on them, but as she started toward one them a ruckus sounded from around the corner. Someone else was coming.

She turned toward the truck. It would take too long to edge along the side so she sprang up onto the trailer. It was easy to hop the four feet to the platform.

"Stop."

Asha turned to see it was a woman with fiery red hair. She was wearing a red jumpsuit, her hands planted firmly on her hips.

"Who are you? What are you doing here?" the woman asked.

"I could ask you the same thing," Asha replied. Although she had said it calmly, her mind was racing . Where was Mick, had he made it out yet? She didn't dare take her eyes off this woman. She seemed very dangerous.

"You made quite a mess here," the woman commented, looking around. "Though it seems to me you might have done it before… at the mall."

Asha stiffened, but didn't reply.

"Don't worry," the woman said. "I don't really care who you are but I would like to know how you found this place."

"I'm psychic, " Asha replied sarcastically.

"Really?" the woman asked, intrigued.

Asha let out a laugh, despite herself.

"Do you work for someone?" the woman asked. "You don't, do you?"

Asha didn't answer. She still didn't know where Mick was. She had to give him more time.

"Why do these kids work for you?" Asha asked.

"They don't 'work' for anyone," the woman said. "The Dragon

is not a company or an organization. We are an idea."

"A pretty messed up idea if you ask me."

"Who are you to judge? You don't know where they've come from. Some have been kicked out of their homes, some don't even have parents, many are ostracised at school. They are the ones no one wants. They are the ones the authorities would rather see in jail or simply gone. The Dragon is the only one to care for them."

"So you turn them into terrorists?"

"We're not terrorists. We fight for freedom."

"Freedom?" Asha asked. "From what?"

"From those who would keep us on our knees. From being told what we must be. From being forced to do *less* than what we are capable of."

"And that justifies attacking innocent people?"

"Those 'innocent' people are part of a system that would never accept us. They are too bound by rules."

"And the graffiti at the schools?"

"People must be made aware. We educate the youth where the system tries to control them. Most of the youth are dominated by the teachers and bullied by those more powerful. We do not accept that. You understand, don't you?"

"What makes you think I could possibly understand?"

"You have incredible abilities, gifts people in position of power would want to take advantage of. But instead of going to them you act on your own. You don't trust them and nor should you. If they knew what you could do they would only seek to control you. Maybe you're more like us than you think."

"I don't enjoy hurting people."

"What we do is not about hurting people. Join us and you'll see."

"You must be joking."

A chorus of loud shouts echoed from behind the corner at the end of the tunnel.

"Just think about it," the woman said.

Asha had to leave, even if she didn't know where Mick was. There was no way she could take on the mob coming down the tunnel. She took one last look at the woman then turned and ran.

She landed on the ramp and rushed up to the main floor of the warehouse. Lily and Mick were nowhere to be seen. A rush of dread flooded her. Out of desperation she threw herself at the large, overhead door, smashing through it. She skidded to a halt on the snow covered ground.

"Asha!"

She snapped her head to the side and caught a glimpse someone huddled near a building.

"Lily?" Asha asked, squinting.

Asha ran toward her and nearly tripped over Mick's leg when she got there. He was sitting on the snow covered ground, gripping his leg. Dots of crimson flecked the ground.

"We have to go!" Asha exclaimed.

"He's hurt his leg!" Lily squeaked, panicking.

Asha hooked one arm around Lily's waist and another around Mick's, just as she had done at the mall. Driving her legs, she hauled them through the alley. She took one step, two steps, three steps and then it was easy.

It was as if Lily and Mick were stuffed dolls and the snow was nothing more than mist. Her breathing slowed and her heart beat lightly in her chest. The wind whipping past her ears was no longer a rush but a light calm breeze. Asha's lips broke into a broad smile.

She ran, dodging old cars and oil drums, pushing harder and harder until the surrounding buildings were one long blur.

She didn't know how long she had been running when a faint voice wafted up to her. She looked to the side and saw Mick's white face; his mouth was moving but she couldn't hear what he said.

She stopped, tripped, and the three of them slammed into the ice covered pavement. Lily let out a low moan.

Asha jumped to her feet, spinning around, certain that The Dragon was chasing them, but no one was there.

"What were you saying?" Asha asked when Mick was finally able to sit up.

"That was awesome!" he exclaimed, "I was trying to tell you to slow down because I thought maybe you would end up dropping us — which you kinda did — but that was awesome!"

"Sorry about that," Asha said. She turned to Lily who was just getting to her knees. "Are you hurt?"

"Not really," Lily said. "Where are they? Where are we?"

"I don't know," Asha replied. "I just ran."

The hear familiar sounds of forklift and trucks echoed in the distance.

"We should get to the bridge," Asha said.

"We need to take a look at Mick's leg first," Lily replied, anxiously.

The three of them stumbled ahead until they cleared the bulk of the warehouses and stopped at the first major intersection. There was a steel bench on the corner. They helped Mick over to it.

"What happened?" Asha asked as Mick sat down gently.

"When those guys started shooting I tried to bolt out of there but I gouged my leg on some steel."

He gingerly pulled apart a tear in his pants to reveal a large gash.

"Asha, can you take these?" Lily asked, holding out Asha's glasses.

Asha took them and put them on. For a moment the world around her got blurrier, so blurry she could barely see Lily's face, then gradually everything came into focus.

"I don't think we can go back across the bridge with you like this," Lily said.

"Take the LR33," Mick said through gritted teeth. "It'll take a lot longer and we'll have to transfer to the LR2."

"Let's go," Asha replied.

She grabbed onto Mick's arm and, with as much strength as she could muster, hauled him to his feet. How had he become so heavy all of a sudden?

"Oh no!" Lily gasped, pointing at Asha's leg. "Your jeans."

Asha looked down at her leg; there was a tear running down the side from her hip to her knee.

"Damn it," Asha moaned.

"Forget about it," Mick said. "We have to go."

The trio walked toward the LR33 station, Mick hopping on one leg with Asha and Lily supporting him.

"I was right about one thing," Mick said as he hobbled along. "They are definitely up to something."

9
THE HYDRO PLANT

"Asha," Lily called, jolting her awake.

She sat bolt upright and looked around, blinking. She was on the LR9 car; Lily sat on one side of her. Mick, whose leg was much better than it had been yesterday, reclined across from them, his feet up on the seat beside him. The rest of the car was completely empty.

Asha hadn't gotten very much sleep last night and was exhausted. After making sure Lily and Mick arrived home safely, she had sat in the apartment waiting for any news about the attack on the bridge. She wasn't surprised to hear their announcement..

"We are chaos. We are anarchy. We are The Dragon. The assault on the West Bridge was only a small demonstration of our power. Your heroes are gone. We cannot be stopped. We are in your offices, your schools, your homes. You will know despair. You will know fear."

That notice had kept her up most of the night, worrying. After yesterday's events she wasn't sure what she should do.

"Where are we?" she asked. She had fallen asleep with her torn jeans in her lap and they had fallen to the floor; she picked them up and folded them back up. The jeans hadn't done their "funky critter thing", as Mick put it, since they had been torn and Asha thought they were wrecked for good. Only Lily's constant assurances that her mother could fix them kept Asha from losing hope.

"We're almost there," Lily said. "Mick was just telling me how he had called the police about that warehouse."

"What happened? What did they say?" Asha asked.

"They didn't believe me," Mick answered, frowning.

"What? Why not?"

Mick leaned back and said, "Well, when I got home I found the police anonymous tip line. You'd think that thing would be easy to find but I had to dig around quite a bit to get it.

"Anyway, I get the number and call it. This woman picks up and I tell her that I've found out where The Dragon has been hiding and I give her the location, telling her it's right near the West Bridge. There's silence on the phone and then the woman says, "How old are you?"

"I tell her I'm fourteen.

"Then she says, "Listen, kid. We don't have time for pranks."

"I told her it wasn't a prank but she kept on repeating that she didn't have time for this.

"After the nine hundredth time, she says, "Get off the line now, kid. If you call back we'll have your call traced and you'll be charged with harassing an enforcement officer."

"Then she just hung up!"

"How could she not believe you?" Asha asked.

"Because she's stupid," Mick spat.

"Are you going to tell your brother?" Lily suggested.

"Oh, that's a great idea," Mick said sarcastically. "He would tell my mom and dad and then I'd really be in it."

"Someone has to know," Lily said. "You have to tell him."

"No way," Mick said, shaking his head.

"Lily's right, Mick," Asha said. "But maybe you can keep out the whole fighting and running part, though. Just tell him we stumbled onto it."

"Seriously?" Mick asked. "You want me to tell him we just 'stumbled' onto the number one terrorist group's secret hideout?"

"It kind of happened that way, anyway. Plus, I don't think it's their secret hideout. Probably just a staging area," Lily said.

"No," Mick said, crossing his arms. "I don't care what it was."

"Mick," Asha said. "Just do it."

Mick glared at the two of them then heaved a dramatic sigh. "Fine," he said.

"You can use my phone," Lily offered, handing it to him.

"Give me a minute," he said. He stood up and walked to the front of the car, slightly limping.

"I really hope they get there in time," Lily said. "They've probably left already, though. At least the police will have something to go on."

"Let's hope," Asha said. "I really don't want to cross paths with those guys again."

"How did you do it?" Lily asked. "Stop them, get us out of there. It was incredible."

"I really don't know," Asha admitted. "I kind of just went on automatic when Mick yelled. It's like I just knew what to do."

"Incredible," Lily repeated.

Mick walked back to his seat near the girls and said, "Well, they're going to look at it right away. I told him the place and area. With the giant hole in the wall they should be able to find it."

"What else did you tell him?" Asha asked, concerned.

"Don't worry. I just told him about what we found. He said we might need to make some official statements but it's no big deal. I should hear back from him in a bit."

"What were they doing there, though?" Lily asked. "And what was so special about that truck that they'd need to hide it like that?"

Mick leaned forward, and with a slight glint in his eye, said, "I know."

"What? How?" Lily asked.

"After that woman hung up on me. I went over the whole thing and I thought something felt weird about it. I mean, why would The Dragon go back to that truck when they could just steal another one. Then I remembered that they took something off of it

"I think they wanted to get rid of the truck so no one would realize they had taken something from it. If that was true then maybe the accident at the bridge wasn't an accident at all. Maybe they set the whole thing up so they could easily get what was on that truck."

"I don't know, Mick," Lily replied, doubtful. "If they wanted something on that truck why not just steal it from where the truck got it."

"You see, breaking into a place and stealing something like that might draw attention."

"And blowing up half a bridge and stealing a big truck wouldn't?" Asha asked.

"It would, but at least people wouldn't suspect that something else was going on. If they broke into a storage yard, people would ask *why* they had broken into that specific yard. But if they staged an attack, then people would simply think The Dragon was being The Dragon.

"I think The Dragon knew that truck was going to be on the bridge at that time. Same with the armoured truck. So they planned that they would crash a car into the armoured truck and pretend that was their ultimate goal. Instead, they were using it as cover so they could actually steal the hauling truck without people thinking they stole it for any other reason than a getaway vehicle."

"That seems pretty weak," Asha said.

"Not when you know what they stole," Mick countered.

"What was it?" Lily asked.

Mick looked from Lily to Asha, excited. "Copper wire. Twelve *huge* spools of copper wire."

"Copper wire?" Asha repeated. "Why would they steal that?"

"Exactly!" Mick exclaimed. "Why steal something like that? If that truck really was just a getaway vehicle why not just take it, drive it, and abandon it?"

"How did you find this out?" Asha asked, still not convinced.

"I searched through the news releases about it and found the name of the company that owned the truck. It's a place that manufactures and supplies communication and electrical cables for commercial buildings. I gave them a quick call and told them I worked for the school news group and I was doing a story on the attack. I asked if they had got their truck back, I knew they hadn't, and that's when the guy starts telling me about how they lost quite a bit of copper wire from it. When I asked him how much he told me they had lost twelve spools.

"Seeing how easy it was for me to just call up this place and get information I don't think it would be that hard for The Dragon to know it was going to be at the bridge at that time."

"Why would they want that copper cable?" Asha wondered.

Mick simply shrugged his shoulders.

"They could be building something," Lily answered. "Something big and electrical."

"Like what?"

"I couldn't say," Lily answered. "But something electrical is the only thing I can think of for using the copper. And since there's a lot of wire it's probably something big. They probably wouldn't need to sell it — though it is pretty valuable — they could steal money whenever they want."

"It's a weapon," Mick said. "Unless they're going to build a gazillion copper bracelets."

If The Dragon was making a weapon the size Lily thought it would mean the whole city could be in a lot of trouble.

"We're here," Lily said, standing up as the LR car slowed to a halt.

They exited the car into another cold gust of blowing wind. Both Asha and Mick craned their heads to look up at the massive building.

The HAAS Integrations building towered above them; an imposing structure of glass, concrete and steel. It was taller than Veda Zhi, much taller.

"Wow, *that* is a tall building," Mick said.

"What floor is your mom's office on?" Asha asked.

"Near the top," Lily replied.

Lily led them through a revolving door in the main entrance. It was pleasantly warm inside and people moved around at a brisk pace, heedless of the frigid temperatures outside. The main foyer was large and lit very much like Veda Zhi; there were no lights to speak of, the walls simply glowed. Like Veda Zhi the floor was made of polished marble, only here it was black; it reflected a dark version of the three of them as Lily lead them to the reception desk in the centre.

"Three to see Eva Donovan," Lily said confidently as she approached.

The desk was a large circle with five receptionists at the centre helping people. One of the women behind the desk looked up at them.

"Names," she said evenly.

"Lily Donovan, Asha Anderson, and Mick Gallows."

The woman touched the screen in front of her in a series of light taps, and seeing something that met her approval, nodded.

She reached into a drawer beside her, pulled out three transparent badges clipped to lanyards, and handed them to Lily who handed one each to Asha and Mick.

Asha slipped the lanyard over her head. The pass badge had some information written on it: her name, the date, and an expiry date. The top right corner had a gold square in it.

Lily led them across the reception area to a row of elevators. She swiped her badge and the doors opened.

A few minutes after they boarded the elevator it stopped.

"You have reached your destination," a soft voice announced and the door opened.

Lily stepped out the door and turned to her right with Mick and Asha close behind. A wall of opaque glass blocked their way.

"Security glass," Lily said as she waved her pass badge before her. Out of nowhere the dark outline of a rectangle appeared in the wall. "Bulletproof and explosion proof. HAAS has all the best security."

The rectangle in the wall swung in on one side revealing a large hallway, which crossed in front of them. Lily strode right in; Asha and Mick followed cautiously after.

"Lily," a familiar voice called from the left.

Mrs. Donovan walked toward them, wearing a white lab coat that billowed out behind her.

"Asha. Mick," Mrs. Donovan greeted them.

"Hi, Mrs. Donovan," Asha replied.

"Mrs. D!" Mick exclaimed and raised his hand for her to slap. Mrs. Donovan looked at him curiously. "Don't leave me hangin'!"

Mrs. Donovan gave him a reluctant high-five.

"Awesome," Mick said with a grin and gave her a wink.

"Mick, you're such a freak!" Lily exclaimed, embarrassed.

"So," Mrs. Donovan said, releasing her daughter. "Lily told me about your little adventure."

Asha and Mick both gave a start and glared at Lily. Lily gave her head a quick shake, her eyes wide, as if to say she hadn't said anything.

"Can I see them?" Mrs. Donovan asked .

It took a moment before Asha realized Mrs. Donovan was talking about the jeans in her hands; she had been so distracted that she forgot she had them. Lily's mom took them from her and examined them for a moment, then said, "Follow me."

They followed her down the hallway, back the way she had come, past row upon row of glass walls. Asha guessed that the glass walls were the same as the one that let them into this hall; she imagined that if she had the right pass card a dark rectangle outline would form from the glass and she could walk right in.

"Is all this your lab, Mrs. D?" Mick asked, gawking.

"No," Lily's mom said. "My lab is just up here."

They reached the end of the hall where, as with the rest of the hallway, there was a wall of glass blocking them. Mrs. Donovan waved her pass card, but instead of revealing a rectangular outline the glass showed a translucent pad. Lily's mom put her hand to it; a faint light glowed behind it and then blinked out. The familiar rectangular outline formed in the wall. It opened revealing a large room beyond.

Once inside, Asha realized she had been mistaken. What she had thought of as one large room was actually two; there was the lab itself on the left and an office or meeting area on the right, complete with desks and leather couches. On the far wall opposite the main door a huge window overlooked the city.

On the lab side of the room there was a long counter and a long row of filing cabinets and storage closets. Mrs. Donovan headed straight for the lab area and stood in front of a microscope that was sitting on it. She flicked a switch on the device and put the torn leg of the jeans under the lens. She peered into the eyepiece and slowly moved the leg back and forth, pulling the fabric tight.

"Hmmm," she said after a long moment. "This is a very serious tear."

"Can it be fixed?" Asha asked, concerned. Lily's mom was the only person who could help her; if she couldn't fix it, Asha didn't know who could.

"I'll take a closer look," Mrs. Donovan said. "Lily, I'll need the nanite spanner. I think I left it on my desk."

Lily hurried to the other side of the room but soon called out, "It's not here!"

Mrs. Donovan stood up to go to the office, but Mick stopped her. "I'll go, Mrs. D. I have a knack for finding things," he said and hurried over to help Lily.

An uncomfortable silence followed as Asha and Mrs. Donovan waited for the pair to come back.

"You can see the Hydro Plant from here," Mrs. Donovan said

conversationally. "Did you want to take a look?"

Asha followed her to the window and looked out over the south side of the city.

It was an impressive sight. To her left the city sprawled out as far as she could see, the main ring roads extending out in ever wider arcs.

The river, to her right, split the city of Ascension's Cross down the middle in a wide, clean strip of water. In the summertime it would be a fast moving torrent, but now, in the grip of winter, it had frozen over.

"Did you know when the settlers first came to this area two hundred years ago they named this river Ascension?" Mrs. Donovan said. "They built the first ferry not long after. It was a small thing, not more than a wooden raft they pulled across with ropes. They used it primarily to move livestock and grain. As the people started living close to the ferry they eventually named the town that grew up there Ascension's Cross."

Then she pointed and said, "There's the Hydro Plant."

A short distance away Asha saw the Hydro Plant. Like Veda Zhi, it was almost completely covered in glass window panes; unlike Veda Zhi with its slow spiral and elegant curves, the Hydro Plant was very much a gigantic cube. It wasn't nearly as tall as the HAAS building, but it was nearly three times as large. From where she stood she could easily see the pyramid-shaped sunroofs that let daylight into the building.

"Have you ever been inside?" Mrs. Donovan asked.

Asha shook her head. Her father had said that he wished she could see the place but that security was too strict to let her in. After seeing the security at HAAS Asha began to seriously doubt that; after all, Lily's mom had been able to get Asha, Lily, and Mick in to see her lab and HAAS had the best security possible.

"I've been inside," Mrs. Donovan continued. "It's really quite impressive. Did you know this plant provides all the power for the entire city, including the Light Rail system?"

Asha replied with a non-committal grunt.

"HAAS did the entire security for the Plant: cameras, alarms, access control, everything. HAAS did it in secret. They worked nights so no one knew exactly what security measures they were taking. At least that's what I've been told."

"So that's what HAAS does? Security?"

"Well, yes. But we do a lot more than that. The security applications is just one area. We also do scientific research and development — that's what I do, medical technologies, robotics. Some military applications as well."

"Military? Like guns and bombs?"

"I really can't talk about that. It's classified."

"With all these Dragon attacks aren't you concerned about it at all?"

"We are. We're keeping a close eye to see if we need to be more concerned. But most of the important stuff — the intellectual property, the designs, the prototypes — are secure. Very secure."

"What do you mean?"

"We have a storage facility in the subbasement. It's surrounded by multiple levels of concrete and steel. There aren't any data lines in there. It's completely sealed off. Nothing short of a nuclear bomb can get through."

"Wow," Asha said. She couldn't imagine what it had taken to even build something like that.

"Your father told us about what happened to your mother. I'm sorry."

Asha's gut gave a small lurch at the mention of her mother .

"I don't know if could have been brave enough to run into a burning building to save someone," Mrs. Donovan said.

"Yeah, me neither," Asha replied.

A vision of her mother sprinting past her flashed in her mind and then was gone. She felt an ache stab in her chest.

"I think it's just that I have too much to lose."

"What do you mean?"

"Well, there's my career and the work I do. And, of course, there's Lily. Yes, I think more than anything I couldn't stand to lose her."

Asha stared at the woman; she was looking out the window with such a longing gaze that Asha felt she was intruding on a personal moment.

"Your father said she was a teacher," Mrs. Donovan said, turning to Asha.

"Substitute teacher, actually," Asha corrected her.

"Right," Mrs. Donovan replied. "She was brave but I don't think I could choose someone else over Lily. I guess that makes me selfish."

Had her mother chosen someone else over her?

"Found them!" Lily called. She was waving a wand like device in her hand.

"I would have found it," Mick said, coming up beside them. "But who puts a nanite spanner beside a coffee machine?"

"Obviously, I do," Mrs. Donovan replied. She took the device from Lily's hand and went over to the microscope where the jeans still lay.

"This is a *great* view," Mick said.

"I've seen it," Lily said dismissively, although Asha had a good idea Lily was secretly proud of it.

Her phone rang and she answered it.

"It's your brother," Lily said, offering the phone to Mick.

"Put it on speaker."

"Go ahead," Lily said.

"Hey guys," Richard's voice came through the phone. "My officers checked out the warehouse."

"And?" Mick asked.

"There's nothing there."

"What?" Asha demanded.

"Sorry, we can't find anything. Are you sure you have the right place?"

"Of course, I'm sure!" Mick exclaimed. "Didn't they see the giant hole in the wall?"

"They didn't find anything like that."

"Did they look for the rusted hinge? The tracks? The ring in the floor?"

"They checked everything. They combed the entire area. There's nothing."

"Did they —"

"Mick," Richard interrupted. "Look. I get you're trying to help. But they didn't find anything. I have to go."

He disconnected the call.

"He doesn't sound too happy," Lily said.

"You think?" Mick asked, sarcastically.

"How could they cover that up? All that damage to the building? The floor? The truck?" Asha asked.

"This is bad," Mick said, running his hands down his face.

"Can you three come over here? " Mrs. Donovan called.

What now? Asha thought.

"I can't fix these," Mrs. Donovan said when they joined her. "The damage is too severe."

"You can't do anything?" Asha asked.

"You might be able to find a tech shop that can handle it, if you're lucky. There might be one downtown near home."

"Okay," Lily said, dejected. "Thanks, Mom."

"I have more work to take care of," Mrs. Donovan said then walked to her desk.

"Is she mad at us?" Asha asked as soon as Lily's mom was out of earshot. "She kind of just blew us off. And before she sort of said something."

"No," Lily said. "Sorry, I should have told you. When she's working she doesn't really have a filter. Some people think she's being rude but that's not it. She's basically working in her head — complex calculations, formulas, algorithms, theories — all while talking to you. She doesn't mean anything by it. Sometimes the message gets garbled, if you know what I mean. What did she say?"

"Nothing," Asha said, relieved.

"What are we going to do about The Dragon, Asha?" Mick demanded.

"Why are you asking me?"

"You're the big time hero."

"I'm not a hero," Asha snapped. "Stop saying that."

"Mick, leave her alone." Lily said. "There's nothing else we can do. Just to let it go."

*

Asha shuffled along the sidewalk, head down and frustrated; her torn jeans rolled underneath her arm. She had just spent the past hour canvassing the downtown stores, trying desperately to find someone, anyone, to fix her jeans. She had tried clothing stores, tailors, even electronic shops but the answer was always no. She had found one store that sold something similar but they had told her it would cost a couple hundred just to look at them. That was money she didn't have.

She had finally decided to just go home when she was bumped out of her daze. She looked up to find the woman from the gift shop standing in front of her, wrapped up tightly in a plaid wool jacket.

"Sorry," Asha apologized. "I didn't see you."

"Oh, that's quite all right," the woman said. "I remember you from the other day. It's Asha isn't it?"

"That's right. I'm sorry, I've forgotten yours."

"Elizabeth," the woman said. "That's okay. Sometimes I can't remember my own, either."

She laughed which made Asha smile.

"How were the gifts? Did your friends enjoy them?"

"Yes. A lot, thank you."

"I had a feeling about them. What are you doing now? More post-Christmas shopping?"

"Actually, I need to get these fixed," Asha said, showing her the jeans. "Kind of tore them."

"Nothing a needle and thread can't cure, I think."

"These are kind of special. NanOLED technology. I haven't been able to find anyone who can do it that doesn't cost a fortune."

"Can I see them?" Elizabeth asked, holding out her gloved hands.

After Asha handed them over. Elizabeth turned them ran a finger over the tear. "I think I might know someone who can help. Would you mind if I took these for a while?"

"Really?" Asha asked. "What would it cost?"

"Nothing, I think. I'm owed a few favours," Elizabeth replied with a wink.

"Yes!" Asha exclaimed. "That would be awesome."

Elizabeth rolled up the jeans tighter and put them under her arm.

"Other than that how are you? You're looking a bit off."

"Guess I'm just uneasy about the whole Dragon thing," Asha said.

She didn't want to let on about everything that was going on, but the woman had such a concerned look about her Asha couldn't resist saying something.

"There's been some vandalism at my school. People have been painting Dragon symbols everywhere. We don't know who is doing it."

Elizabeth regarded her for a moment then said, "Don't judge them too harshly, Asha. Not everyone is lucky enough to have people who care for them. The Dragon speaks to that, plays on it.

People can't help wanting to be accepted.

"Just today I ran across one of them. Nothing violent or scary mind you. I was on the west side, just picking some stuff up from a hardware supply store and I walked past one of them. He was sitting in the alley just across the road, kind of hiding behind a garbage bin. He had one of those tattoos on his face.

"I asked if I could do anything and he just stared at me, eyes wide. I had a spare sandwich in my bag so I gave it to him. He seemed surprised and kind of spooked so I just left him."

"Did you report him?"

"No, but by the time I would have he would have been long gone anyway. I think it's hard sometimes, trying to figure out what you're supposed to do. I imagine that boy is doing just that. He probably isn't evil; just a kid trying to get by. Hopefully, that little act of kindness will give him something else to think about."

"You're nicer than I would have been," Asha admitted; she probably would have hurt the boy had she seen him.

Elizabeth shrugged and said, "I like to help. That's how I roll."

"How you roll?"

"You kids don't say that now? Maybe I'm losing touch."

Asha smiled and shook her head.

"I have to run. I don't know how you can walk around in just a sweater but I'm freezing. Swing by the shop when you have a chance sometime. Maybe these jeans will be fixed."

"Will do."

Elizabeth turned around and hurried away down the street. Asha walked in the opposite direction, a little bit of a bounce in her step.

*

Asha returned to school after the holiday break to some very disturbing news.

"This week the whole school will be taking a trip to the Hydro Plant."

The classroom buzzed with excitement, Lily most of all.

"That's awesome!" Lily exclaimed, nudging Asha with her elbow.

Asha was unable to hide her disappointment. "Not really."

"Why not?" Lily asked.

Asha just shook her head. Of all the places the entire school could be going on a field trip to, why did it have to be the Hydro Plant?

"I thought since your dad worked there you would be excited to go."

"He doesn't have an amazing job, Lily."

"Still… "

"Can we just drop it? It doesn't matter."

"Okay," Lily said, backing off the subject..

Asha felt guilty she had been so short with Lily; she couldn't help it though. She just couldn't understand why bad things kept happening to her.

*

"I want everyone on their best behaviour today," Ms. Lowen said.

They were on their way to the Hydro Plant, an event Asha had been dreading ever since she had heard about it. The students were crammed onto a yellow school bus; Ms. Lowen had to holler over the noise.

"I don't want any messing around and don't wander off. If security tazes you it's not my fault."

The bus pulled up to the Hydro Plant a few minutes later and the students eagerly filed out. More buses stopped at the curb, forming a line that stretched the length of the building.

"Is your dad working today?" Lily asked as they walked to the main entrance.

"Yeah," Asha said. Why did he have to have such a stupid job? Why couldn't he do interesting stuff like work with Nanoids or something respectable like drive a tow truck?

From this vantage point the building seemed like it was made entirely of glass. All the walls were translucent, lit from within by unknown sources. The place was nearly twelve stories high and massively wide.

When they approached the front entrance's row of rotating doors, Asha felt an odd vibration under her feet. It started slowly, like the ebb and flow of waves on a beach, but quickly built to a low, powerful thrum. An uneasy, queasy feeling rose up in her; she stopped and gripped her stomach.

"What's wrong?" Lily asked.

"I don't know," Asha answered. "I feel dizzy."

"Do you need to sit down?" Lily asked. "They'll probably have chairs in there."

"Maybe," Asha replied.

"Do you need mouth to mouth resuscitation?" Mick piped in. "Because I can totally do that."

"Knock it off, Mick," Lily said. She turned back to Asha and asked, "Can you go on?"

The rest of the students had already filed in through the revolving doors. The three of them were the last ones still outside.

She gingerly took a few steps, and once she was sure she wasn't going to throw up, walked faster, keeping pace with Lily and Mick as they went through the main doors.

As Asha left her rotating door she saw that there were actually two sets of doors, one outer and one inner. Between them, on either side of the entrance security personnel sat behind glass windows. A huge sign above each read "ALL VISITORS MUST CHECK IN WITH SECURITY. NO EXCEPTIONS."

"Mr. A!" Mick hollered and waved. Asha looked to where he was waving and saw her dad waving back from behind a window. He motioned for them to come to him.

"How are you guys?" her father asked, his voice distorted by the amplifier mounted in the glass. Directly below it was a little hole, barely big enough for a hand.

"Awesome," Mick said, reaching through the hole bumping his fist against Asha's father's.

"Good," Lily replied, smiling.

Asha nodded. The sight of her father standing behind the glass made her uncomfortable. She looked around to make sure none of the other kids were watching.

"Not too strict with your own security policies?" Mick asked, pointing up at the sign above him.

"You'll be getting passes in the main lobby," Asha's father explained. "We just didn't want a bunch kids freezing outside while we handed them out. I really hope you enjoy the tour. Security will be coming with you, but that shouldn't affect it very much. You'd better go, they'll be waiting for you."

Lily and Mick turned and headed for a door, Lily leading the way.

"You doing okay?" her father asked. "You don't look too good."

"Felt a bit sick before coming here," she replied. She saw his worried look and hastily added, "I'm fine now."

"You sure?"

"Yeah," Asha replied, then she saw Lily and Mick disappear through the door and said, "I better catch up."

"Sure thing. I'll see you later."

The main lobby looked very much like the one in the HAAS building. The ceiling was high and the space was wide and open. Like Veda Zhi, the walls glowed but instead of an off yellow colour, the ones here glowed a bright white. The floor was a dark, black marble, and in the centre of it sat a large, round reception desk, complete with a few stressed-looking receptionists. The rest of the students had gathered around this desk and were being handed plastic badges. Asha spotted Lily and Mick and went over to them.

"Here's yours," Lily said, handing her a badge when she approached.

"ATTENTION!" Ms. Lowen hollered, her voice cutting through the noise of the chatting students. When the din had died down she continued. "We're going to start the tour soon. Mr. Sherman will be our main guide" — she indicated a tall man standing beside her —"and others will join us on the way. But first, a few rules.

"Remember that we are guests here, so don't touch anything without permission." She looked directly at Trevor McKnight and Andrew Hasting. "And don't run off anywhere. Because this is a secure installation, Security will be accompanying us for the duration. They should be — Ah! Here they come."

Five uniformed security officers approached, Asha's father among them. She thought he might wave at her or do something to draw attention to her, but all he did was look at her as he passed. He stood with the tour guide and Ms. Lowen.

"The Hydro Plant is the first fusion reactor power plant in the world. It creates electricity that powers just about everything we use, from the lights in our homes to the Light Rail system to the RC bots in your school," the tour guide informed them. "This tour will show you how we generate this power and how we distribute it."

They passed offices with leather furniture, large rooms containing equipment, a gigantic cafeteria; there was even an arboretum filled with lush trees and other plants. They were going in a circle, around the perimeter of the plant, she caught the occasional glimpse of daylight through an office window. Underneath it all, that vibration moved beneath her feet.

It was a quite some time before they finally made their way to the centre of the plant. This is where the tour had been heading and the guides had been building it up. The students were led into a huge room. The back wall of the room was one huge glass window, looking into another, massive room. In the centre of the room, beyond the glass, four huge, thick pillars rose up from the floor to the ceiling. A giant sunroof let in the day's light, metal support beams crisscrossed all the way up. Blue electrical sparks shot from each pillar. It danced from edge to edge, lighting up the room. The entire area was a vast, changing, spider's web of jagged light.

The room was divided in two by a wide aisle; on the far side two men stood before a control panel. They were covered from head to toe in a grey, metal mesh material. Electricity struck them over and over; they seemed unfazed by it. From this side of the glass the zapping and cracking was muted and faint but Asha imagined on the other side it would be as loud as a thunderstorm.

The tour guide spoke over the hum of the students. "This is the Extraction Room. Don't be concerned, this window is made of twelve-inch-thick non-conductive glass which means you can't be hurt by the electric current in that room. You should see two men in the centre of the room doing maintenance on a panel. They are wearing special suits. Does anyone know what they're called?"

Lily shot up her hand. When the guide nodded in her direction Lily said, "Those are Faraday suits. They protect the men by redirecting electric fields."

"Good!" the guide exclaimed. "Most of you might be familiar with a fission power plant. That is where we break an atom apart. Doing that releases a lot of energy. The problem is that this type of reaction can produce radiation and, if not handled correctly, can be dangerous to contain. If you have heard of a power plant called Chernobyl you will know that it suffered a meltdown; it was a *fission* reactor that had major problems causing a huge radioactive fallout that made thousands of people flee their homes.

"This fusion process is much safer. We smash atoms together, fusing them. This releases a lot of energy without the threat of radioactive fallout. In this room you can see some of this energy being released and converted to electricity through these four collecting pillars."

The guide continued, talking about electrons, cathodes, and other things, but Asha wasn't listening. The vibration had begun to drop lower. It pulsed faster, each time becoming more powerful. Asha could feel the pulse not just in her feet but in her legs and chest as well.

The vibration hit its lowest tone yet. The feel of it made Asha's headache. She clamped her hands to her head and tried to sit down. Before she could move, a thick jet of electricity struck the glass where she was standing and ran all the way down the room. Kids screamed and jumped back, desperate to get away. The electricity struck again and again, loud cracking sounds racing across the glass. A blue arc shot out from the glass and struck Asha in the chest.

She screamed, a thousand pricks of red-hot needles running through her body. She twitched violently and her arm shot out, smashing the wall. Asha grabbed her arm and fled, pushing aside students and teachers.

She hurried down the hall, not sure where she was going. Her chest throbbed with pain, as if she had just been hit by a battering ram; her arm kept trying to twitch, to spasm out of control, but she held it tight. Breathing was hard, next to impossible. Her legs wobbled and shook, trying to support her weight. None of it mattered. The only thing she wanted was to be away from that room, away from this building with its insane hum.

Miraculously, she found herself in the main lobby. She hurried past the reception desk, ignoring the calls of the receptionists, and out through the two sets of revolving doors. The cold air outside hit her like a wave; snow blasted her in the face. She hurried back to her bus and stood beside it, one hand propping her up.

Slowly, painfully, she began to breathe.

"Asha!" someone called from behind her. She looked over her shoulder to see her father rushing toward her, followed closely by Lily and Mick. "What happened?" her dad demanded, putting his hand on her shoulder.

"Spasm," she managed to say. "Had to get out."

"Are you okay?" he asked, "Do you need anything? Do you need to sit down? We can go to the Security Office."

What Asha needed was to be left alone but she couldn't say it; instead she shook her head.

"How about we just get her on the bus, Mr. Anderson?" Lily suggested. "The tour's pretty much over, right?"

Her dad looked at Lily doubtfully saying, "It is but... "

"No, it's fine," Asha said, straightening up. It hurt to do it, but if she couldn't convince her father she was okay he would badger to go back inside, and that was something she could not do. "I guess all that electricity kinda freaked me out."

Her father nodded. "I was hoping it wouldn't, but sometimes it happens."

"We should get you on the bus," Lily said.

Mick pounded on the bus door with a tight fist yelling, "Open up! We got an inbound casualty here! We need access! Stat!"

"Mick!" Lily hissed as the bus driver opened the door.

Ignoring the pair, Asha's father said, "I can stay with you if you want, until your teacher comes."

"No, I'm good," Asha replied.

"We'll take good care of her, Mr. A," Mick said. "We have the finest in medical technology on this bus. I know there's gum under the seats we can make use of. I think I even saw an old finger bandage, used but fully functional."

"We'll take care of her, Mr. Anderson," Lily said, giving Mick a foul look.

Asha's father considered them for a moment. "Okay, but I'm going to have a quick chat with Ms. Lowen before you leave. I would get them to send you home but I know there's no one to give you a ride and I don't want you taking the LR."

Asha nodded. Her chest felt like she had been punched and it took all her effort not to hunch over. She turned around, climbed aboard the bus, and walked to the back using the seats for support. She sat down and looked out the window in time to see her father finish talking to Lily and Mick before turning around and hurrying away. A moment later Lily and Mick joined her.

"What was that?" Mick asked, sitting down. "I don't know if your dad saw it but that spark jumped through the glass and hit you."

"I saw it too," Lily said.

"I don't know," Asha replied, crossing her arms in front of her. She felt light headed and tired.

She didn't know how long it was before the rest of the students filed onto the bus, but it was soon filled with yammering and laughter. Asha pressed her head against the window, its cool touch pushing back a building headache.

"Head's up," Lily whispered.

Asha dragged herself away from the window in time to see Keri Shaw, Trevor McKnight, and the rest of their gang moving swiftly toward her.

"Enjoy the tour, Asha?" Keri asked, sarcastically.

"Get lost," Lily threatened.

Ignoring her, Keri continued, "I did. I just loved the part where you ran screaming like a baby! I think they should put that on every tour! You could be the main attraction!"

"Yeah, they could —" Crystal started but Keri interrupted her.

"Shut up, will you?" Keri said. "I'm having a conversation with Twitch here."

Lily shot out of her seat and pushed her face into Keri's. "Leave now, or I'll make you," she threatened, towering over the other girl.

"Yeah, beat it," Mick said, standing up behind Lily.

Behind Keri, Trevor scowled but could do nothing; there was only enough room for one person in the aisle.

"What's the matter, Asha? Did all that walking make you tired?" Keri taunted.

Lily gave Keri a hard shove; she stumbled back into Trevor who stumbled back into the others. It took a moment before the group was able to get their balance back.

Trevor lunged forward but Keri held up her hand and said, "Don't bother."

She turned around, a smug grin on her face and herded the others to the front of the bus.

"I can't stand her," Lily said, sitting back down beside Asha.

"You didn't have to do that," Asha said.

"Yeah," Mick agreed. "You should have punched her in the nose instead!" He punched his own hand making a slapping sound.

"ATTENTION!" Keri hollered from the front of the bus, standing in the aisle, her arms raised. When the bus had quieted down Keri continued by saying, "I think this was a very fine trip but I don't think it would have been nearly as good without the help of a couple key people. First, I'd like to thank Twitch, without whom we might have had to endure an uninterrupted an enlightening discussion on fusion power. Thanks, Twitch, for putting others before yourself!"

The students let out a roar of laughter and turned to the back of the bus, clapping and hooting loudly. Asha shrunk lower into the seat. All she wanted to do was to vanish and be left alone.

"And," Keri said, raising her hands. "I'd like to thank Twitch's father. Without him, I'm sure we all would have been tempted to steal a pen or pad of paper and what a shame that would —"

"Sit down, Miss Shaw!" Ms. Lowen ordered. Keri spun around to reveal their teacher fuming and pointing at an open seat. The bus grew very quiet. Keri slowly sat down.

Ms. Lowen hurried to the back of the bus to Asha's seat.

"Your father said we should keep an eye on you, so you'll go to the nurse's station when we get back, okay?"

Asha merely shrugged, hoping the woman would leave.

Ms. Lowen turned on her heel and headed back to the front of the bus. Soon they were on the move, heading back to the school, Lily and Mick chatting quietly.

"At least we can be thankful for one thing," Mick said.

"What's that?" Lily demanded, crossly.

"No Dragon attack today," he replied and gave her a wink.

"Don't jinx it!" Lily snapped.

"Although I wouldn't mind Keri and them being caught in an explosion, if you get what I'm saying," Mick said. "What do you think, Asha?"

Asha didn't say anything. The headache that had been building took hold of her. It throbbed with each beat of her heart, pounding behind her eyes. She couldn't wait to get back to the apartment and into her bed. This had been the worst trip she'd ever been on.

*

That night Asha fell into bed, exhausted and in pain. While she slept, oblivious to the outside world, The Dragon put their plans into motion, and the City of Ascension's Cross would never be the same again.

10
THE DRAGON ATTACKS

Asha awoke the next morning, her chest still slightly sore. After leaving her room she found that her dad had left the radio on and stuck a note to it. In her father's jagged writing, it read:

Asha,

Heard on the radio that they're at it again. Seem to be keeping to it at night and on the Northwest quarter.

Keep safe and I'll see you after school.
Love,
Dad

Asha read the note with a sense of unease and listened intently to the radio as the announcer relayed the news.

"Reports are coming in from the Northwest quadrant of the city about the power outage in the Heritage North neighbourhood last night. The power outage occurred at 3:30A.M. and cut off power to all residences in the area. At the time, residents reported hearing a series of explosions. It is believed that the explosions disabled or destroyed some of the power substations in the area. The power disruption has caused many people to seek shelter from the freezing temperatures as workers try to restore power.

"Police are investigating the events and warn citizens to be vigilant for suspicious activity."

The reports went on but Asha had heard enough. She turned off the radio.

Is that what they're building? A bunch of bombs? It was a big city and there weren't very many of The Dragon, but at the moment it all seemed too possible. At school, she learned that things were much worse than she feared.

More Dragon symbols had been spray painted at the school. Some had been sprayed on the exterior doors, some on the floor; one had been sprayed on Trevor's locker (he had pronounced whoever did it a dead man). The idea that someone could do this and not get caught gave Asha chills.

"The important thing to remember is to be careful," Ms. Lowen lectured after giving a brief review of what everyone already knew. "Make sure that someone knows where you are at all times and can get a hold of you in an emergency.

"Always travel in groups to be safe and if you see anything suspicious don't interfere, call a parent or tell a teacher."

"Question:" Mick said. "Wouldn't staying in groups make us better targets? I mean if shrapnel is flying everywhere isn't it better to be spread out than to bunch up? Although I guess there are the human shield opportunities."

"That's not funny," she scolded. "This is a serious matter and should *not* be taken lightly."

"Will school be cancelled?" Lily asked.

"These are just isolated incidents so, no, it won't be," the teacher replied, which caused most of the class to groan. "Yes, Keri?"

Asha turned to see Keri Shaw sitting primly in her seat with her hand raised.

"Ms. Lowen," she said in a falsely sweet voice. "With the power going off and on, is it true if the lights flicker too fast people can have seizures? You know, the kind where they scream and fall on the floor and can't control their limbs?"

Asha clenched her teeth as the class laughed.

"That's enough," Ms. Lowen warned, calling over the ruckus. "See me after school today, Keri."

"But — " Keri started.

"After school," Ms. Lowen commanded.

A surge of gratitude flooded through Asha. At least there was someone in this school who was willing to do the right thing.

At lunch time, Asha and Lily sat at a table far away from everyone else. Every time she looked up she would catch glimpse of someone staring at her. She had to wonder what Keri Shaw had been saying about her.

"I did some digging," Lily said, after looking around to make sure no one was listening. "There could be any number of things The Dragon could be building, but so far nothing sticks out. I wish I knew what they were up to."

"I can help with that," Mick said, shuffling toward them. "Did you guys know that the explosion last night took out just about everything?"

"Yeah, we heard," Lily answered.

"No," Mick said as he sat down. "I mean it took out everything. Lights, alarms, TVs. It even made people's watches stop."

"I seriously doubt that," Lily said. "Watches run on batteries so the power to them wouldn't be cut."

"It's what I heard," Mick replied.

"Well, whoever told you that is wrong."

"Still," Mick said, pressing on. "Everything was taken out. I was especially interested in the alarms. If they took out all that security stuff then no one would be alerted if something happened. They could take what they want."

"But what about them flying under the radar and the police not knowing they were up to something?" Lily asked. "I thought they were building something 'secret.'"

"This *is* their secret," Mick replied. "If they can build more they can launch them in an area and take what they want."

"How could they have built something like that with only copper wire?" Asha asked. "Wouldn't they need other things?"

"I don't know," Mick said. "Maybe they stole other things without anyone knowing. It might have been during the first couple of attacks; the ones downtown and at the mall. I bet there's a place in the downtown they robbed and another one near or in the mall."

"That would explain why there was only a few of them at each attack," Asha replied. She remembered the man in the jet boots had been alone while there were only four attackers at the mall. "The others could have been trying to get what they needed."

"Yeah," Mick added. "There were so many explosions maybe the store owners couldn't tell something had been stolen. But what could be around there that they needed? I don't think they were looking for costume jewellery or knick-knacks."

"Maybe —" Lily started to say but her phone rang.

She answered it and listened, her face darkening.

"So what are we going to do?" she asked.

Asha looked cautiously over at her wondering what was going on.

"Really?" Lily asked. "Awesome! Okay, I'll talk to you later."

She turned to Asha. "That was my mom. She says she has to work late tonight, maybe all night, and that I can stay at your place. I can get some stuff from home after school. She's already cleared it with your dad!"

"Can I come too?" Mick asked.

"What?" both Asha and Lily asked.

"Sure," he said. "We can have pizza and watch movies. Then we'll have a pillow fight and then we can have hot chocolate with marshmallows and talk about our feelings. It'll be magical!"

"Did you eat glue as a child?" Lily wondered, causing Asha to snicker.

"Forget it," Mick replied, waving his hand. "I'll just stay at home, alone, finding out what The Dragon could have stolen and saving the city all by myself."

"Works for me," Asha replied with mock indifference.

*

Mick's mom gave the three of them a ride from school that afternoon. She dropped Asha and Lily off at Lily's place, since they wouldn't need a ride for the few block's to Asha's apartment. Once again, as Asha and Lily approached the front entrance, the front door unlocked. Inside, the lights had turned on already.

Asha had only been in Lily's house once before, on the day of the attack at the mall. To her left was the living room, clutter-free; to her right was the kitchen, just as pristine. Directly in front a tall staircase led upstairs.

"Come on. You can see my room," Lily said.

They hurried up the stairs to a landing and turned to the right down a short hallway to Lily's room. She opened the door and led Asha in.

It was a huge room, probably twice as large as Asha's. Like the rest of the house, it was perfectly clean. There was a large bed in one corner and a desk in the other. Along the side wall there was a walk-in closet that Asha was sure she could fit her entire room into.

"What do you think?" Lily asked in eager anticipation.

"It's amazing," Asha replied making Lily beam with pride.

"I'll get my stuff," Lily said and ran over to her closet.

While Lily gathered her things, Asha strolled around the room, taking everything in. There was a computer sitting on the desk and beside it Asha saw an open notebook with Lily's neat handwriting on the page. On the edge of the desk there was a picture frame; unlike those in her house the pictures in this one changed occasionally and were mostly three dimensional. Most of the pictures were of Lily and her mother; they were always in a different location — a house, a beach, a mall. Lily always wore the same ecstatic smile. A picture of Lily, Asha, and Mick sitting in a line at Christmas supper appeared. They were all looking across the table at Mick's brother, mouths open wide, frozen in mid-laugh. Asha couldn't remember what they had been laughing at. Another faded in and switched again to one of Lily, her Mom, and another woman.

Lily came up behind her, a suitcase in tow.

"Who's this?" Asha asked, pointing at the picture.

"My mom."

Asha laughed and said, "No, the other woman."

"My mom," Lily repeated. "Her name's Maria. She's a doctor. Mom took her name when they were married. They divorced half a year ago."

"I'm sorry. Do you know why?"

"They both work a lot. It put a strain on their relationship. They were separating when Mom got the offer to work at HAAS. So she moved and I came with her."

"Oh."

A glint of motion from the bedside table caught Asha's attention. Sitting on the table, propped up as if on display, was the Obshida, the "Little Oracle", Asha had given Lily for Christmas. She went over to it and saw a faint and fading swarm of bees. Asha reached out, hoping to see what her inner creature might be, but as soon as she touched it the surface went black. Disappointed, Asha drew her hand back.

"Are you ready to go?" Lily asked, obviously anxious to leave and edging toward the door. "This is going to be so much fun!"

*

"I brought supper," Asha's father said, coming through the door carrying two large pizzas.

"Are we going to watch movies too?" Asha asked, joking.

"Sure, if you want."

"Okay, but I'm really not in the mood for hot chocolate."

"What?" he asked, confused.

Asha gave Lily a knowing look, and the pair broke out in laughter.

While they ate and watched movies Asha's dad disappeared for a while then came back. When it was time for bed Asha understood why. He had moved the inflatable mattress, the one reserved for guests which had been patched a hundred times, into Asha's room. He had also changed the sheets on Asha's bed and made it up insisting that Lily take the bed and saying Asha could use the inflatable one. With both beds in the room there wasn't much room to move.

"Is this your mom?" Lily asked, picking up the picture of Asha' family.

"Yeah," Asha replied. She felt a sudden urge to snatch it away.

"She's beautiful," Lily said. "Except for the age, you could be sisters."

Asha felt a twinge of pride at the compliment.

"It's too bad you lost her. At least you still have your dad. He's pretty cool."

"He was."

"What do you mean?"

"I don't know. He's different now. He used to be like at Mick's party: happy and joking all the time. Everybody loved him. I used to be able to tell him things, too. Not like I could with Mom — I could tell her anything — but I could still talk to him. Now... "

"Not anymore?"

"I don't see him much and when I do he's quiet."

"My mom was like that during the separation and divorce. She was quiet, even quieter than she is now. It's taken a while but she's coming out of it. I think it's something everyone goes through when they lose someone."

"Whenever I bring up my mom he ignores me. I just don't get it."

Lily looked at her, concerned, but said nothing. Instead she looked around the room.

"Is that the planetarium I gave you for Christmas? Have you used it much?" she asked, pointing at the dresser.

Asha nodded although she hadn't actually given it much thought. Since the Christmas party she had been too distracted to consider it. In fact, she didn't remember even putting it on the dresser. Her dad must have put it up when he prepared the room.

"Can we put it on tonight?" Lily asked. She reached over to the device and pressed a button on the back. Dots of light covered the room. "I've never actually seen this one. Most just show pinpricks of light on the ceiling but this one is supposed to actually show the stars and nebulae and such. Did you know you can zoom in on certain ones if you know the name? Of course, most are just computer models but some are real pictures taken from space."

Lily got up, shut off the bedroom light, and crawled into the bed.

"Watch this." In a commanding tone she said, "Enlarge star Vega."

A pinpoint of light across the room quickly grew larger, all the other stars morphing around it. It burned bright in the darkness, its surface warping and roiling. Every once in awhile a flare would burst from the surface, sending flames in great arcs.

"Whoa," Asha whispered.

"Return," Lily commanded, and the red sun zipped away, leaving the slowly turning stars they had seen before.

Lily did this a few more times, sometimes telling Asha about the star, sometimes saying nothing at all. After a while, they just lay and watched the stars move lazily around the room.

Asha was edging on sleep when Lily asked, "He's kind of

strange, isn't he?"

"Who's that?" Asha asked, not really paying attention.

"Mick."

Asha opened her eyes and rolled over to face Lily.

"He acts like everything is just a big joke. He's always getting into trouble."

"I guess," Asha said. "Where did this come from?"

"The hot chocolate thing," Lily said, as if it were obvious.

"You do have to admire his spirit, though," Asha said.

"It's because of his family. He has so many older siblings and they're so much bigger than him I think he tries to compensate. He tries to make up for it by doing dangerous things and he does them without thinking. Still, I think he might settle down, after all that Dragon stuff I think he'll finally get it."

"Get what?"

"Just how dangerous it can be messing with them." Lily answered. "I mean, you're special but he's just a guy."

"What makes me so special?"

"You have all these amazing abilities. Still you should be careful, too. You have to stay away from them. I just wish we knew what was going on with you."

"What *do* you think is going on with me?" Asha asked. She was genuinely curious. If anyone could figure out what was happening to her, it was Lily.

"I don't know. Maybe you've got a hyperactive adrenal gland."

"A what?"

"The adrenal gland release hormones like adrenaline into your body when you're stressed," Lily explained. "It can make you stronger and faster than under normal conditions. I've heard of people who've lifted cars off of loved ones because of it."

"Really?"

"It's true. Although that rarely happens. You seem to do it all the time. Maybe it's some sort of malfunction in your nervous system. Maybe it's something else. In any case, I'm going to find out. *We're* going to find out."

"Lily, you think about this kind of stuff a lot, don't you?" Asha asked.

"Why wouldn't I? You're my best friend," was all Lily said before quietly falling asleep.

*

"Magnets!" Mick exclaimed.

It was the next day, and the three of them were at their lockers just getting ready to leave for the day.

"Magnets?" Asha asked, envisioning the U-shaped pieces of metal she had played around with in elementary school.

"Not just any kind of magnets," Mick replied. "They were something called rare earth magnets. Supposed to be like a super magnet. And they stole resistors and capacitors and a bunch of other stuff."

Lily asked, "How did you find this out?"

"I asked Keith," Mick answered. "He told me they stole lots of stuff during the first two attacks. These were the ones he thought were the most odd but he figured they were in a rush so they grabbed everything they could."

"Rare earth magnets are really strong. With some of them if you put two close together and they were attracted to each other and your finger got between them they would cut it off."

"There's more," Mick said. "The manufacturer for these resistors and such is out of town on the East coast but a supplier for rare earth magnets is right here in the city."

"Have they been hit yet?" Asha asked.

"I don't think so," Mick replied. "I had to dig around quite a bit to find these guys. They're a big storage centre in the Southwest. My brother would have heard of them being robbed, but he didn't mention them."

"What could The Dragon want with magnets?" Asha asked.

"I don't know," Lily answered. "But I can guarantee it's nothing good."

"Something doesn't seem right," Asha said.

"You mean besides the fact that these terrorist dudes are running around and the school's still open?" Mick asked.

"Just because they're out there, it doesn't mean the school has to close," Lily said. "If we give in and stop living our lives The Dragon wins."

"Well —"

"Where's this warehouse where all the magnets are kept?" Asha asked.

"Just over the West Bridge," Mick answered. "Instead of

heading south like we did before, you head north. It's a warehouse called Johnson's Industrial Supply."

"On the west side? I think one of the Dragon was there recently. Someone told me there was a kid with a Dragon tattoo hiding just across the street from that store."

"Wait, you're not planning on going over there?" Lily asked.

"I thought we might check it out."

"But that's the worst place we could go," Lily replied, concerned. "They could be there when we get there."

"I don't think so," Asha replied. "They would have hit it already."

"I have to agree with Lily on this one, Asha," Mick warned. "If they haven't been there already, they're bound to show up sooner or later."

"But we need to check it out," Asha replied.

"The last time we just went to 'check it out' you and Mick were almost killed," Lily said.

"That's a bit of a stretch. We made it out fine."

"*You* made it out of that hole fine," Mick said. "I had to hobble out of there."

"What if this time something worse happens?" Lily asked.

"Come on," Asha pleaded. "We at least have to make sure nothing is happening there."

"We could try telling my brother," Mick suggested.

"That didn't work last time," Asha said. "And you even had some proof. This time it's just a hunch."

"This is a bad idea," Lily warned.

Asha turned to Mick and said, "You always want to check things out. This has to be the least dangerous thing we've done."

"Having your head gashed open and your leg cut through tends to put things in perspective," Mick replied, stiffly.

Asha looked at him in shock; she had expected him to finally relent. Instead, he stood firm, his arms crossed, giving no indication he would do anything but argue.

"I'm going," she said through gritted teeth.

She turned around and walked away, ignoring Mick's calls for her to come back.

She didn't know where she was going, but she knew she had to get away. They didn't understand that bad things were about to happen and they were the only ones who could stop it.

She would go across to the west side, find the supply centre, and see for herself what was going on.

*

"LR2 transfer stop to LR33," a pleasant voice sounded over the speakers.

Asha got to her feet and exited the car into the cool afternoon.

It was much brighter than she would have expected; the sunlight made her blink and she squinted, trying to find the next LR car. Meanwhile, the LR2 car silently took off, leaving Asha behind.

"Looking to transfer?" a man in a reflective vest and hard hat asked, coming toward her. He had a small mole on his chin.

"Yeah," Asha replied.

"You'll have to go on to the next available transfer station, about ten blocks that way," he said, pointing north. "Power Distribution Nodes, we're upgrading them."

If the next station was that far away she wouldn't be able to do this; she would have to walk all that way, wait for the LR33, go over to the West side, look around, and then come all the way back. She wasn't sure how long that would take, but she was certain her father would be home long before that and then she would be in serious trouble.

"When does the next LR2 come back?" Asha asked. "I *can* take the LR2 back, right?"

"It should be about ten minutes," the man replied. "You can take it. We're working on the other routes today."

"I guess I'll just wait," Asha replied.

"Suit yourself," the man replied then turned around and disappeared behind the LR2 shelter.

Asha wasn't sure if she should be disappointed at this turn of events or not. When she had left Lily and Mick at the school she had been so disappointed she didn't care what happened. Now, after having her plans ruined, she was having second thoughts. What if Lily and Mick were right? Maybe this was a sign to just give up on the whole idea.

*

She lay in her bed late that evening and closed her eyes,

thinking. The Dragon was out there. They were putting their plans in motion and the hardware store had something to do with it. She had to do something. But what if Lily and Mick were right? What if it was too dangerous?

It was true that it would be too dangerous for *them*, but this time they wouldn't be with her. Maybe without them there, she could actually do something rather than run away.

Unable to sit in her room any longer, Asha walked out into the darkened hallway. Out of the blackness Asha heard voices floating toward her. The voices came from the kitchen radio; a late night show host sounding out to those people still awake.

She crossed the kitchen, running her hand over the soft fabric of the hooded sweater she had left on a chair, and looked out the small window. The darkness of the evening had given way to full night.

A severe warning beep came from the radio followed by a sombre voice.

"This is the Emergency Broadcast System. Approximately ten minutes ago Police Officers confronted members of The Dragon just off of the West Bridge. These members opened fire on the Police Officers and then fled South in a stolen vehicle, unleashing gunfire at the pursuing officers.

"During the pursuit the vehicle collided with a light standard causing the members to flee. They have taken refuge in a firearms and ammunition supply store and refuse to surrender to authorities.

"Police have cordoned off the area in a five-block radius, and citizens are warned not to approach the scene. We repeat, citizens are warned not to approach this area.

"Further updates will be given through the Emergency Broadcast System. This message will repeat... "

The message did repeat but Asha didn't pay attention to it. Instead, she looked out the kitchen window, envisioning what was happening far across the river. In her mind she saw police cruisers with their lights flashing surrounding a small gun store. The police hid behind their cars, using them as shields in case The Dragon opened fire. Inside, the fugitives scurried around the shop, gathering all the weapons they could and securing their positions at the barred windows.

She imagined an officer talking through an amplifier, ordering The Dragon to surrender. In response, a barrage of bullets slammed into the cruisers forcing everyone to duck for cover.

Asha's heart skipped faster, soon it would be pounding.

The police would fire back, their guns blazing, the explosions echoing through the air. In houses and apartments all through the neighbourhood, she saw families cowering in fear; mothers and fathers covering their sons and daughters with their bodies.

Asha had had enough, she knew what she had to do. She grabbed her sweater, put on her shoes, and rushed to the door. Heedless of any sound she was making, she left the apartment, letting the door close on its own.

Outside, it seemed calm but Asha knew this was far from the truth. Across the river there was a situation that was going from bad to worse. The only problem was how she was going to get there in time to stop it.

She could take the LR and transfer to another route to go over the West Bridge but LR service at this time of night was spotty, and if she did get to the Police standoff she would probably be too late. She would have to go on foot.

She started off with a light jog, her breath visibly puffing out of her mouth at a slow, regular pace. Obviously this wouldn't do—at this pace she would get there by next Sunday. She sped up to a run, her footfalls kicking tufts of snow up into the air. Her legs felt heavy, as if they were filled with wet concrete. The cars and street passed by no faster than when she had been jogging.

You have to do this, she told her body. *You ran fast with Lily and Mick, you can do this.*

She closed her eyes tight and pushed harder, willing herself to move fast, to do what she had done at that warehouse, to be the one who was —

Light flashed and the weight left her body. She opened her eyes, a part of her recognizing that the bright light moved with her as she ran, the streetlights blooming. She was running but it was effortless; the air, that seconds ago had dragged her back, gave way. There was no harsh impact with each footfall; her breath was calm and sure.

It's like flying.

A smile broke out on her face and she pushed harder.

With this burst of effort she started to feel her legs but only a little; her breath seemed heavier but only a bit, like she had walked up a set of steps not run a dozen blocks.

Asha stepped on a patch of ice hidden under a skiff of snow, but rather than slip her foot merely touched it, like a feather on the wind, and then she was past it. She avoided each obstacle — pothole, snowdrift, broken bottle — as easily as the one before, never stopping, never slowing.

Asha pushed harder and harder, her breath heavier and heavier, moving so fast she doubted any vehicle could keep up to her.

She approached the West Bridge. Blocking her path across the lanes, two police cruisers pointed nose to nose with about only feet between them, yellow tape tied between their bumpers. Two police officers sat in the front of each car, trying to keep warm.

Asha broke through the tape and sped down the centre of the bridge. As she approached the road and was about to turn South her body finally started to slow.

Her breathing was so ragged and heavy that Asha thought she might pass out. She skidded to a stop and fell to her knees, her legs weak, her head swimming. Her breath hitched in her chest and she gasped, trying to pull in short gulps of air. Darkness threatened to engulf her.

No. Not this time.

Through sheer force of will she kept herself awake and managed to get a few, quick breaths in. Asha, still trying to compose herself, looked around and found she was kneeling in the intersection right off the bridge. To the south, her left, were the warehouses she had seen before — when Lily and Mick had been with her. That was the direction the Emergency Broadcast had said The Dragon had gone. She listened carefully and thought she could hear gunfire in the distance, but she couldn't be sure.

Asha rose shakily to her feet and started walking South. She only got a few steps when she stopped dead in her tracks. The Dragon had driven south, away from this area. They had stolen a car, crashed it, and then holed up in a gun shop. But there was something else in this area, and it took a moment before Asha realized what it was: Johnson's Industrial Supply, the store where Mick thought the magnets were. If she was right, it was probably the same store where Elizabeth had seen the boy with the Dragon tattoo as well, the one she had given a sandwich to. He had probably been staking the place out.

Asha looked North. The Dragon had used distraction before; that was how they stole everything. They would keep people busy by making trouble somewhere and then steal from another place.

If she was right, the police would have to handle the situation to the south. With a great effort, she started walking north, toward where she thought the hardware supply store might be.

Whereas before, on her mad dash to the West Bridge, she had run down the street and not really cared who saw her, now she felt totally exposed. In an effort to hide she clung close to the buildings, pressing her back against them.

She hadn't gone more than a couple blocks when she saw the outline of Johnson's Industrial Supply. The building shaped like a warehouse, big and square, but its front face had a curved lip at the top. It swooped up in a lazy arc giving the place a more grand appearance. She hid in the alley directly across from it.

The store had a row of glass doors all along the front, each probably locked and alarmed for the night. Inside it was pitch dark.

Should she go in and check it out? Should she just wait and see if something happened? But what if nothing was going on, what if she'd been wrong?

A white flash of light winked on and off in the store. Asha blinked once to clear her eyes, then it happened again.

She looked up and down the street, to make sure no one was watching, then darted across the road, crouching low. She pressed herself against the neighbouring store and slipped into the dark alley beside it.

She tiptoed down the alley, running her hand along the side of the supply store to guide her. At the far end of the alley Asha peeked around the corner of the building. The lot behind the store was dimly lit but she could still make out numerous racks and pallets, most of them covered in snow.

The building had three garage-style doors, all of them as tall as the building itself. Nestled between each door was a regular door. All of them were shut except the middle one, which was ajar. Soft, dim light spilled around the edges.

Asha knew it was no use hiding behind the building. If she wanted to find out what was going on she would have to get closer to that door.

With her heartbeat pounding, she crouched low and shuffled toward the door. There was nothing. There were no voices, no clanging metal; no muted footfalls.

Asha took a deep, steadying breath and slipped inside.

She entered into the main storage area of the store, cautiously stepping on the concrete floor as if an alarm would sound at any moment. It was just as dim in here as it had been outside, only a few of the overhead lights had been left on, but she was still able to make out the full size of the building.

Racks stacked up to the roof and on each level a product of some kind; industrial valves, gears, and tubes on one set of shelves; on another, there was some sort of coiled up tubing of varying sizes. But apart from that she didn't have a clue what most of this stuff was. Lily would know, but then again, if Lily was there she would be constantly complaining that they shouldn't be there at all.

Asha figured that ahead, at the end of this storage area, would be the display area and the source of the blinking light.

She moved down the centre aisle, keeping her ears tuned for any trouble. About ten feet in front of her there was another aisle this one running across her path. She approached it with caution, keeping close to the shelves, and soon heard voices.

A group of people gathered in the intersection ahead. Most were teenagers, some no older than she was. Each carried a gun. Two men she recognized from the mall attack, one shorter, on taller. Of the remaining men, one was the man with the ridiculously large gun. The last was a giant of a man; even in this dim light his metal arms gleamed. He towered over all the rest, his arms crossed over his massive chest, his face scowling, sweat beaded on his bald head. Anger boiled up in Asha at the sight of him.

"Take what I tell you to take," he ordered. "Make sure you get what's on the list. Take anything else you want but don't miss anything. Check your list with Fitch and Hinch."

"How much time do we have, Toro?" Fitch asked.

"The other guys will be able to hold out for another hour," Toro said. "They better not screw this up."

"Don't be so dramatic," a woman's voice called. Out of the darkness the woman in red sauntered up to them.

Pointing at Fitch and Hinch Athena said, "You two go guard the back door."

The duo hurried down the aisle, passing by Asha on the other side of the rack she was crouched behind.

"The rest of you know what to do," Athena ordered and the rest dispersed.

Only Toro and Athena were left standing in the intersection.

"When are we going to quit messing around?" Toro demanded. "I'm getting impatient."

"This is the last job, Toro. I promise."

"We should use what we have right now. Use it and take everything in this area."

"Like I said before," the woman replied, her voice smooth and calm. "With what we get here and the work our people have been doing around town we will have the entire city. In less than a week it will all be ours."

Toro glared at her, the gears of his mind slowly turning.

"Why are you doing this?" he asked. "You're able to get all these people, all these weapons, all this tech." He flexed a metal clad hand. "You can get all this stuff. So why do it? Why do you need us?"

"Yes, I can get this stuff," she said. "I can get pretty much anything. But getting *things* is not what I want. I've spent a long time trying to understand why, in a city as great as Ascension's Cross, a city whose technological power dwarfs any other place in the world, so many people are still so marginalized.

"People like you and your friends who are only trying to survive, thrown in prison. These children tormented by cruel lives at home and a school system that ignores their need for protection. All bullied, pushed around, hated by the popular and self-righteous.

"This city needs a change; its citizens must be shown what it means to be on their own, to be forgotten, cast aside like so many others have been. You will be a part of that. We won't let anyone stand in our way."

"And what about this kid who's been messing with us?"

"She won't be a problem," Athena replied. "Soon we'll have free reign of the city."

"For how long?" Toro demanded, leaning down toward her. "How long before they call in extra cops or even the army?"

"It doesn't matter how many they bring. With what we're going to do there will be no turning back. They won't be able to stop —"

The lights in the building burst on, flooding the area with bright, white light.

"HEY!" a voice yelled from the back of the building.

Asha spun around to see Hitch and Finch running up the aisle behind her, panic etched on their faces; their guns hung lazily at their sides. She had been so interested in Athena and Toro's conversation that she had forgotten how visible she actually was.

"There!" Athena cried out and Asha spun back toward her to see the woman pointing a finger in her direction. Toro was already moving toward her.

Asha turned around and ran toward the oncoming Fitch and Hinch. Their faces changed first from shock, then to disbelief. They tried to raise their guns, but in a moment Asha was upon them.

She grabbed Finch by the shirt and threw him across the aisle. He crashed into the racks and fell to the floor, with a thud. The rack started to sway.

Asha turned to Hitch, but he was already running away, pumping his arms for all they were worth.

A heavy sound of explosions filled the air; bullets embedded in the steel racks around her. Asha bolted toward the back door, dodging from one side of the aisle to the other. She felt the heat of a bullet tear past her head. She neared the back door but it was closed, one of the teens blocked her way.

He raised the machine gun to his shoulder and pulled the trigger.

Like in the warehouse before, time slowed. She twisted to the side in mid-step, just in time to feel the heat of a bullets rip past her and tear into the floor. Asha didn't wait for him to fire again.

She grabbed onto his face and threw him back, slamming him into the door. He struck it with a loud bang and he let out a harsh gasp.

She ducked instinctively as a bullet tore through the air. She rounded to see a boy and a girl rushing at her, weapons drawn.

Asha launched herself toward the wall and, planting her foot on it, pushed off hard with all her strength. She flew toward the two attackers. Landing in a dive just before them, she planted her hands on the cold concrete, and rolled over her shoulder. The girl was just in front of her so Asha kicked out, catching her on the knee. She howled in pain and buckled to the side.

In one fluid motion, Asha rose to her feet and pushed the boy's gun to the side, his arms flying wide open. Asha drove her palm into his chest. He let out a *woof!* and soared back, slamming into the concrete and sliding a few feet before coming to a stop.

Asha ran in the opposite direction. She passed row on row of ceiling-high racks, knowing that at each aisle that she could encounter more Dragon members.

She was wasn't afraid. More than that, she was enjoying this. Maybe it was the fact that she had taken out so many Dragon members already or perhaps it was simply that she didn't have to worry about protecting anyone. Either way, she knew this was what she was supposed to be doing. Everything just felt right.

She reached the last aisle closest to the wall and turned, running toward the front of the building. A boy appeared directly ahead pointing a machine gun at her. He raised it up, but before Asha could even think about dodging she heard a familiar click come from behind her. She leapt to the side just as a bang sounded from behind her. At the same time the boy in front of her pulled the trigger on his machine gun. The sound was deafening. With heavy thuds, bullets hit the floor and rack where Asha had been standing.

She was trapped. Behind and in front of her they were advancing, on either side of her there was a wall and a tall rack of shelves.

Crouching low Asha threw herself at the rack, straightening her body flat and diving hands first through the shelf closest to her. She knocked over stacks of gears before her foot snagged on the edge of the bottom shelf, making her fall to the ground on the other side.

An explosion of gunfire trailed her and Asha flattened herself to the ground. She was pinned down and time was running out. Soon they would be close enough to get a clear shot.

She looked up, twisting her head to see how tall the rack was and an idea struck her. She rolled to the shelf, and took a deep breath. She would only get one chance.

Asha jumped to her feet and slammed her back against the rack, hooking her hands under the bottom shelf. She drove her feet into the ground and pushed against the rack with all her strength. It began to tilt. She could hear the two attackers running closer. She closed her eyes and pushed harder.

A surge of power burst through her limbs and she opened her eyes, letting out a yell with the effort. The rack swayed lazily, and then began to tip. Asha lifted harder, the bottom edge of the shelf on her side raising off the ground. One inch, two inches, six inches, and finally a foot. It let out a low groan in protest.

The Dragon members let out shocked screams. She watched as

each skidded to a halt, their heads craned up. They tried to turn around, to flee back the way they had come, but it was too late. With a horrendous crash the rack tipped all the way over, spilling its contents down onto them followed by the rack itself, breaking apart as it toppled over. Like an avalanche, the whole mass swept over them.

When the tangled mass finally settled Asha had to wonder if she had lost her hearing. The entire shop was dead silent. She looked up and down the aisle. She hadn't only tipped over this section of the rack but also all those down the line to the next intersection. From the back of the shop onward there was a glaring hole where shelves should have been. In its place was jumble of metal, wood, and other broken things.

I did it.

She was still alive and unhurt.

Asha ran toward the front of the shop, certain that the rest had run out that way. She knew that Toro and the woman in red were the leaders; if she could just stop them this would be over, here and now.

The front part of the shop was really just an extension of the rear. There was no wall separating the two, only a high desk that ran the width of the building. Beyond, in the showroom, there were spinning racks and display cases holding odds and ends.

Asha put on a burst of speed; she would have to hurry to catch the others. They were probably down the street by now, scared off by the thunder of gunfire and crashing shelves. But she wouldn't let them get —

Cold metal clamped around her arms from behind, gripping hard enough she couldn't even scream. She was hurled through the air, her arms and legs flailing wildly. With a jarring thud she hit the side wall, her back cracking against a hard, metal box. She fell to the concrete floor and gasped madly, trying to draw breath; all she could do was make a weak huffing sound.

She was savagely yanked to her feet by her hair.

"Where do you think you're going?" Toro growled, scowling at her through squinted eyes.

He drew back one metal arm and drove his fist at her head. She twisted away as it grazed her cheek, fighting against the pull of her hair. His fist crashed through the metal box she had hit, sending sparks flying. He pulled his hand back revealing a tangle of wires. A spark leapt from the box and touched Asha's arm making her cry out in pain; it was like a thousand red hot needles jabbed into her arm.

Toro jerked the arm holding Asha by the hair. She screamed again, certain her hair was going to be ripped from her scalp. His pull sent her flying through the air again, weightless and helpless, over the high desk. Her back skimmed the ceiling, smashing into the lights hanging from above, until she crashed into a display case at the end of the room. She landed hard, what air she had managed to get driven from her lungs.

Asha tried to force her body to move, but it wouldn't obey. Her arm, the one that had been shocked, felt dead; her head throbbed where she was sure he had ripped the hair out. Her breath still would not come.

A cold metal hand gripped her throat and she was heaved off the ground, her feet dangling limply below her. Toro's massive face loomed in front of her.

"You've interfered with us for the last time," he threatened through gritted teeth.

Asha choked, the man's steel fingers squeezed so hard she could feel her windpipe start to break. The store went a dark grey and she felt herself slipping away. A few more seconds and she would be dead.

Out of desperation, Asha threw a weak kick at his chest, certain it was the last thing she would ever do. Her foot connected and his hand opened. He flew back and slammed into the desk. Asha dropped to the floor, coughing, her throat on fire. She heaved in a breath, trying desperately to force air into her lungs.

Metal hands grabbed her again, the steel fingers digging into the flesh of her upper arms. She was heaved off the ground and thrown through the air. She crashed through the doors, glass shattering around her and she was engulfed in the cold winter night. She hit the ice so hard her head cracked through to the concrete. Bright white lights danced in the slowly growing darkness.

Asha forced herself to raise her head. Through the haze of snow and darkness she could make out that she had been thrown across the street. In the hole of the door stood the man with the gigantic gun; Toro loomed behind him. Asha tried to stand up, to get her legs underneath her, but they wouldn't move.

A horn, soft and distant sang out a warning, signalling the oncoming explosion.

With a flash, the gun lit up. The air warped from the heat as it ejected a stream of intense light. Asha tried to turn, but she was frozen in the glare of that killing weapon.

A tow truck, pulling a car and blaring its horn, cut across her view. Half a heartbeat later the rear of the car exploded, the street lit up in a gigantic ball of fire. The shock wave hit Asha first, then the heat and flame.

The tow truck swerved, swaying left and right as the driver hit the brakes. It skidded on the ice and careened out of control, slamming into a parked car.

Toro and the man with the gigantic gun stared in awe at the fiery wreckage.

MOVE! NOW!

She staggered to her feet and unsteadily turned around. She lumbered to the alley she had hid in when she first saw the lights in the warehouse.

She stumbled down the alley, working her way up from a limping jog to a run. She pushed herself harder, fighting the pain. She turned down another alley and another, looking desperately for a way out. Then she saw it and she nearly wept.

Up ahead in LR33 stop, as if it knew she needed it, sat an LR pod.

She forced herself over to it and boarded the car just as it started to move. It cleared the station, leaving the warehouse, and The Dragon, behind.

11
FALLING DOWN

Asha awoke with a yell, certain Toro, was in her room. She shot out of bed, hurling her covers to distract him. The blankets fell to the floor as Asha's feet landed on the carpet. She spun around to the left, arms up, ready to defend herself . There was no one there. Frantically, she spun around to the right, ducking low, only to see that there was no one there either. She was alone.

She looked over at the alarm clock; it was still five minutes before her alarm would go off. She reached over and switched off the alarm.

All Asha wanted now was to lie back down and sleep. Her body was drained and her arm still hurt where the spark had struck her. She could move it now, but it was stiff and weak. Her throat hurt, it burned and was sore to the touch.

She put on her glasses and left the room, heading off to the bathroom. She flicked on the light switch and was greeted with a shocking sight. In the mirror, she saw her face bruised and bloody. There were tiny cuts on it along one side, red and inflamed. On the other, just under the hairline, was a light bruise. Dirt and grime covered her face. Worst of all was her neck.

Encircling her throat where Toro's hands had dug deep cut dark, purple bands. She gingerly touched one and hissed at the pain. She had been lucky, if that was the word she could use, had he squeezed any harder he would have killed her.

She knew she couldn't go to school like this and considered staying at the apartment. She could call in sick and just stay put. But of course, that would lead to questions and then her father would want to see her. He would take one look at her and know that something besides a stuffy nose was wrong. She didn't want to deal with that. At least at school the teachers mostly minded their own business.

In the end, Asha tried her best to clean herself up. She washed her face, gingerly scrubbing around the cuts and the bruises. She was only able to gently run the cloth over her throat, just enough to brush off any lingering dirt. She tried her best to cover up the cuts and bruises on her face. Her throat was another story; no matter how she did it, those deep bruises wouldn't fade. She decided that she would have to wear something to cover her neck and then realized she was still wearing the torn clothes from the night before.

She went back to her room and got changed into fresh clothes, or at least not filthy and ruined ones. She put on her hooded sweater and zipped it up all the way to her chin, which mostly covered her neck. By pulling the hood over her head and face she was able to hide just about all of her injuries.

Asha left the apartment soon after, not even bothering to find something to eat.

*

She arrived at school earlier than usual, stopping by her locker only long enough to pick up her books. She wandered back toward her homeroom, stopping in front of the Tube. There was a lush forest scene this time, the trees and ground covered with bright, white snow. A shadow of a deer ambled far away in the distance.

A black symbol flashed onto the screen: it was The Dragon. The voice that came from the Tube eerie and ominous.

"We are chaos. We are anarchy. We are The Dragon. Your heroes are gone. We cannot be stopped. We are in your offices, your schools, your homes. You will know despair. You will know fear. Our time has come."

Then the Tube went black. Asha waited, wondering if it would activate again. It didn't.

How could someone have done that? They would have had to access the computer in the administration office. Maybe it was a teacher. Maybe it was the gym teacher, Mr. Tan, he certainly seemed to really not like kids, judging by the way he had yelled at her. Or the Science teacher, Mr. Speiger. How many times did he have to put up with unruly students like Keri and Trevor. And what about Mr. Jones with kids always going into the nurse's station and messing with his posters like Mick did. It could have been any one of them.

Students filled the area quickly. Soon she was being bumped and pushed. Her arm hurt each time and Asha finally had to move out of the traffic flow. She walked to her home room and took her seat.

"Did you see that?" Lily asked as she sat down beside Asha.

Asha replied with only a nod, staring down at her desk.

"What's with the hood?"

"Nothing," Asha answered, curtly.

"Come on," Lily said, leaning ahead and peering around the edge of the hood. "What's with — " She drew in a sharp gasp. "What happened?"

"Nothing, I'm fine," Asha replied, turning away from her. Why couldn't Lily just leave it be? She always had to know everything.

"What happened?" Lily repeated, reaching over to push Asha's hood away.

"I said, I'm fine!" Asha snapped and slapped Lily's hand away.

Lily hissed in pain and held her hand tightly against her chest. Asha felt a surge of guilt. She hadn't meant to hurt Lily, she just wanted her to stop. She was about apologize when Mick entered the room. His normal, happy smile was gone.

Five minutes passed, then ten. Fifteen minutes went by and still Ms. Lowen had not arrived. The class was impatient and everyone was talking loudly. It all grated on Asha's ears, the noise of it drilling into her skull like a dull ice pick. A wadded up piece of paper hit her in the back of the head and she didn't even so much as flinch. She had to get out.

Asha went to stand up, to leave, when Ms. Lowen entered the room.

"ENOUGH!" the teacher commanded and, remarkably, the class quieted. She hurried over to her desk and put the papers she was carrying down on her desk. She kept her back to the class.

Asha had never seen Ms. Lowen this agitated before.

When the teacher turned around she was composed.

"I want everyone to remain calm," she stated. "I have bad news. The Dragon has attacked again."

Lily raised her hand and patiently waited.

"Yes, Lily?" the teacher asked.

"Where did they attack?"

"Everywhere."

No one shuffled their feet, no one threw wads of paper, no one breathed.

Ms. Lowen continued. "There have been a series of attacks all around the city. At last count there were ten."

Ten? That was more than all the attacks so far combined.

"What kind of attacks?" Lily asked, this time not even bothering to raise her hand or wait for permission to speak.

"Bombings and gunfire," Ms. Lowen answered. "Classes have been cancelled."

Despite the gravity of the situation a collective gasp of excitement washed through the room.

"Your parents are being notified and all the buses are being recalled," Ms. Lowen added. "You are to stay in the school until your bus arrives or your ride comes to pick you up. Teachers will ensure each of you is safely on the way home. Please, go to your lockers and collect your things so you can be ready to leave as soon as possible."

The buzz inside the classroom was nothing compared to out in the main area; it was packed wall to wall with students. Lily pushed her way through the crowd. Asha tried to keep up but the constant flow of students pushing at her from all sides held her back. When she finally caught up at their lockers, Lily and Mick were in a heated debate.

"What do you mean?" Lily asked him.

Asha stepped between them and opened her locker. She took out some of the books she would need for homework and tossed them in her backpack. When she closed the door again the pair had grown silent. She looked first at Lily, who showed only concern, then back to Mick.

"This is all your fault," he said to Asha.

"What are you talking about?"

"You know what I'm talking about!" Mick shouted, slamming his locker door shut.

The area around them grew silent as the crowd turned to see what this new drama was about.

Lily took one look around at the crowd and moved down the hallway saying, "Come on." When neither Asha nor Mick moved, she grabbed them both by the shoulders in a remarkably strong grip and pushed them ahead of her.

Asha shrugged off Lily's hand, irritated at being pushed around. Surprisingly, Mick let himself be lead forward. Lily found an empty classroom doorway and pushed both Asha and Mick into it.

"What's this all about?" Lily demanded, rounding on Mick.

"Why don't you ask *her*?" Mick replied through gritted teeth. His pale skin was growing redder by the moment.

"What are you —?"

"You were there last night, weren't you?" Mick demanded. "At the warehouse."

Asha was taken aback; she'd never seen him like this before.

Mick took her silence as proof and nodding his head, exclaimed, "I knew it! After we told you not to go, you went anyway!"

"Is this true?" Lily asked, turning to Asha.

"Yes," Asha answered. "What's the problem?"

"See, I told you!" Mick said.

"We told you it was too dangerous," Lily said. "Why would you go if it was so dangerous?"

"I went there to stop them. Like I said I would."

"Well, nice job on that one," Mick replied, sarcastically. "Now you've got them blowing up the city."

Furious, Asha rounded on him. "At least I tried to do something."

"You really showed them. I guess all those cuts and bruises must have really scared them off. Or are you going to tell us we should see the other guys?"

"What's your problem?" Asha demanded, glaring at him. It wasn't her fault The Dragon decided to start attacking again. From what she had heard at the supply store they were going to do it anyway.

"My *problem* is you! You're reckless and you're going to get everyone killed!"

"Reckless?" Asha repeated. "Who's the one who wanted to investigate the disappearing truck?"

"Yeah, well getting shot at kinda puts things into perspective," Mick retorted. "At least for normal people."

"What would you know about being normal?"

"Whoa, guys," Lily interjected. "Let's just take a break here. There's no need — "

"My dad was almost killed because of you!" Mick yelled, pointing an accusing finger at Asha.

"What are you talking about?"

"Tell me you don't remember a tow truck saving your life last night."

Asha took a step back, surprised. How did he know about that?

"What?" Lily asked, looking from Asha to Mick.

"It seems Little Miss Big Time Hero over here got in over her head at the store. My dad had just finished picking up a car that had stalled on the west side. He gets into his tow truck, starts it up, and heads down the street. All of a sudden, a person crashes out of a window ahead of him, like they've been thrown, and hits the pavement.

"He looks over and there's two guys, one with metal arms and one with a big gun pointed right at the person in the street. So, thinking it's the poor guy who owns the place who's on the ground he hits the gas and blares his horn. The guy with the gun turns just as he drives by and then the gun goes off.

"It tears through the car and the car explodes! Then he loses control of the truck and smashes into a building and blacks out!"

"Is he all right?" Lily asked, shocked.

"By the time he came to, everyone was gone, the car was still on fire, and the Police — those that weren't still at that shootout — were arriving. He's pretty banged up — probably a concussion — the car and truck's have got thousands worth of damage, and the tow company might fire him for getting involved, but other than that he's perfect. Now do you remember it, Asha, or did you lose your memory when that guy threw you through the window?"

Asha didn't say a word. Having had the whole night played out before here was terrible enough, doubly so now that she knew Mick's father had been the one that saved her.

"Why didn't you tell me?" Lily demanded, turning to Asha.

"Why should I? You didn't want any part of what I was doing yesterday."

"And I was right, wasn't I?" Lily shot back. "Look what happened."

Asha clamped her mouth shut, wanting to shout, wanting to fight. But she knew it was no use.

"Y'know, her mom was right about you," Mick said.

"Oh yeah?" Asha replied calmly, on the outside at least. On the inside, though, her blood was boiling. "What did she say?"

"She said anyone who would let jeans that cost five hundred be ripped like that was too reckless." He looked intently at her then added his final parting shot. "She said you get that from your mother."

It was like Asha had been slapped in the face. The anger that had been building ever since Lily and Mick started in on her drained in an instant. She took another step back, looking to Lily for support. But Lily, who backed her no matter what, was looking down at the floor.

There was nothing she could say, it was clear what they thought of her. She turned on her heel and rushed away, roughly pushing students out of her way.

She managed to get to the main entrance, but the entire area was so packed with students that she would have waited ages to get out. Instead, she continued on to the next side exit.

She was just approaching the lockers opposite the doors when a familiar, but very unwelcome, group approached her. Keri Shaw, Trevor McKnight, and the three others confronted her, making a semi-circle around her and cornering her to the lockers.

"Twitch! I heard you had a fight with Lily and your boyfriend," Keri said in mock concern. "Do you need a hug?"

The others laughed heartily at this, which drew a smug smile from Keri. Asha couldn't understand how they had heard about the fight already.

Keri must have seen the confused look on Asha's face because she said, "News travels fast in here, especially when it's about the school's biggest freak."

Crystal stepped up beside her and said, "We heard —"

"Will you shut up already?" Keri spat. "How many times do I have to tell you?"

Crystal looked hurt. Asha didn't care.

She tried to step to the side, toward the door, but Trevor and Andrew blocked her way, their arms crossed over their chests. A rush of laughter bubbled up inside her. She had narrowly missed being killed by The Dragon, real and dangerous criminals with real and dangerous weapons, and here were junior high thugs trying to intimidate her. She suppressed the laugh but a smile broke out on her face nonetheless.

"What's so funny?" Keri demanded.

Asha knew nothing she said would do any good here. "Nothing."

"How rude," Keri said. "Although I can't say I was surprised, anyone whose mother would abandon her must not have been raised properly."

"What did you say?" Asha threatened.

"It's sad really," Keri continued. "That a mother would be so desperate to escape her own child that she would resort to suicide."

Asha's arm began to twitch.

"Because that's what she did, you know? You are such a loser she couldn't bear it anymore. She was so desperate to get away from you that she actually threw herself into a burning building! I imagine the pain was terrible, but it was probably nothing compared to —"

Asha's hand shot out and clamped tightly around Keri neck. She heaved the girl to the side and slammed her into a pair of lockers.

Keri's hands clamped onto Asha's arm, her eyes wide with terror.

"Say it again," Asha growled, squeezing tighter. Keri let out a whimper.

Trevor and Andrew grabbed onto Asha's free arm and shoulder. She rotated her arm, breaking their hold, and pushed Trevor in the chest. He stumbled into Andrew and the pair fell back into the other two girls.

She squeezed harder on Keri's throat. All that came out of Keri's mouth was a sputter.

"HEY!" someone called.

A hand gripped Asha's shoulder and pulled. She spun and, with her free hand, hit them with the back of her fist. They gave a hiss and stepped back far enough for Asha to see who it was.

"Let her go," Mr. Jones warned, clutching his arm where Asha had hit him. "Now."

Asha took one last look at Keri's quickly reddening face and her teary eyes. Asha let her go; the girl fell to the floor coughing and gasping for air.

Asha turned around, only to meet the serious face of Mr. Jones and a swarm of students gathered around him.

She charged through the crowd, kids jumping back to clear way for her, and headed straight for the exit. Mr. Jones yelled something but Asha ignored him.

If he *was* the one vandalizing the school, if he was the one who had put that message on the Tube, then this was his fault, too.

She threw open the doors and raced away from the school.

*

The rage she had felt at the school hadn't lessened by the time she got to the apartment. If anything, it had grown. Before, with Keri, she had acted without thinking, spurred by the girl's comments. Now, though, she had time to think about all that had happened and it made her feel worse. Lily and Mick hated her for something that wasn't her fault, and by now the entire school knew about how she had attacked Keri, although, that wasn't entirely her fault either.

The one bit of silver lining in this day was that she didn't have to be at school, and judging by the looks of things she wouldn't have to go again for a long time.

After calling her dad and letting him know she was back home she went to her room and laid down on the bed atop the covers. Toro, the woman in red, and Keri Shaw, they were all the same; they hurt people because they could and they enjoyed it. Rather than make her angrier, the thought left Asha feeling drained. How was she supposed to deal with that? How was she supposed to *stop* people like that?

I can't. I can't stop them.

Asha wanted to argue, to say there had to be a way, but there was no point. She had known it from the moment Toro had thrown her through that window; it was impossible.

That was how she fell asleep, with thoughts of The Dragon, Mick and Lily, and Keri Shaw and her friends bouncing around in her head; and below it all a vision of her mother running into the burning house, leaving her behind.

*

She watches as he balances the camera on the picnic table. Asha and her mother are sitting beneath a tree while her father sets up the camera for the picture. The park is alive with sights and sounds of summer. Kids scream chasing each other, parents call to their children, birds call from trees. "Careful!" her mother yells.

The sun is bright in the sky and beams down on her face through the trees; shadows of leaves dance on her face. "Got it!" her father calls back and rushes toward them.

He's just about there when he slips. Like a cartoon character his feet fly into the air, his arms flail, his mouth makes a gigantic 'O' of surprise. He lands on the ground and her mother lets out a loud, light laugh. Asha laughs, not at her father, but at her mother laughing at him.

"Hurry!" her mother calls and he gets up, laughing, and rushes over to them.

"Watch it! Here it comes!"

There is a bright flash of white light and then the sounds stop. The children stop. The birds stop. The sunlight stops. Asha stands up and looks around. Her parents are gone. She turns back and all the children are gone. And the birds. Everything is dim.

"Careful," a high voice says behind her. Asha turns to look but no one is there. "Watch it. Here it comes."

A low thud presses into her as if a giant hand has pushed at her chest. The trees shake. The ground trembles. Lightning rips through the sky and the camera on the picnic table sparks and crackles. The flash tears apart the dimness of the day and all Asha can do is watch as it engulfs her.

*

Asha jolted awake. Her head was still groggy from the sleep and she willed herself to focus. She tried to move but found she was covered in a light blanket; she didn't remember crawling under one.

How long had she been sleeping? Judging by the light it was edging on evening. She crawled out of bed, throwing off the blanket, and left the room.

In the kitchen the radio was silent, thank goodness. Asha glanced out the window, the dull grey light seemed to be lifting, perhaps aided by the streetlights as they grew brighter one by one. That was one thing about this city, you were never short of light.

A rumbling in her stomach distracted Asha from the window. How long had it been since she'd eaten? She was about to head to the fridge when a scrap of paper on the table caught her eye. She picked it up and nearly dropped it even as she read the first line. It was from her father; in his messy handwriting, it read:

Ash,

Tried to wake you up last night but you were really out of it. Rough day at school? Left some pasta and sauce in the fridge from last night. Hope that'll tide you over till supper. Will probably be late again today. Training didn't go so well yesterday, new guys kept getting lost, but we'll manage. School's cancelled today so stay inside and keep safe. I'll call you when I have the chance to check in.

Dad

It's tomorrow morning? Asha thought. She reread the note again and it certainly seemed that way. How could she have slept that long?

As if to confirm the fact that she had slept for nearly an entire day her stomach growled violently again. Obeying it, Asha went to the fridge and found the food her father had made last night neatly packaged away. She heated it and ate ravenously.

When her food was done Asha found herself wondering what she should do with her day. There was homework, of course, and although she dreaded doing any kind of work she knew she was falling behind. All the running around, getting shot at and getting thrown through windows, had been too distracting when it came to schoolwork.

Resigned, Asha found her backpack, she had dropped it on the floor by the door when she came in yesterday, and sat down on the couch. After having to deal with all that stuff before, doing homework would be a breeze. And while she didn't have Lily to help her anymore, she thought she should be able to do it without too much trouble.

The only problem was, whenever Asha tried to focus on her work, her mind would blank out. She wouldn't *black* out, she could see everything around her and hear the sounds of the street outside, but she certainly wasn't thinking about anything. She would try to focus on the words, but one moment she would be reading and the next she would be staring at the wall.

Asha finally gave up on trying to work at all. Instead, she went to the bathroom, hoping that washing her face with some cold water would clear her head. When she turned on the light, though, she was met with a surprise.

The cuts on her face were nearly gone; whereas yesterday they had been red and angry, today they were faded pink. The zipper of her hooded sweater had come undone a bit; she pulled the collar to the side. The bruises there had faded as well, now they were only slightly darker than her own skin. It seemed her body healed quickly.

Asha returned to the living room, but the sight of the homework there made her feel worse.

I could go for a walk, Asha thought. *Just a short one to clear my mind.*

Asha did walk around the apartment complex, a couple times in fact, but it didn't make any difference. Instead of going back inside, she walked toward the downtown area, not really paying attention to where she was going.

The past half year came back to her, accompanying her on her journey, and this time, rather than block it out, rather than deny anything that had happened to her, she let it consume her.

The image of her mother running into the burning house came to her. It was probably because Keri Shaw's words had cut her so deep. Her mother *had* left her; she *had* run away only to die in a fire that was started by people too heartless to care what they were doing. Some people had felt sorry for Asha then, some people had wanted to comfort her, to let her know they were there for her and she had simply pushed them away, confident that she could handle everything herself. She had no clue what had given her this idea, and only now did she realize how stupid it had been. Of course, she couldn't handle everything by herself, she was only a kid.

And why had she thought that she could return to school only a month after she had been in the hospital? A month after her mother had died? Any normal person would have done it right. They would have taken the time to work it through and to heal. But then again, she wasn't normal.

Then she had moved out of her house; she had to leave her home and move to this city into a rundown apartment. Her father had taken a job where he saw her less and really, could she blame him? After all, who would want to be around someone as strange and abnormal as her? The thought didn't please her, but she knew it was true, he wasn't around as much anymore and she knew it was because of what she had become: a twitching, moody girl who could only remind him of what he had lost.

And, of course, there was her condition; this weird thing that had made her a stranger in her own body. She had been hoping to figure it out, that maybe her pain had been for a reason and that she could finally be something worthwhile, but that hadn't been the case. Instead of doing good, she had nearly gotten people killed, including herself. It wasn't The Dragon's fault she had decided to try and stop them. If she was honest with herself she had made them out to be a bigger threat than they had been. Sure, they had stolen things and blown a few holes in a few walls but so what? Up until she had confronted them, they hadn't terrorized the city in huge waves of destruction. They had only started that when they were threatened by *her*. The whole thing was her fault, just like Mick said.

A loud horn made her jump. A blue car swerved toward her, its tires slipping on the ice. Asha froze, confused about why a car was on the sidewalk. The car rushed toward her and Asha threw up her hands in a vain attempt to stop it. At the last moment the driver swung the car to the side and cut around her, missing her by a hair. The car swayed dangerously from side to side until the driver got it under control. She expected the car to stop, for the driver to get out and ask if she was hurt; instead it kept going as if Asha had merely been a chunk of debris, narrowly avoided. It was only then that Asha realized she was standing in the middle of the road.

She hadn't recognized she was on the street because there were no cars. There were no trucks or taxis or vans or anything. The street was completely empty. What was more, she was downtown amongst the stores and shops, but they all seemed abandoned.

Far down the street, in the direction the car had come from, a great plume of billowing grey smoke stretched to the sky. It rose before being whisked away by the cold, winter wind.

Asha finished crossing the road, never taking her eyes off that plume of smoke. She didn't know how far away it was, but clearly it was close enough that everyone had fled, everyone who hadn't stayed home, that is.

"I really do hope they deal with that soon," a voice behind her said, giving Asha a start..

She spun around to come face to face with Elizabeth.

"It's been going for an hour now," the woman said conversationally, as if she were discussing the weather. "Would you like to come in?"

She indicated a door with her open arm. It was only then that Asha realized she was standing outside the woman's shop.

Asha didn't want to be rude, but she didn't really feel like going inside.

The woman seemed to sense this because she dropped her arm and said, "On second thought, I could stand to get some fresh air."

"You said it started an hour ago?" Asha asked, turning back to the smoke.

"Yes. I had been doing okay, people stopping in and checking things out, until that explosion. They all left of course. Kind of put a damper on things."

"Why didn't you leave?"

"I really don't think there's anything to worry about here."

"Nothing to worry about?" Asha asked.

"I'm sure the fire will be out sooner or later, although I do hope it's the former and not the latter."

"You're not worried about The Dragon?"

"Those guys?" the woman said. She waved her hand in the air dismissively. "They're a joke."

"I don't think the police are having much luck stopping them."

"They police are good at making sure all the day to day stuff runs smoothly, but this is something else entirely."

"Then why aren't you worried about The Dragon?"

The woman looked at Asha out of the corner of her eye, a sly grin creeping up on her lips; it was a look Mick might have given her.

"There's someone else out there, keeping these guys in check."

Asha grew uneasy.

"Someone has been throwing monkey wrenches into The Dragon's machine. First someone took out their flying jet-boot man, then someone stopped them at the mall. A couple of days ago they foiled a robbery at a supply store."

Asha took a step away from the woman. Her unease had turned to fear, fear that this woman might know something about *her*.

"I know what you're thinking," the woman said

Dread washed over Asha.

The woman edged closer. "You're thinking Captain Stoneman is back."

Asha's mouth dropped open.

"Yes, I thought so. Maybe undercover," the woman agreed, as if Asha's reaction were proof enough of her suspicions. "He served this city well for a number of years but I don't think it's him. As they say, all good things must come to an end."

Asha's dread slipped away — the woman didn't know anything after all.

"Are you all right?" Elizabeth asked. "You seem a bit, preoccupied."

Asha shrugged. She didn't know what to say.

"You can tell me. Promise I won't tell anyone. Scout's honour," she said holding up her hand in a salute.

"You're a scout?"

"I'm a lot of things."

"I messed up," Asha admitted. "People got hurt."

"I see," Elizabeth said, sombrely. "How bad?"

"Pretty bad."

"It was all your fault?" the woman asked, concerned.

"Pretty much."

"And there's no way to fix it?"

"I don't think so."

Elizabeth stood in silence, staring at the cloud of billowing smoke spreading across the sky.

"Do you know Alexander Stoneman's story?" she asked.

"Kind of," Asha said. "He volunteered for an experimental program. The police gave him a fancy armoured suit. They trained him to be some sort of super cop. I think they even gave him performance enhancing drugs. That's about it."

"Yes," the woman said. "But do you know the story of Alexander Stoneman?"

"Alexander Stoneman *was* Captain Stoneman," Asha replied.

"True," the woman admitted. "But he was Alexander Stoneman first."

Asha stared at the woman, confused.

"He was a boy, about your age. Loved movies. Westerns, sci-fi, action, super hero, romance. They were magic to him. He would see a show again and again until his parents told him it was enough, and then he would sneak in and watch it again. He loved being taken to those other worlds. He would have lived in a theatre if he could have.

"Then his parents were murdered."

A sharp pang twinged in Asha's chest.

"It happened right here, where you're standing."

Seeing the surprise in Asha's face the woman added, "Strange, I know. Alexander had dragged them to a show at the theatre just across the street."

Asha looked across the street, but only saw an art gallery. She supposed it could have been a movie theatre at one time.

"When the movies was over, before they could get back in their car, two men rushed at them. His mother and father tried to fight them off, but the men had knives. They stabbed the father and when the mother yelled at them to stop they turned and stabbed her through the heart. The two of them fell to the ground. Alexander dropped with them to the sidewalk, screaming.

"One of the two men grabbed the keys from his father's hands and then they were gone. The boy was left with his parents, trying desperately to stop the blood flow with his bare hands. It didn't make a difference."

In her mind's eye Asha could see it all; the screaming boy, the glinting knives, the blood.

"Were they caught?"

"No."

"No?" Asha demanded. "Why not?"

The woman only shrugged. "Who knows?"

"What happened to him?"

"Alexander died right there."

Asha's eyes widened in shock.

"Not like that. But the happy boy, the one who loved movies. He was gone. I think he thought it was his fault. After all, he had dragged them to the movie."

"How could it have been his fault? He was just a kid."

"Like you?" the woman asked. When Asha didn't reply Elizabeth continued. "He was put into foster care, he had no one else, and that's where he spent the rest of his childhood. Alone and unwanted."

"How did he get through it?" Asha asked.

"Hope."

"Hope?"

"It happened a year later. He was in school but he was never really *there*. His grades were passable, but only just. He was withdrawn, had no friends, he was very much a loner.

"Then one day they were having a career day at the school and a police officer gave a presentation. The officer talked of dedication, of serving the public, of *protecting* others. I don't know exactly what he said, but Alexander took notice. It was in that moment that Captain Stoneman was born.

"He dedicated himself to that one goal: he pushed himself to get perfect grades, joined sports to make himself fit, led debate clubs to better his public speaking. He did anything that would make him a perfect police officer. It took him all his teen years and into his twenties to grow into the man we knew as Captain Stoneman. He had a special suit, years of training, performance enhancing drugs, but beneath all of that was the will that made him special."

"Why did he do it?"

"Hope is a powerful thing, Asha. People will do anything, even at a cost to themselves if it means a chance at something better. He found that "something" in helping people and in doing so gave hope to countless others.

"But now Captain Stoneman's time has passed and he has gone over to the other side."

Asha hadn't known any of this; all this time she had hated him for what happened to her mother. Could he really have been the great man everyone made him out to be?

"We've been waiting for someone to take his place and, as they say, all good things come to those who wait," the woman continued.

"I thought you said all good things must come to an end."

"So I did!" she replied, clearly surprised. "But that doesn't mean only one can be true. It's all about balance."

"Balance?"

"Everything seeks balance, Asha."

The woman looked seriously at Asha then, with absolute certainty, proclaimed, "We have a new protector. The Dragon will be stopped. It's only a matter of time."

Asha wished she could believe the woman, but knew what she said wasn't true; there was no new protector. Asha was the only one who could possibly stop The Dragon and she was not going to interfere with them ever again.

The faint wail of fire trucks and police vehicles approached. They would arrive soon and, quite frankly, Asha had no desire to talk to anyone else.

"Wait here a second," Elizabeth said.

She disappeared into the shop and re-emerged a minute later carrying a cloth bag which she handed to Asha.

"What's this?"

"Open it when you get home."

"I really should get going," Asha said, apologetically.

The woman showed no signs of disappointment or surprise. Instead, she simply nodded. "I guess I should close up, too. I don't suppose many people will be stopping by, and it is getting late."

"What time is it?" Asha asked, not really caring.

"About four-thirty."

Four-thirty? Had she really been walking for hours?

"Thanks," Asha said and turned to leave. Although she didn't know where she was going she knew she didn't want to be here any longer.

The fire trucks were coming up around a bend; she could see their flashing lights reflected on the buildings as they approached. Asha hurriedly crossed the street before the vehicles could arrive.

"Good luck finding your way," Elizabeth called.

Asha looked back to see the woman give a brief wave before turning around and going into her shop.

Asha wondered where she should go next. Clearly there was no place open she could go to and it was getting late. She decided she should just head home. She didn't want to go, but what choice did she have?

Asha was halfway down the block and on her way home by the time the fire trucks and police cars arrived at the burning building. She knew they would be too late to make any difference.

*

On her way downtown Asha must have taken a long, meandering route because she arrived at the apartment only a short while after leaving Elizabeth's store. She unlocked the door and stepped into the apartment. Silence greeted her.

She took off her sweater, letting the door shut behind her, and stepped into the darkened living room, dropping the bag Elizabeth had given her on the floor.

"What are you doing?" a low voice called from the black, making her jump. Her father loomed out of the darkness before flipping on the light. He was still wearing his security guard uniform.

"Don't do that!" Asha gasped. "You scared the life out of me. What are you doing here? I thought you were going to be late."

"I called during my lunch break," he replied. "You didn't answer."

"I went out for a walk," Asha said.

"When I clearly told you to stay inside and not leave?" he demanded.

"I couldn't stay in here any longer. It was driving me insane, okay?"

"No, it's not okay," her father shot back. "I tried calling you three times in a hour and you still didn't answer. Then I thought you might have gone to Lily's, so I called her mom. You weren't there. So I called Mick's house and you weren't there either."

"I told you I went for a walk."

"I also got a call from your school today. From Mr. Jones."

Asha gave a start, her eyes widening.

"Yeah, him. He said he was too busy with the school evacuation to call me yesterday. He said he had to stop you from hurting another girl."

"That wasn't my fault! Keri and her friends were bullying me, I was just trying to defend myself."

Her father stood silently. When he spoke again his voice was low. "After I talked to Mr. Jones, I tried calling you again, but you still didn't pick up. So I left work and drove straight here. I got home around one o'clock."

He tried to speak calmly, but Asha could not deny the tremor in his voice. "You weren't here so I thought you might have gone for a walk around the block. I scoured the area, but I couldn't find you."

"I went for a long walk."

His face darkened. "I called the police."

"What? Why?"

"They said there was nothing they could do right then. It seems they're too busy dealing with a bunch of psychos terrorizing the city to look for a fourteen year old girl who should have been at home."

She was starting to see his point. Just another thing she'd messed up.

"I'm worried about you."

"I'm sure," Asha said, sarcastically.

"What?"

"Forget it," she said, waving her hand. She turned around to go to her room, wondering how much more of this horrible life she would have to endure.

"Asha Anderson," her father commanded. "We're dealing with this now," he said before turning on his heel and walking into the living room.

Asha hesitated then followed him, not wanting to, but helpless to do otherwise. When he got to the couch he turned to face her.

"You can't go on like this. You have to start getting things back on track. I know it's been hard and we've gone through a lot, but this is no way to live your life. You can't just keep doing whatever you feel like and not have any consequences."

"Like Mom did?" she shot.

He scowled. "Leave her out of this. She has nothing —"

"She has *everything* to do with this!" Asha shouted. "This is all her fault!"

"You don't know what you're saying."

"She left me on the street and ran into a burning building! She left me there alone! And now I'm a freak. My arms and legs flip out or I collapse and blackout and everyone laughs at me. Everyone!"

Asha wanted to stop, to just walk away, to go to her room, to go anywhere but she couldn't.

"Everything I do goes wrong. People get hurt or people get mad or I get hurt.

"I used to have a home, a real home. You keep calling this place our home, but it's not. This is where we moved to because you didn't like our real one and decided to bring us here.

"Even you don't want to be around me. You stay longer and longer at work and I know it's because you think I'm weird or because you can't stand to be around me! You don't even want our pictures up you're so ashamed of me.

"Do you think Mom would have wanted me to be cautious? To be a good girl and do what I'm told? Mom was more reckless than anyone. She could have stayed out and called for help. She could have *not* gone into a building that was going to explode at any second. But instead, she chose a stranger over me. I used to have everything!"

She looked at her father through blurry eyes and finally said, "I used to be happy."

There it was. All that she had been feeling all these months laid bare, all the things she had kept hidden, even from herself, out in the open. Asha raised her hand to her face, taking off her glasses, and brushed the tears from her cheek.

"Sit down," her father said. His tone was calm, there was no hint of anger. Through the haze of tears she saw his face, tired and weary.

Asha backed up to the couch and sat down, staring up at him. He ran his hand through his hair and heaved a heavy sigh. He sat down on the coffee table in front of her.

"You're right," he said. "Mom did choose, but she didn't choose a stranger over you. She made a choice to try and help someone." He looked off to the side then added. "She chose to help someone, and I hate her for it."

How could he say something like that?

"I don't know what she was thinking when she ran into that house, but I do know she wasn't thinking about us. Sometimes I wonder how she could have left me to manage on my own and why she didn't think of that before she wanted to be a hero. And it's those times I miss her the most."

He shifted his gaze from beside Asha to his hands.

"Some days I wake up in the morning and I can't move to get out of bed. I know the day is going to be hard and that I'm going to be wanting her to be alive so badly it will hurt. I *know* it will and there will be nothing I can do about it. I just want to give up, to let it all go away.

"Do you know what makes me get up? Even when I know it will be a horrible day?"

Asha shook her head.

"I think of you. I think of how I know you will get up, like you do every morning. I think of how you will somehow make it through the day even though you have it far worse than I ever will.

"So I get up. I move and I start the day. And it does hurt just like I knew it would and sometimes I want to quit it all, just like I knew I would. But at least I'm moving and that's a start."

He took a deep breath and steadied himself.

"I don't know when things are going to get better. But I do know *you* need to make the choice to make it that way.

"It's hard, but you need to let go of the fact that Mom died too soon and hold onto the time she was with us; to recognize that this apartment may not be as nice as our old house but it can still be our home; to understand that you are the one who decides that you are important, not some kids at school.

"I wish I could make everything better, but I can't. It's up to you."

Asha tried to hold his gaze but couldn't.

He smiled and said, "I believe in you."

The phone rang, startling them both. Her father gave a weak chuckle then stood up. He picked up the phone receiver and greeted the person on the other line, but soon his face fell.

"Can't someone else do it?" he asked. There was a pause then he said, "Well, I am kind of busy right — " Another pause. "Okay, yeah." he said as he hung up the phone.

"What is it?" Asha asked.

"That was my boss. A couple of the guards at work haven't come in for their shift. So it's just him and a bunch of new guys there. They need me to come in."

"Now?" Asha asked.

"I know, but I did cut out of work early to find you," he said. "I'll just head over there and see what's up. Maybe, the others are just late."

"Is it safe?" Asha asked, thinking of all the explosions around the city. In her mind she saw a great plume of smoke darkening the sky.

"You've seen the Plant," he said, handing her the phone. "The place is like a fortress when it's locked down. It's probably the safest place in the city. Will you be okay here by yourself?"

Asha considered saying no and, of course, he would stay. But that would be a lie; if there was one person who could take care of herself it was her. Instead, she gave him a simple nod.

"If you want to talk a bit when I get back we can do that," he said, almost apologizing.

He gathered up his things — his coat and gloves, wallet and keys — and walked to the living room entrance.

"Keep this door locked and don't leave," he said, then added "You'll listen to me this time, right?"

"Yeah." She had no desire to walk around the city any more; she was exhausted. There was no way she was going to leave the apartment.

"I'll see you later."

The door shut. She was alone.

He believed in her, that's what he had said. He believed she could be happy and all she had to do was choose to do it. The idea seemed ridiculous, the thought that she could make her life better just by choosing to do it. It was like defying gravity just by willing yourself to or stopping time just by wishing it.

Asha stood up, went to the balcony door, slid it open, and stood outside. It should have been freezing outside, but here it was actually warm; perhaps there was an updraft or maybe it was just the building itself giving off heat.

The phone rang once again and Asha considered not answering it, it was probably her father's work wondering if he had left yet and when he would arrive. She answered it anyway.

"Hello," she said.

The other end of the line was silent.

"Hello?"

Nothing but quiet, muffled breathing.

Irritated, she said, "Hell — "

"Asha?" a desperate voice whispered from the other side.

"Lily?"

"They're here!" Lily's voice quavered.

"Who — "

"At Mom's work! The Dragon!"

A shock ran down Asha's spine.

"Mick tried to call the police but they don't answer! No one does! You're the only — "

A bang echoed from across the line.

"Asha —"

The line went dead. There was no buzzing sound or crackling voices. Just silence.

"Lily!" she screamed.

The terror she had heard in Lily's voice was now in her own. Lily was in danger and there was no one to help her. She couldn't get a hold of the police and even if they got there, they wouldn't be able to do anything. Her father was long gone by now and had told her to stay put. And every time Asha tried to do something the situation just got worse. Look at what had happened to Mick's dad, look what happened to Keri Shaw. She had to do something but knew she couldn't.

Once more a vision of her mother running into the burning house flashed across her mind; she saw the woman turn to her, saw something she should have recognized a long time ago.

The phone slipped out of her hand, her fingers letting it slide out of her grip. Before it crashed to the floor Asha made her choice.

12
THE HAAS BUILDING

Asha Anderson stood on the snow covered balcony of her apartment and looked North, to the HAAS building, to Lily and Mick.

She had considered running as soon as she dropped the phone, just heading out the door and sprinting all the way to the HAAS building like she had sprinted to the West Bridge before. She knew it wouldn't work though; if she ran all that way she would be dead tired by the time she got there and she would be of no use to anyone. It was time to start being smarter.

She had only one option: the LR2. It was still running regularly and would take her right to the HAAS building.

She turned on the spot and looked up. It was ten feet to the roof. She closed her eyes, envisioning the leap it would take.

Her eyes flashed open and with a mighty push, she launched herself toward the roof. She reached out her hand, caught the ledge, and pulled herself up.

She sprinted across the roof, but rather than slow down near the edge, she leapt. She landed on the roof of the next building, rolling on the snow. In one movement she was up and running again. The LR2 was only a few blocks away, it would take her where she needed to go.

Asha was in luck; she arrived at the LR2 stop just as the capsule was leaving. She jumped and landed on the roof with a loud thud, crouching to cushion her landing.

The car quickly picked up speed and was soon zipping through the city. She only hoped she wouldn't be too late.

*

Outside, the HAAS building was quiet. Asha stood at the main doors, looking up into the black sky, trying to see the massive building's roof. It was lost in the darkness.

How was she going to get inside? The last time she was here she had just walked in the front door with Lily and Mick, but she doubted that would work now. She walked up to one of the revolving doors and pushed. It spun easily.

She had expected the place to be locked up tight since it was after hours. She had also expected extra security measures to have been taken since The Dragon had come. Cautiously, she walked through the door.

The main lobby lights were low; it looked like she was walking on a sea of black, the marble floor reflecting light in a soft glow. The reception desk in the centre of the room sat empty except for a lone woman. The place was eerily silent.

Asha approached the desk, her footsteps echoing loudly.

"Can I help you?" the woman asked, pleasantly, when Asha arrived at the desk.

"Uh… yeah… " Asha stammered. She had expected the place to be a disaster zone, like the rest of the places in the city that The Dragon had attacked.

"I'm looking for someone," Asha said, cautiously.

"I'm sorry, but the building is empty."

"Are you sure?"

"Positive."

There was something strange here. A building this size was never empty. Lily's mom was here often enough to prove that. The woman fidgeted in her seat.

"Can I use your washroom?" Asha asked, hoping that if she could get by this woman she could find Lily.

"No, sorry. But you can try the convenience store down the road," the woman said, pointing at the door. Her sleeve pulled back to reveal a dragon shaped tattoo.

The lights flared. The woman's eyes narrowed and her other arm shot out from under the desk. A moment later Asha was face to face with a very large pistol.

Asha twisted to the side, grabbed onto the woman's wrist, and wrenched it up.

The woman let out a scream of pain before the gun fired with a loud boom. Asha twisted her arm harder and felt the bones snap. The gun toppled out of her hand and onto the floor. Asha pulled the woman close, grabbed her by the jacket and threw her back. She soared through the air and hit the back of the reception desk with a crack, tumbling over backwards.

The doors surrounding the lobby flew open and a horde Dragon members rushed in, all of them with dragon tattoos on their faces, all of them armed, and all of them certainly dangerous; many of them were teenagers.

Asha managed to jump over the desk and land in its centre before she was surrounded.

"Don't move!" yelled a man with a mole on his face. He looked suspiciously familiar.

Her heart beat rapidly, but it was a steady beat, as if counting down the seconds. She was ready for whatever came; Lily and Mick needed her.

Asha scanned the room for an exit, a way to get out without doing what she knew she was going to have to do.

"Fire!" the man yelled, his finger slowly squeezing on the trigger of his gun.

Asha flattened herself to the floor as the gun fired, the bullets hit the desk with a dull thud. An instant later the others joined in.

Explosions ripped the air, each one tearing deeper in the steel of the desk. Above her head computer monitors exploded in showers of sparks, paper shot up high into the air.

Asha sprung up into a crouch. She grabbed the bases of two chairs and heaved them over the edge of the desk and followed them. As they soared through the air over the desk, so did she, leaping high. The chairs smashed into two of the attackers, knocking them off their feet and sending them sprawling onto their backs. Asha landed a moment later where the two had been standing, picked up one of the chairs and hurled it again, striking a girl in the legs sending her sprawling onto the floor.

Another rushed at her. With a desperate jump she launched herself toward him, driving her fist into his chest. He fell back into the desk, his gun firing high into the ceiling, his arms flailing madly about.

She spun around to find a girl directly behind her, a machine gun primed and ready. Asha reached out and grabbed the gun barrel in a tight grip and yanked it out of her hands. She swung the weapon in a wide arc catching the girl at the base of her neck with the butt of the gun. The other girl crumpled to the floor.

In front of her a boy her age screamed and charged at her. She launched herself forward, landing in a diving roll just before him, and swung the gun at his knee. He let out a yell of pain and dropped to the floor, clutching his leg.

A blur of motion caught her eye as a second boy rounded the desk, firing at her. Asha swung her arm and an instant later the gun was cutting through the air, tumbling end over end like a pinwheel. It struck him square in the chest, sending him flying.

The remaining members intensified their attack; they grouped together on the far side of the desk and fired heavily, pinning Asha to the floor. She rolled to the desk, trying to gain cover from the hail of bullets. She couldn't hold out much longer; eventually one of them was going to get a lucky shot and it would be over. She decided to not let that happen.

She gripped the desk with both hands and then, driving with her legs, tore it off the floor. The anchors holding the desk to the marble floor snapped and Asha hurled it. The Dragon members could only stand and watch, stunned, as the huge bulk of steel bore down on them. It crashed down hard, knocking them back and pinning them beneath it. The force of it drove them along the floor until it came to a screeching halt near the far wall.

Silence blanketed the room.

Asha looked around the room and was shocked to see the state of it. The main desk was torn in two, the one side still standing nearly shredded. Holes punctured the floor, walls, and ceiling; the glass windows at the front had been shattered. All about the floor, people lay scattered. A couple of them rolled back and forth in pain, the rest lay motionless.

Asha ran to the elevator ready to hammer the call, button but then she realized the elevators didn't have them; you had to swipe a badge to do anything. Besides, from the look of them with all the bullet holes, she doubted they were in any shape to operate. She had to find a way up. If she couldn't do that soon — There! She saw a sign just above a door that read "Stairs".

A dull thudding sound echoed through the lobby. More Dragon members were on their way.

She rushed over to the door and tried the doorknob; it was locked. She took a step back and kicked it as hard as she could. It exploded inward, as if it had been hit by a car; the hinges tore out of the frame as the door itself crashed into the wall behind it.

Then the lights went out.

She ran up the stairs, her feet pounding the concrete steps as hard as they could. She took two steps at a time, then three. The signs for each floor blurred passed: 1,2,3,5,8,13.

Asha reached the the right floor in little time. Lily had said they were in the building and she had probably been her mom's office when she called.

She left the stairwell, the elevators to her right motionless. There was a faint glow coming from somewhere, perhaps the emergency lighting systems had kicked in. Everything *looked* normal so far, but as she approached the barrier wall Asha knew things were far from okay.

The wall, which was usually a solid blank sheet, had a door shaped rectangular hole in it. Asha didn't know much about the technology behind the wall, but she was pretty sure the wall filled itself in once someone had gone through it. She inched closer to it and poked her head through. Like the elevator hallway, this one was dark and empty.

She jogged toward the end of the hallway, keeping her eyes peeled for any sign of motion; the glow of the emergency lights went with her.

When she reached the door to the lab Asha rushed through it, but as she entered she skidded to a halt. The room was in shambles.

Equipment was strewn about the floor, the fridge and couch from the office were tipped over, Lily's Mom's desk had been thrown across her office. Papers littered the area.

"Lily?"

"Asha?" a quiet voice called out.

From behind the couch in the office area, Lily's head poked up followed quickly by Mick's.

"I told you it was her!" Mick exclaimed, coming around to the front side of the couch.

"What are you guys doing back there?"

"Just hanging out," Mick replied. "Y'know, catching up on old times."

Asha tiptoed around the mess toward them, careful not to step on anything.

"We were hiding from The Dragon," Lily said. "A couple guys chased us in here so we hid."

"They were they chasing you?"

"Yeah," Mick replied. "I think they wanted my autograph but no way was I going to give it to them. I mean first you do that for them then they get your phone number then they're stalking you — "

"Yes, they were chasing us," Lily said, cutting him off.

"They're here because their big thing is happening tonight!" Mick exclaimed. "They tore this place apart looking for us. We hid in the office next door and then came here when we left."

"How do you know their 'big thing' is happening tonight?"

"Because they said so," Lily replied.

Asha held up her hands and said, "Okay, hold on. Just start from the beginning."

"Well, yesterday, after we, you know... fought," Lily said, ashamed.

"It's okay," Asha said. "Go on."

"Well, after, I got to wondering just what The Dragon was building. I mean, they just about killed you trying to get what they were looking for so they must have wanted it really bad.

"I had been searching online at home, but I couldn't really find anything. HAAS has designed and created lots of stuff and I thought they might have a record of it and maybe it could help. Then Mick said he would like to go. So today, Mick and I caught a ride here with my Mom — "

Lily stopped in mid-sentence her face flushed with fear.

"Oh, my — Mom!" she gasped.

"Where is she?" Asha asked.

"I don't know!" Lily shrieked. "Mick and I had been sitting at the computer, looking over things when she went out. She had been gone a while so we went to see what she was up to. We got up to the elevators and saw a couple of Dragon members standing there, so we hid. They must have spotted us because just as we hid they started trashing the place looking for us.

"What if she's been hurt or — " Lily's voice cracked and she gave Asha a pleading look.

"We'll find her," Asha assured her; they would search every room in every floor if they had to. "We just have to be care —"

A white hot laser tore through the door and scorched the ceiling.

"Hide!" Asha hollered, pushing Lily and Mick toward the couch.

An instant later another jet of white light demolished what was left of the door.

She stood turned back to see the man with the ridiculously large gun standing in the doorway.

Desperate, she grabbed a table and threw it at him. It soared through the air, tumbling end over end. He fired, cutting it clean in half. One chunk hit him in the shoulder and he spun; the beam of the gun sliced through the air, barely missing Asha's head.

She picked up a chair and threw it, then another; each time the gun lit them on fire. Asha gripped onto a desk and heaved it at him as if it were a cardboard box. She rushed at him, reaching him just as the desk crashed to the floor.

He tried to fire at her again but never got the chance. Asha knocked the weapon away with one hand and drove her other fist drove into his face. He flew back, out the door and into the hallway. He crashed to the floor, his body skidding along the surface until it came to a dead stop.

Two figures rushed up the hallway shouting. They skirted the man lying on the floor and thundered their way toward her.

Asha stepped ahead to meet them. Hitch and Finch skidded to a halt a moment later. The pair stared at the carnage of the room and then at Asha.

"You guys really don't want to do this," she warned.

The men looked at her in shock then at each other, eyes wide. They held their stares for a second then turned and ran, stumbling down the hallway and pushing each other out of the way.

Asha hurried back to the couch where Lily and Mick were hiding. They had to get out of here and find Lily's mom.

"Well done," a high voice called from behind her.

Asha spun around. Standing in the doorway was the woman in red.

*

"Very well done," the woman in red said, then she began to clap. "Bravo."

Asha took a step toward the woman, but she held up her hand.

"I don't think so," Athena said. In her hand she revealed a small spherical device with a blinking red light on the top.

"What's that?" Asha demanded.

"Just a little insurance. If I push this little blinking light, well, let's just say you're not going to be too happy and neither will a few million other people."

"What do you want?"

"I've told you already. Join us. Be free."

"After all that I've done to you, how can you expect that?"

"You are young. You don't always understand what you are doing. We accept that. How many others can say the same?"

"Is this the same speech you give to all the kids you sucker into joining you?"

"I haven't 'suckered' anyone into anything. I have only shown them the truth. And look at what they have done. Youth no older than yourself, with no special skills or abilities, have shown this city the true meaning of freedom.

"I've watched you these past couple of months and I see greatness. Captain Stoneman was the same and look what happened to him, died fighting the 'good' fight. I don't want the same to happen to you.

"Tonight, we are going to finally bring this city to its knees. Ascension's Cross, the City of Lights, will dwell in darkness. We will rampage through it, take what we want, *do* what we want. Join us and you can be a part of it."

"You're insane," Asha said.

The pair stood staring at each other, the seconds ticking away, neither of them moving.

Finally the woman spoke. "You're not going to join me, are you?"

The question was ridiculous.

"No."

"I didn't think so," the woman admitted, but she was studying Asha closely. "You have no idea what is coming, little girl. Events are in motion that cannot be undone and what happens in this city is only the beginning. Choose your side wisely if you want to survive."

"Survive what?"

The woman merely grinned and then slipped to the side.

A huge figure filled the doorway. Toro, his steel arms glinting in the glow of the emergency lights, glared at her.

"Toro here has been dying to meet you again," the woman said as he stepped into the room, his footsteps echoing ominously.

The woman slipped behind him and through the doorway.

"Oh, and little girl," she called, peeking around the man's massive body. She held up the device with the blinking light and pressed down with her thumb; it let out a beep. "I'd say you have about five minutes, give or take."

A moment later she was gone.

Toro scowled at her, his face hard as granite. His voice rumbled when he spoke. "Now it's just you and me."

Asha stepped back as the goliath of a man stalked into the room. He towered over her, his massive body trembling the floor with each powerful step.

"I've been waiting for this," he rumbled. He punched one metal hand with a steel fist; it made a dull metallic thump.

"OH MY — " a woman cried from behind him.

Toro spun around revealing Mrs. Donovan standing in the doorway.

"RUN!" Asha screamed.

Time slowed; Asha could count each step, she could hear the rise and fall of each of Mrs. Donovan's breaths.

Lily's mom tried to stumble back when she realized the huge man was coming at her, but she backed into the door frame instead. With lightning speed he shot out a steel hand and caught her by the arm.

"LET HER GO!" Asha commanded.

For a moment it looked like he might indeed let her go; his hand started to relax and his face went slack. Then his arm twitched and he tossed her. She flew high in the air, her shoulder grazing the ceiling, her high pitched scream echoing.

Asha leapt, hoping desperately that she had timed her jump right. She reached out her arms, her hands touched the woman's jacket and she clamped on has hard as she could. Together, the pair of them tumbled over the work counter; Asha spun in mid-air, rolling them. She hit the row of cabinets, taking the force of their fall with her back. Then they crashed to the floor.

Cold, metal hands gripped Asha by the shoulders and then *she* was soaring through the air, her arms pin wheeling and her legs kicking wildly. She crashed hard into what was left of Lily's mom's desk.

Stunned, Asha could only wonder at how fast he had moved; she had only taken her eyes off Toro for a second.

Asha rolled to the side as a metal hand drove toward her. It punched a hole through the desk, the sound it made when it hit the floor like an explosion.

"You're mine!" Toro yelled and clamped a hand on her shoulder.

Asha grabbed onto his arm, the one holding onto her shoulder, and squeezed; the steel underneath crumpled under her hand, the look on his face changing from triumph to shock.

"No, *you're* mine!" Asha yelled. Then she ran.

She sprinted toward the door, dragging the man with her. He struggled roughly, his bulk swaying Asha from her path. Desperate, he swung his other arm around and gripped her in a bear-hug. Their combined weight was too much and she stumbled forward.

Asha had been aiming for the door, to get him out and away from the room. Instead, they fell through the wall, tearing through the steel posts.

She clasped her hands around the man's back and lifted, driving him through the next wall like a battering ram. Then another and another. She pushed them through walls, tables and chairs, filing cabinets and counters.

The final wall gave through and Asha slammed him through a set of metal doors.For a moment she and the man seemed to float in mid-air above the gaping hole of the elevator shaft.

Then they toppled over and together they fell.

Something hard rammed into her back and she bounced to the other side of the elevator shaft and hit a metal beam then another. They plunged down, bouncing and smashing as they went.

They crashed into another door so hard she felt her teeth rattle.

She hit the floor at a roll, unable to stop the force of her fall.

*

GET UP! a voice screamed in her head, tearing through the black.

Asha's eyes shot open. She was lying on her back, pain screaming in every part of her body. She rolled to her side to see where she was; it was a room about the size of Mrs. Donovan's lab but completely empty. A bay of windows ran the width of the room.

A low groan echoed through in the silence. Asha forced herself to roll over and came face to face with Toro. He was lying crumpled up with his eyes shut; a huge gash cut across his cheek through his dragon tattoo.

Asha sucked in a hiss of breath and his eyes fluttered open. She skittered backwards on all fours, fighting the pain, desperate to get away from him. She was barely able to stand on two shaky legs.

Toro let out another groan. He pressed his hand against the floor and pushed himself up, getting his feet underneath him. His left arm dangled uselessly from his shoulder, torn apart by Asha and the fall.

"That was fun," he rumbled. "You put up a good fight, kid, but you're done. What do you think?"

Asha clamped her mouth shut.

"That's what I thought," he said. "Maybe when I'm done with you I'll go upstairs and have a bit more fun with that woman," he threatened. He took another step then added with a knowing grin, "And with whoever else is left up there."

Asha shot forward.

Her feet pounded the floor, her legs driving her ahead. Her vision narrowed on the man. She could feel her heartbeat pulsing in her temples, beating out the pace of her feet, pushing her on toward him.

Toro saw her rushing at him and swung his steel hand in an arc to fend her off.

With a scream she tackled him, his body folding in half, and together they crashed through the window. The glass shattered, a cold gust of wind swept her face, and then they were airborne.

For a moment, they hung weightless, like feathers on a breeze, then gravity took hold and they plummeted. Toro squirmed and Asha lost her grip. She grabbed onto the front of his shirt with both hands, wrapping them in the fabric.

They hit the ground a second later.

Even with the man under her the impact of the hit rattled Asha's skull. A loud boom echoed in her ears; snow shot up into the air.

Asha held onto him tightly, ready to fight, ready to do whatever it took to stop him. His eyes were half open, his mouth a gaping maw. He didn't move.

With an effort, she released her grip on him.

That's when Asha saw them.

A crowd had formed at the base of the HAAS building. People had packed themselves in to get a better view of the events inside. Police officers raised their hands up in an attempt to hold them back while others rushed to set up a barricade.

Now, however, no one moved. Coats fluttered in the wind, yellow tape flapped lazily in an officer's hands, voices called on handheld radios but were not answered, somewhere in the distance she could make out the low bark of a large dog. It was as if they were all frozen.

Asha turned back to the HAAS building and saw the window she and the man had fallen through. It was only the fourth floor so she ran forward and, with a push, launched herself up. Her jump landed her at the first floor windows, so she jumped, clearing the next floors, and caught the fourth ledge with her free hand.

She pulled herself to through the broken window and rushed for the stairs.

13
THE PULSE

"Asha!" Mick exclaimed as she rushed through the door.

"How is she?" Asha asked, running over to Lily. She had her mother's head in her lap.

Lily's mom's face was a pale white except for a dark puffiness around her right eye and cheek. Lily gently brushed her mom's hair with her hand.

"She's breathing but, I can't wake her up," Lily replied, her face anxious. "She had been mumbling nonsense when I got to her, not even words, really. Then her eyes kind of fluttered and she passed out. I can't mover her."

"I can," Asha replied.

She bent down and slipped her hands under the woman's light frame.

"Wait," Mick said.

"We have to get her out of here," Asha said.

"I know," he replied. "But you heard what that other woman said and we don't know how long we've got before whatever it is they're doing is going to happen."

"But what about my mom?" Lily pleaded.

"If they do something terrible to this city it won't matter what happens to her. We have to do something."

"Like what?" Asha asked. "We don't even know what they are planning."

"But we can figure it out."

Asha knew he was right, but Mrs. Donovan still needed help. She didn't know how long Lily's mom had been out or how hurt she was. Again, it seemed, Asha would have to make a choice: save Lily's mom or save the city.

She let out a deep sigh then stood up and said, "Okay, Mick. What do we do?"

Mick started to pace. "What do we know? They're here at the HAAS building so we know it has something to do with that. HAAS does security for a lot of places. Maybe they're going to shut down security on a bunch of places and do one big heist."

"I don't think so," Asha replied. "If they were going to do that why did they go to all that trouble stealing all that copper and then magnets and whatever else from the warehouse? I'm sure everything is run by computers so they could flick a switch if they wanted to shut down security."

"Maybe it's inside HAAS itself," Mick offered. "You said you took out a bunch of guys in the lobby, maybe they were doing something and you caught them off guard."

"Maybe," Asha said, but she wasn't entirely convinced.

"Lily," Mick said, walking over to the girl sitting on the floor. "Do you know of anything going on in this building that they would be interested in?"

Lily merely shook her head and continued to brush her mother's hair with her hand.

"Come on, think!"

"I don't know!" Lily shot back, turning to face him and scowling. "Why are we even talking about this? She needs help!"

Mick crouched down beside her. "We will help her but we need your help first."

"Do you promise?" Lily asked, skeptically.

"Promise," Mick replied. He brought up his hand to place it on her shoulder; a shot of static electricity jumped from his hand and zapped her.

"Mick!" she screamed. "What's wrong with you?"

An image flashed across Asha's mind of Ms. Lowen zapping

Asha's hand on the first day of school, then another of that poster Mick had drawn, the one with the bear — ONLY BEARS CAN STOP THE SPREAD OF POSTERS — then one of Mr. Jones saying something about electricity. What had it been?

She squeezed her eyes shut, pushing everything away except that one image. He had said he taught Linguistics and Asha had replied that she knew Lily. Then he had said he taught Special Projects. There was a kid in there doing something with electricity. It was an electro-something. Why couldn't she remember the name?

"Electro mini," she mumbled, trying to coax the name out of her memory. "Electro man, electro-mag, electro — "

"Electromagnetic," Lily said.

"Yes!" Asha exclaimed, opening her eyes. "Electromagnetic! Mr. Jones told me about it ages ago! Electromagnetic something."

"Pulse," Lily stated flatly. "Electromagnetic pulse."

"Yes!" Asha cried. "That's it!"

"What's that?" Mick asked.

"EMP. It's a rapid expansion of electromagnetic energy. I saw a small scale demo in the Special Projects class a while ago," Lily said. "If it's a big enough charge it can disrupt electrical signals."

"So?" Mick asked.

"So," Lily said, exasperated. "If you have a *really* big one you could do a *lot* of damage. All the electrical systems would be fried in the area: phones, RCs, all the stuff that keeps places warm in the winter, lights, everything."

"How big of an area?" Asha demanded.

"Depends on the size, maybe a few blocks."

"Like before on the north side!" Mick exclaimed. "They could have done one there. Everything was shut down, even watches."

"Could it be used across the city?" Asha asked. "That woman said something about the city and darkness."

"You'd have to have a very big device to do that," Lily said. "It would have to be four times the size of this building and you'd need a massive source of power to make it work."

"Maybe that's what they were doing here," Mick said.

"Do you *see* copper strewn about the place?" Lily asked.

"What about a lot of small ones, placed all over the city?" Asha asked. "Could that do it?"

"Maybe, but you'd need to connect them all so they are timed to go off one after another so the pulse wouldn't take out any of the devices. Plus you'd still need to power them."

Things were starting to fall in place. The Dragon had been building these devices, Asha knew it. They had been putting them all over the city. Then they came here, at least some of them. She had recognized the guy with the mole. She had recognized him from the —

"The LR."

"Pardon?" Mick asked.

"They're using the LR," Asha replied. "They were working on the power distribution nodes."

Lily said, "Of course!"

"Distribution nodes?" Mick asked.

"The cone shaped things," Lily said. "They distribute power through the entire Light Rail system and they're all connected. Some could be converted to EMPs."

"We can't run around the city trying to stop them all!" Mick exclaimed. "There must be thousands!"

"There has to be a central device the pulse is starting from," Lily answered. "One node that controls all the others, but it would have to be connected to them all."

"Well, we can't search each one," Mick said.

A sinking feeling fell into Asha's gut. How could she have been so blind? Hadn't she been standing in this very room when she had been told about it? Hadn't she been standing at that very window overlooking the city talking to the woman who was now lying unconscious on the floor? Didn't she *live* with someone who talked about it all the time?

"It's at the Hydro Plant," Asha said.

*

"The Hydro Plant supplies direct power for the entire Light Rail system," Asha explained. "That's what your mom said, Lily, and the tour guide at the plant, and my — "

Her dad would be there by now, checking in to replace someone who hadn't come in. It was a good bet that person had been a member of The Dragon and had just been scoping the place out, feeding information back to the others. Her father would have no idea something was wrong until it was too late.

"What's wrong?" Lily asked.

"Where would it be, the EMP?" Asha demanded.

"I don't know," Lily sighed. "The place is so big it could be anywhere in there."

"Think about what we know," Asha prompted. "We know the device takes lots of power and would take up quite a bit of room. Where could it be?"

"The Extraction room," Mick said. "That's where it will be."

"How do you know that?" Asha asked, surprised.

"The tour guide said it used the most power in the entire plant although that was small compared to the amount they got out. Plus it's a very big room."

It made sense, and quite frankly, Asha had no other ideas.

"Go get help for Mrs. Donovan. There are police outside."

"Wait, what are you going to do?" he asked.

"I'm going to the plant to stop that thing from going off," Asha replied.

"Hold on a second! Let's talk about this!"

"There's no time! I wasted enough fighting that metal armed man and we've spent more of it to figure this out. It could go off any second and my dad is in there."

"Asha," Lily said, carefully. "Remember the lightning, the electric charges. You were hit with one through the protective glass. You could barely walk after. Now you want to go into a room filled with that. It could *kill* you."

Lily was right; she was always right.

"I have to," Asha stated and turned to the window.

Mick grabbed her arm and fiercely pulled her around "Are you crazy? Didn't you hear what she said?"

"I have to stop it," Asha said, wrenching her arm out of his grip. "Don't you get it? If that thing goes off this entire city will be without power. That means no security systems, no backup systems, no lights, no running water, no heat. All of this in the middle of winter. How many people will be hurt? How many people will die? And what about my dad? Should I just leave him in there? Would you?"

Mick had no answer and Asha didn't wait for one.

She would have to get over there in a hurry, but that meant rushing down all those stairs and dashing through to the Hydro Plant. Asha feared there wasn't time for that. She rushed over to the window and stared out at the Hydro Plant. It seemed so close, but it was so far away, its skylights lit up from inside with bright, pulsing, blue light. If only she had jet boots she could just fly over there, one quick boost and it would all be over. One. Quick. Boost.

She knew what she had to do.

She grabbed a nearby chair, lifted it over her head and hurled it at the window. The glass shattered and a cold gust of wind buffeted her body.

"Get her help," Asha ordered turning to Mick and pointing at Mrs. Donovan.

He nodded grimly.

Asha ran to the far side of the room, trying to get as much distance as she could. She would need all the speed she could get; she had never done anything like this, never gone so far.

"Asha," Lily called to her. "The Faraday suits. The mesh ones. They're your only chance."

Asha gave her a nod and turned to the hole in the window.

Asha crouched down, like a sprinter in a race, and focused on the hole in the window. She let it fill her mind, let the shape of it draw her in, let the feel of the wind caress her skin. The room shrank, its walls closed in, the mess melted away, until all that was left was that one empty spot into the darkness of the night.

She pushed off on one foot, rushing forward. One step. Two steps. Three steps. Four. Her body lightened. Five steps. Six. Her foot touched the ledge of the window, glass crunching beneath her shoes.

Then, she leapt.

Asha flew through the air, the cold wind tugging at her. At first, her jump had shot her high but then she began to fall down toward the Hydro Plant's roof.

She tore through the skylight, the force jolting her. She tumbled and spun, knocking against concrete walls and steel cross beams until she fell into a wide open area. The floor sped toward her, rushing up in a wall of solid cement. She rolled herself toward it, getting her legs underneath her before it was too late. A split second later she touched down in a crouch, the concrete shattering beneath her feet.

A wave of dizziness washed over her, she closed her eyes and forced the feeling away.

Above her, countless strands of electricity arced and raced, crackling and spitting, the sound so loud Asha thought her mind would split from the force of it.

She tore her eyes from the sight, desperately searching for the suits Lily had spoken of. If she could just get in one she might be all right. Maybe they put them away after each time they used them. They could be in a storage area somewhere in the building. That would make the most sense if they wanted to keep —

Asha spotted them; a feeling of dread washed over her. Across the room the tattered remains of the suits lay spread across the floor.

Looming behind them, centred between the four pillars supporting the roof of the huge room sat a gigantic machine. It was unlike anything she had ever seen.

It rose halfway to the ceiling and stretched out wide, the bulk of it a mass of steel. Rusted metal beams had been welded together to support the structure; bare copper wires looped around it in a tangled mess. On one side there was a clump of magnets nearly the size of Asha herself, and on the other a grid of eerily blinking red lights. Most disturbing of all was the sound. A dull pulse, a vibration so low she felt it more than heard it. It dug into her mind, making her dizzy.

An arc of blue lightning shot out, striking the wall behind her. The electrical sparks pulsed at the same speed as the machine, joined in a deadly dance of devastating destruction.

Asha knew the lightning couldn't be powering the device. If it was it would be an unreliable supply. She edged around it, keeping low to avoid any stray sparks that might come her way. The pulsing grew more intense; slow at first then faster and faster until it was moving at a breakneck pace.

Halfway to the other side of the machine she spotted it: a long, black cable connected to the far wall. It had to be at least two feet thick and was connected to a panel in the far wall.

The pulse sped faster. The lights on the device blinked quicker. It was building up to something.

Asha rushed the rest of the way around the machine, the blue lightning striking it over and over. She kept her eyes on the cable, looking for ways she might be able to unplug it, either from the wall or the machine itself. The closer she got, the more impossible that seemed. The end attached to the wall had been welded to the panel; a giant steel plate was attached to the cable and there were great blotches of hardened, molten metal joining it to the wall. The other end of the cable, the one at the machine, entered into the device through an opening.

Then the lightning hit her.

*

She fell to her knees, clutching her chest in agony. Another arc slammed into her, this time hitting her shoulder, wrenching her down toward the floor. Then another, and another, and another.

The lightning rained down on her, paralyzing her with pain.

It arced between her fingers, tearing through her legs and arms, each strike like a knife slicing into her skin.

Asha prayed for the darkness to take her, like when the seizures came, desperate to make it stop. She didn't care how.

The pulse beat maddeningly in her head. Any moment now the machine would let out its deadly signal and everything would be over. Would she feel it, the impact of a force so powerful it could destroy millions of lives? Could it be any worse than now?

The darkness would not come. No matter how much she wanted it, it would not save her. Asha forced her eyes open. The cable was only a few feet away. It lay there, taunting her, knowing she would never reach it.

She forced herself to stand up and the lightning worsened. It ripped through her, almost driving her to the ground again.

She took a step and the lightning blanketed her, washing through her in a giant wave. It felt as if her skin was being ripped from her bones. She would have screamed if she could.

She took another step, and the pulse grew louder. The lighting powered over her, tearing into her head.

She took another step and her foot hit something.

Asha forced herself to open her eyes and found they already were. She willed them to work, to see what she had hit, and there it was: the black cable.

She fell to the floor, smashing her knees on the concrete.

The power of the pulse and lighting grew. The machine knew she was there to destroy it.

She gripped the cable with numb hands, the only way she knew she was touching it was by looking at it.

The pulse was now one steady beat, Asha could feel a build-up of energy coming from the machine, pure and massive. It was happening.

She pulled the cable, trusting that her hands were strong enough, focusing on the end by the panel. It didn't budge.

She tried again focusing on the machine end. It wouldn't move.

A massive surge came from the machine.

Asha gripped the cable in both hands, they couldn't even make it all the way around. She began to pull.

Every part of her screamed for her to stop. Lighting struck her, the air spinning in a hurricane of electricity.

Asha forced her hands apart and a small tear formed in the cable, revealing bright copper. She pulled harder and the gap grew larger.

The machine screamed out a massive beat.

Asha dragged air into her lungs and with one final pull, let out a yell of effort.

The cable tore in half, electricity spilled out like a waterfall, slamming into her. The machine gave out a cry of despair, a sound Asha could feel somewhere in the back of her mind.

The broken cable poured its energy into her and then, when she could endure no more, the darkness finally took her.

*

She is alone in the silence of the black. She cannot speak. She cannot see. She is lost.

For one, fleeting moment a voice whispers to her, a song carried on the wind of a sweet, five note chime:

Watch it. Here it comes.

Then it is gone and from that darkness something else comes to her, something hungry, something terrifying, something altogether wrong. She tries to shy away from it, to run, but there is no place to hide.

It wraps itself around her, it digs into her, a formless invading malice.

She knows she cannot stop it and she prays to be saved. But there is nowhere to go. The void is all that exists and it is the void.

It is Chaos. It is Anarchy. It is the End. In that darkness, it speaks not with words, but with deathly purpose.

You have no idea what is coming, little girl.

*

Asha's eyes flew open and she gasped. She was lying flat on her back, the cold concrete pressing against her.

Two guards stood over her.

"You okay?" one of them asked.

Asha wasn't sure. The last thing she remembered was trying to pull apart the power cable, electricity pouring into her. Gingerly, she sat up. When she didn't fall over, she gathered her feet underneath her and stood. She braced herself for the wave of dizziness she thought would come, but nothing happened. She didn't fall over or even stumble.

The device at the centre of the pillars sat still and silent. Whereas before it had been a living, pulsing creature, now it was simply a mass of wires and metal, nothing more.

"What happened here?" the other guard asked, astonished.

"I had to stop it," Asha said.

"*You* did this?" the first guard asked.

The other guard opened her mouth to speak, but Asha held up her hand; she had more important things to take care of. "Where's my da—" she started then cut herself off short. "I mean, is anyone missing?"

"No," the man said, shaking his head. "We were locked in the security office but managed to get free. They rounded up the other guards and put them in the cafeteria. They were all accounted for."

Asha turned toward the main doors, eager to get to them and find her father.

"Wait!" the woman called. "Someone *is* missing. Tom. Tom Anderson."

Asha spun around. "Where is he?"

"He didn't come in. He was called and didn't show up. The Dragon arrived just after he said he was coming in. He probably didn't even know they were here."

A flood of relief washed over her. He wasn't there, which meant he was probably safe.

"Call the police," Asha said. "I know there are some over at the

HAAS building so it shouldn't take them long to get here."

She had to get home, she had to know he wasn't hurt. Asha looked up to see the broken skylight and clear black sky above. That would be the quickest way.

She leapt up and was gone.

*

Asha hopped down to from the roof to her balcony and rushed into the apartment.

"Dad?" she called.

No answer.

She went from room to room, searching for him, finally ending up in the bathroom, only to be greeted with a grisly sight. The mirror reflected a disheveled girl.

Her shirt was so torn she had to wonder that it was able to stay on. There was a giant circle-shaped burn on her chest. Miraculously, she didn't have a scratch on her.

Ignoring how she looked for the moment, she stopped to think. If her father wasn't here and he wasn't at the plant then where was he? More than likely he had been blocked somewhere along the way, but she couldn't be sure. She would have to go and find him.

She rushed to the entrance, put on the sweater she had dropped there only a few hours before and hurried to the balcony door. She was just stepping out onto the balcony when the apartment door opened. Her father came through, his security uniform as clean as ever.

"Dad!" she exclaimed and rushed over to him, throwing her arms around him in a tight hug.

"Whoa!" he gasped. "Too tight!"

"Sorry," she apologized, letting him go. "Where were you?"

"Got stopped just before getting to work by a police barricade. Had to come back home; it took forever. Did you hear about the attack? Looks like The Dragon bit off more than they could chew this time. Seems someone cleaned their clocks good. It's been all over the news. Are you all right?"

Asha answered by hugging him again. This time she didn't let him go.

14
THE CIRCLE OF NINE

The light tik-tak of the woman's footfalls echoed down the corridor. She walked with confidence, passing through the doorway into the chamber beyond without a moment's hesitation. The room was massive, the echoes of her footsteps on the marble floor lost in its depths. Dim, crimson light seeped from the walls. A bright spotlight lit a circle on the floor.

Athena, the woman in red, stepped into it.

Stone stairs rose from the floor before her to a short pyramid. Above the plateau, arranged in a semi-circle, eight monitor screens hovered motionless; each showed a shrouded figure. Some she knew not at all, others she knew quite well.

Centred among the screens stood a man.

"Your report."

"The Dragon Initiative has completed and we have collected all the necessary information. You will all receive the report in the next hour."

"Your findings."

"While the ultimate result of The Dragon Initiative was not achieved, the scenario did expose potential benefits.

"Recruits to The Dragon Initiative performed satisfactorily, particularly those liberated from the Violent Offenders Centre. The children served their purpose well; however, more study needs to be conducted in order to evaluate their roles."

"And what of this… girl?" the man demanded.

"Her appearance and subsequent interference was unfortunate, yet not without value. I suggest she be monitored and studied, if possible."

"Do you believe she can be converted to an asset?"

"Definitely."

"Further recommendations?"

"We should implement the Alternative immediately."

The man pressed his fingers together, deep in thought. Beside him the silent figures shifted.

"Very well. Proceed," he ordered.

The woman in red grinned.

15
BETTER DAYS

The day was surprisingly bright; sunlight filtered through the window and landed where Asha sat on her bed, books and papers strewn about in a jumbled mess.

She was finally doing her homework. With everything that had been happening she hadn't realized just how far behind she was. There were essays due and math assignments she hadn't even begun to understand. Normally, she wouldn't enjoy doing any kind of homework, but she threw herself into it, happy to be thinking about simpler things.

She was so engrossed in her work that she was startled when her bedroom door swung open. Mick charged into her room followed closely by Lily.

"Mick!" Lily said. "You can't just go barging into a girl's room!"

"What? She's dressed," Mick replied defensively, reaching behind Lily and shutting the door.

Lily fumed at him then turned to Asha. "Your dad let us in. Why is he putting up all those pictures in the living room?"

"I guess he thought it was time."

"Hey, you're wearing the jeans." Lily said.

Asha looked at her legs in time to see the shape of an eagle soar out of sight. They had been in the bag Elizabeth had given to her.

"Yeah, they're just like new. How's your mom doing?" Asha asked. She hadn't heard any news about Mrs. Donovan in the last day or so.

"She's okay," Lily said. "They released her from the hospital yesterday and she was already back at work today. There's a huge mess in her lab to clean up. "

"I'll say," Mick said. "You should have seen that place after you left, Asha. It was worse than *this* room."

"Very funny, Mick," Asha replied. "How's your dad? I haven't heard anything about him, since, you know, that day."

"Oh, he's fine. He just got a bump on the head, but he's better. The towing company didn't fire him after all. Apparently, they have insurance to cover that kind of thing so no harm done I guess."

"Good," Asha replied, relieved.

"What's your dad doing here, anyway?" Mick asked. "It's the middle of the day. Shouldn't he be at work?"

Lily cleared off a spot on the edge of the bed, moving papers around gingerly, and sat down while Mick explored Asha's room.

"There's police at the Plant," Asha explained. "Some of the guards my dad was training were Dragon members, so there's an investigation going into that, too.

"They're tracking down all the Power Distribution Nodes that The Dragon modified. I still don't know how The Dragon got that machine into the place without being seen. It was massive."

Mick answered, "There's a tunnel running from HAAS to the Hydro Plant, like the one in the abandoned warehouse. When HAAS was setting up security for the Plant they made the tunnel so people wouldn't know what they were doing. The Dragon used it to run their parts to the Plant without being noticed. That's why they were at HAAS to start with."

"How do you know that?" Lily asked.

Mick shrugged. "My brother," as if the answer was obvious. "Did you guys hear, the police caught quite a few Dragon members already. They were all just sitting outside office buildings in vans, waiting."

"Why?" Asha asked.

"Each building had a storage bunker. Like HAAS they stored all their top secret stuff like designs, schematics, prototypes in secured bunkers in their buildings. Turns out The Dragon was going to steal that stuff and sell it to the highest bidder."

"That was their plan?" Asha asked. "Cripple the city then steal tech secrets and sell them?"

"Some of those designs can be worth billions to the right buyer," Lily said. "Not to mention all of the military tech they would have been after. If they had gotten away with it they would be some of the most powerful people in the world. Plus, the EMP wouldn't have affected anything in those bunkers. Nothing short of a nuclear bomb can get through them.

"Still, it's good the police got them. Hopefully, this time they can keep them in Violent Offenders Centre for good this time."

The room fell silent, but Asha didn't mind. She was content to just sit in the light with Lily and Mick and not worry about anything.

"Hey, I figured it out," Lily said.

"What's that?" Asha asked.

"About all that super stuff you can do. Your body is adapting."

"To what?"

"To dangerous situations. Most animals adapt to environmental conditions."

"Yeah, but I think those animals are born with that ability," Mick replied.

"True," Lily admitted. "But I think when that transformer hit you, Asha, it kind of jump started something in your body. Like a car battery that's gone dead and someone gave it a boost. It would explain all the seizures you've been having. Remember the frogs in Science? Where Trevor and them were zapping it?"

"Yeah" Asha replied, disgusted.

"When they jolted it with electrical current the frog's limbs twitched. After they took away the current, the frog's limbs sometimes keep twitching."

"So you think I'm like a dead frog?"

"No, just that your body may still be storing that electrical energy somehow and it's helping you to adapt to stressful situations. It uses the energy from the electricity to make your muscles stronger. It uses that energy to heal you faster."

"How much will I change?" Asha asked.

"I don't know," Lily replied. "I guess we'll just have to see."

In her mind, Asha saw herself changing to a frog like creature, able to leap tall buildings in a single hop.

"Speaking of school," Lily said, snapping her fingers. "I got all your homework."

"Oh, that's just wonderful," Mick said, rolling his eyes. "She takes a couple days off after saving the city and you have to ruin it."

Asha let out a groan and said, "I'm already so far behind... "

"I'll help," Lily assured her. "You'll be caught up in no time."

"What about everyone else? How am I going to explain everything to them?" Asha asked.

"Why would you need to?" Mick asked, distracted. He was playing with the light up flower on Asha's dresser.

"I crashed that guy out the window. Someone had to have recognized me."

"I don't see how," Mick replied. "Not with all that glowing."

"Glowing?"

"Yeah, you were glowing again," Mick answered.

"Again?"

Lily and Mick glanced at each other, then Lily turned to Asha. "When you do your thing you glow."

"You mean, like, I sparkle?"

"No, nothing crazy like that," Mick laughed.

"Are you guys serious?" Asha asked.

"How do you think you were able to find us in the HAAS building? All the lights had gone out by the time you got to us," Lily answered.

"The emergency lights came on," Asha explained.

"There were no emergency lights," Mick replied. "They took out everything in that building. The Dragon did *not* want to be caught."

"No one could have recognized you," Lily assured her. "Whenever you glow it's impossible to see your face. I only know it's you because I've seen it start to happen. I still have to squint at you, even then I can't really see you."

"But why?" Asha asked, turning to Lily, hoping for an explanation.

"I don't know," Lily answered, shaking her head. "I've been trying to figure it out, but I've got nothing."

"Did you eat glow in the dark paint as a child?" Mick asked.

Despite herself, Asha let out a laugh.

"And I wouldn't worry about Keri and them for a while," Mick said. "They're already having to deal with the fallout from Crystal to even think about you."

"What fallout?"

"Didn't you hear? The police arrested her at school."

"What for?" Asha asked, shocked.

"She was the one vandalizing the place, spraying those Dragon symbols everywhere. Even put that video on the Tube."

"You're kidding."

"Nope. They received a tip and Mr. Jones searched her locker. Found all sorts of stuff. Spray paint. A copy of the video that was on the Tube on a drive. A gun. Police handcuffed her and took her away."

"Who tipped them off?"

"I have no idea," Mick said.

"It was me," Lily admitted.

"What?" Mick asked, incredulous. "How did you know it was her?"

"Did you see the way Keri and the rest of them treated her?" Lily asked. "They yelled at her and were mean all time. She might have looked like one of the popular crowd, but she was treated like garbage, always being told to shut up.

"She worked in the administration office. She had access to the video systems and the Tube computer. I knew a teacher couldn't have been doing those things and she was the only one left. So, when we got back to school, I followed her for a bit and caught a glimpse in her locker and saw the paint cans. I called in an anonymous tip right after."

"So much for the profile," Asha said. "Why would she do that? I mean, we're harassed more than that and we didn't do what she did."

"She didn't have any real friends. Not like us," Mick said.

Asha smiled. She couldn't help herself.

"Let's forget about that," Lily said. "I don't want to talk about it anymore. How are you, Asha?"

"I'm all right, I guess," Asha answered. "I'm a bit stiff, but I'm getting better."

"After having that much electricity run through you, I'm surprised you're not worse off. You should be dead."

"Should be, but I'm not. Guess what. No more spasms."

"Weird. I mean, that's not a bad thing. I'm just surprised."

All through their exchange Mick had been silent, but now he seemed to be agitated. He kept darting his eyes between the two girls.

"What?" Asha demanded.

Mick held his tongue for a moment before blurting, "We have something for you! We thought you could use a little pick me up so we went to the mall and we bought it for you. C'mon, Lily, give it to her."

Lily reluctantly ruffled through her backpack and pulled out a plastic bag. Asha took it gently.

"You guys didn't have to," Asha said.

"Just open it," Mick replied. He was nearly vibrating.

Asha slipped her hand into the bag and pulled out a folded piece of white fabric. She gently unfolded it and held it up in front of her. It was a t-shirt with red sleeves; written on the front in bold letters was the word 'HERO'.

"Mick picked it out," Lily said, apologetically.

"Isn't it awesome?" Mick asked. "I knew you should have it the moment I saw it, 'cause you're a big time hero and all now."

Asha stood up, her body protesting from having not moved in a while. She held up the shirt to her front; it fell past her hips.

"Maybe you'll grow into it?" Lily suggested.

Asha was at a loss for words.

Lily frantically said, "You don't like it. I told Mick it was a dumb idea. I wanted to get you one of those mini-RCs. You know they have them with a built in sorting function they could have this place straightened up in a flash. In fact, we could go right —"

Asha bent down and wrapped her arms around Lily, squeezing her tightly.

"Whoa!" Mick exclaimed. "Get a room!"

Asha reached out and, without letting go of Lily, grabbed him and pulled him into the hug.

"Thank you," she said.

"So," Mick said awkwardly, straightening up and pulling at his shirt. "What now?"

"What do you mean?" Lily asked, standing up after Asha released her.

"We're young, we're free. It's a beautiful day. What do we do now?"

"I guess I can go out for a bit," Asha said.

Lily, on the other hand, gave him a wary look. "What are you up to, Mick?"

"Me? Nothing," he said, innocently.

Lily stared at him skeptically.

"Okay," he relented. "Have you guys ever heard of the Crypt?"

"The Crypt?" the girls asked in unison.

"Yeah, they're a big crime organization from the east. Like across the world East. Bigger than The Dragon was here."

"What about them?" Lily asked.

A sly grin twitched on Mick's lips.

Asha's heart beat faster, with each pulse the room grew brighter.

Mick leaned forward and said, "Come a little closer, ladies. You're gonna love this."

Asha hung on every word.

ABOUT THE AUTHOR

Dustin Archibald lives in Grande Prairie, Alberta with his wife (Tracy), son (Logan), and miniature poodle (Tootsie). He is a writer, editor, tinkerer, entrepreneur, Kung Fu instructor, and maker of strange things.

Find more information at:
dcarchibald.com

Made in the USA
Lexington, KY
25 November 2019

57685851R00126